IF I Only KNEW

if i only knew - special edition

corinne michaels

If I Only Knew

Cover Design:
Sarah Hansen, Okay Creations

dedication

Christy Peckham, even though I tell you I hate you . . . I totally love you.
Thank you for putting up with my crazy and being an amazing friend.
(I'll deny this if you ever repeat it.)

prologue

. . .

Danielle

"I'M GETTING MARRIED!" My sister, Amy, screeches into the phone as I'm driving home from grocery shopping.

"What?" I ask, almost veering off the road.

"Javier proposed, and I said yes!"

"Oh! Wow! That's . . . great! Yay!" I say with fake enthusiasm.

My sister is the last person in the world who should be getting married. First, she's never had a job, paid a bill, or been a contributing member of society. Second, I'm pretty sure her now fiancé . . . is gay.

"Javier picked out the most amazing ring, Danni. Like, it sparkles in the light and sends these rainbows everywhere when I move. Oh, and he wants to get married in a month!"

"What's the rush?" I ask.

She sighs, and I picture her staring at her ring. "He thinks it would be better to do it now instead of waiting."

I roll my eyes and bite my tongue. Today isn't the day to have an opinion on this. She's clearly excited and nothing good will come of me telling her that he doesn't love her, and there's some ulterior motive—like a green card.

So, for now, I'll be the good sister and keep my trap shut.

"Well, I love you and I know Peter and the kids will be excited," I say, staring at the traffic ahead of me.

I look at the clock and start to worry a little. I have to get my fifteen-year-old hellion daughter, Ava, and my sweet five-year-old son, Parker, from school in twenty minutes. Plus drop this stuff back at home so all my frozen food doesn't thaw. My thumb taps on the wheel as I barely move an inch.

"I love you too! Gah! I'm just so happy!"

My phone beeps, "Amy hold on, it's Peter's cell."

I swap the call over, thankful that I can stop trying to pretend my sister is making an even halfway decent decision. I love her to the moon, but she lives in the stars. Peter and I have never understood her. "Hi, babe. I can't wait to tell you my sister's latest bullshit. She's getting married to that idiot! Can you even believe that? How dumb is she?"

"Umm, is this Mrs. Bergen?"

"Yes? Who is this?" I ask when it's not my husband's voice on the other end.

The male clears his voice. "This is Officer VanDyken with the Tampa Police department."

My heart starts to race and my throat goes dry. "Is everything okay?"

"Ma'am, I'm going to need you to come down to the station."

A sense of dread fills my veins. Peter works with some shady people and there have been times when he's done some things that I've thought were a little weird, but he says it's for the protection of his clients.

"Which one?"

He tells me the address and I make a quick U-turn to head that way. I have no idea if Peter is in trouble, but I range from worried to pissed off. I hate his job. It was part of the reason we almost divorced three years ago. Well, that and Parker, who unexpectedly graced us with his presence and sent our lives into a tailspin.

I send a quick text to my best friend, Kristin.

Me: Can you get the kids? I just got a call from the TPD asking me to come down. I have no idea what happened but I'm freaking out because I won't make it to pick them up.

Kristin: Of course. I have to get Finn and Aubrey anyway, I'll swing by and grab them.

Me: Thank you!

Kristin: Is he in trouble or arrested?

That's the question of the day.

Me: I have no idea. I swear, if this is about the case he's been working on and he got arrested for hiding the client or some shit . . . I'm going to kill him.

Kristin: Call Heather! Don't talk to anyone until you've talked to her.

I didn't even think about that. Heather has been a Tampa police officer for a long time. She knows everyone.

Me: Thank you! I'll grab the kids as soon as I'm done.

Kristin: No worries. We'll entertain them.

Or Ava will drive Kristin nuts, but she's usually only the devil for me. She's fifteen and a load of freaking fun. She knows everything. Hates everyone who is not her father, and thinks I'm the worst person on the face of the earth. Which has made for some lovely family dinners.

Then there's my sweet baby, Parker. He's the angel to the demon spawn I birthed first. I know as a mother we're not supposed to have favorites, but that kid makes it hard not to. He loves me, still thinking I'm wonderful, and I can't imagine a world without him.

While he was never in the plan, he was the best mistake I ever made.

I push the button to send a voice message to Heather.

Me: Hey, can you meet me at the station? Something happened with Peter.

The roads going this way aren't busy, and I make it there before Heather returns my text. Shit. I call Peter's assistant's cell phone, but it goes to voicemail. *Figures.* The one time she doesn't have the damn thing permanently glued to her hand.

I decide I'm just going to have to go in and deal with it. I know where he keeps the extra money in case we ever need it for something like this. I'll bail him out and then I'm going to beat him with his own torn-off arms.

When I get through the doors, Heather is standing there. "Hey!" I say, relief flowing through me. "I tried to message you."

"Hey." Her smile is small.

"Thank God you're here. Did you find out what Peter did? I wasn't sure the protocol on bailing someone out . . ."

She nods. "Danni," her voice is soft. "I . . . it's not . . . this isn't like that."

"What?" I ask as my throat goes dry. "Like what? I can't get him out? Did he do something really bad? Jesus Christ! He did, didn't he?"

Fear starts to fill my body as I wonder what the hell is going on. Heather doesn't look me in the eyes. Instead, she releases a deep breath and her eyes fill will tears. This can't be good. She's not a crier and definitely not over Peter. My best friends accept my husband, but they'll never forgive him for all that happened years ago.

If she's on the verge of tears, this isn't bad, it's worse than bad.

Heather steps forward. "Danni, Peter was shot at his office earlier today and," her lip trembles.

I hear the words, but I don't want to believe them.

"Why am I here then?" I start to step back. "I should be at the hospital!"

"Danielle," she says in her police voice. "He's not at the hospital."

"Why not?" I scream out. "Why didn't you take him there? Why the hell am I here?"

"Because I wanted to be the one to tell you . . ."

One sentence says it all.

"Don't say it," I beg. "Don't tell me because it's not true. It can't be true!"

"He's gone, honey." She steps forward and I start to crumble, but she catches me. We crumple to the floor as she holds me in her arms. "I'm so sorry. I'm so so sorry. We tried everything. I got the call, I was on scene as soon as I could, but there was no saving him."

one

...

Danielle

sixteen months later

"I LIKE THIS PROPERTY, Callum. The land is already partially cleared. It's a prime location for this project," I explain with my best authoritative voice.

The price tag may be a little bigger than he wants, but it's a great piece of land. In the last year, I've found that my boss doesn't often question me. He knows I'm good at my job, even if I only work part-time, and the fact that he happens to be my dear friend Nicole's husband give us a sense of trust. My work ethic has only further solidified that.

"It's a lot of money, Danni. A lot more than I told you I was willing to spend," his eyes are hard, but with an edge of softness. His British accent makes him sound sterner than he really is. I imagine if I was anyone else, he'd have none of the kindness I see.

"I know." I sit in the chair. "If you were to go with the other lot, I think you'll lose money. There's too much competition in that part of the town for the types of stores you're looking to build, but this one has a thriving community that is desperate for options. The price tag might be a little higher, but the return will be as well."

Living here my whole life, I have a great sense of the people. My job is to scour the surrounding area to find land for Dovetail Enterprises to develop on at the lowest price, and to assist on special projects like this one.

Normally, Dovetail would find an aging development, knock it down, and build a new high-rise or something fancy. This time, Callum wants to build a community by cleaning up one that's a little run down. He's a good man, and it's part of why I wanted to work for him.

"I see." Callum looks at the survey a little closer.

Instead of giving him the cheaper option, I hoped he'd see the value this one could offer. It was a risk, but he's a smart man who can spot a good opportunity.

I lived here before my husband moved us out to the suburbs, when we could only afford to live in the crappy part of town. I remember our first place, which was only a few blocks from this property, with a new baby. We were so broke, being parents much sooner than we planned, and pretending we had our shit together. Peter was an associate at his firm and I had just started in real estate. We were making pennies, paying student loans, and then once Ava was walking, he insisted we get out of there and we became even broker thanks to our house payment.

As soon as I think of Peter, my chest aches. I miss him.

I miss him so much sometimes that I can't breathe.

No amount of time has eased the pain that sits inside of me, festering, clawing up my throat until I choke on it. I've gotten very good at hiding my agony.

My friends keep saying how great I'm doing, and how they're proud of the woman they see, but they're not there at night when I break. When I long for the smell of his cologne on the pillow next to me. When I can't stop the tears and bury my head in my pillow to muffle the sobs.

Tears start to prick as my thoughts get away from me.

"Danielle?" Callum calls my attention.

"Sorry," I shake my head, shoving down the emotions. "I think you'll be making a mistake if you pass this one over, Callum, I really do."

"Is that your professional opinion?" he asks.

"Yes."

"If you were sitting in my chair, you would pay the extra half-million dollars?"

If I had half a million dollars I wouldn't ever want to part with it, but I know based on what Callum has paid for projects before, the high price tag won't hurt him.

"Yes."

"Okay, get the offer in."

My eyes widen a little that he listened and I didn't have to push him harder. I was ready to start breaking out all kinds of statistics, comparatives, and where we could save cash in other areas.

"I'll get this wrapped up for you today," I say with a smile.

"There's something else we need to discuss," Callum says and steeples his fingers.

Callum Huxley is an intimidating man, even with our existing friendship. He's fair, but at the same time, he puts up with zero bullshit, which baffles me daily on how he's married to Nicole. She's chock full of crazy bullshit, but they balance each other in a way that makes me jealous. Peter and I never had that.

Sure, we loved each other, but if it wasn't for becoming pregnant with Ava, we never would've gotten married at twenty-three. However, our life was on track finally. We were doing great, happier than we'd been in years.

And then he was stolen from me.

I pull myself back to professional mode. "Of course, what's going on?"

He leans back in his chair. "Are you happy at Dovetail?"

"Yes, it's been a great experience." I smile.

This job gave me purpose, a reason to fight each day, get up, shower, eat, and live again. Of course, my kids kept me functioning, but when they went to school . . .

I would curl in a ball on the couch, eat ice cream, and cry watching some horribly made romance movie that ended with people riding off into the sunset.

That was until Kristin showed up, smacked me around a bit, and made me get my shit straight. I was offered a position here, and it was like someone reminded me how to exist again.

"As you know, my brother, Milo, has stayed in London," Callum says with a heavy sigh. "I hoped he would get his head of out his arse, but . . . Milo refuses to grow up. I'm looking to fill the position of Senior Vice President of Acquisitions and Logistics."

"Oh, great," I say. "Do you want me to help you find someone?"

He laughs. "No, I want you to take that role."

My jaw falls slack. "What?" He's crazy. I've only been here a little over a year. I'm freaking part-time. "Callum, you can't be serious."

He smirks. "I very much am. You're qualified, smart, driven, and you bring me quality projects each time."

"I haven't been here long enough," I tell him.

"That is not important to me."

He leans back in his chair, watching me. I don't know what to say. "I'm part-time here. I have the kids and . . ."

"I will need you to be full-time, but I'm very aware of your situation, Danielle. I'm perfectly accepting of you needing to work from home at times, but when I'm away on travel or holiday, I will need you to step in. There's a generous salary boost, as well as other luxuries." He hands me an envelope. "All of the details are in there. Think about it."

I take it in my hands as I get to my feet. "I'll think about it," I promise.

I head home for my next job as an epically failing mother

before their bus is due, pushing the conversation with Callum to the back of my mind. My daughter is let out of school an hour before Parker, and she watches him until I get there. Of course, she loves to remind me how she should be getting paid for "doing my job". I fucking love teenagers. Dealing with Ava is much like being a bomb disposal officer. You approach the device, hoping it won't go off before you're able to contain it. However, I'm not trained like they are, and usually we have an explosion just by me smiling at her—or breathing.

The drive from Dovetail isn't long, but I take my time, wanting to savor the small slice of quiet before I'm bombarded again. Between Parker's karate, Ava's dance classes, and having no help, I'm already ready for bed.

When I pull into the drive of the house I spent the last thirteen years in, I sigh. Small things are starting to become noticeable. The lattice on the front of the porch is falling to the side a little. Peter would've fixed that already. The gutters need to be cleaned after being filled with twigs and leaves from the last storm we had. And the yard has more brown patches than ever before. I never remember to water the stupid lawn. That was Peter's thing. No matter how busy he was at the firm, he loved to have the winning green grass on the street.

The timer is set on the bomb.

I can feel it counting down with each step I take.

Three.

Two.

One.

Please don't detonate.

"Hi guys," I say as I open the door.

"Mommy!" Parker yells as he runs towards me.

I catch him in my arms and kiss the top of his head. "Hi, my little Spiderman," I try to put him down, but he clings to me. "Oh, you're getting heavy."

"I'm growing up."

"You sure are."

Parker's blue eyes meet mine, and I thank God for giving me him. Peter and I were done after Ava. I wanted to go back to work, he had recently made partner, and our lives were good. I made my appointment to see the doctor to have a procedure to ensure no more babies, and low and behold, I was already pregnant.

After a lot of tears, anger, and accusations, we finally accepted it. It was the best gift we never wanted.

"I got an A on my test," Parker beams, handing me the paper.

"Wow! Good job, dude."

Parker's pride is oozing off him. I love that he works as hard as he does.

"Thanks, Mom."

"Where's Ava?" I ask, noticing her absence from the living room.

"She's out back. She told me to stay here."

I look to the ceiling, knowing no matter what I find, it won't be good. "Finish your homework and I'll be right back."

He nods.

Making my way through the house, I hear her voice on the patio. When I get out there, the cigarette smoke punches me in the face. "My mom is such a bitch. She's so stupid and I'll sneak out tonight once she goes to sleep," Ava laughs into the phone.

We'll see who's stupid. I grab the phone from her ear, putting it to mine. "Ava can't meet you tonight because her stupid mother caught her, but don't worry. In a month when she's ungrounded…" I level her with a glare. "She'll tell you all about the bitch her mother is then."

"Mom!" she screams.

I grab the cigarette from her hand, dropping it to the ground. "Don't talk, Ava. Don't even say a goddamn word to me. Your phone is gone. You will go to school, dance, and home. That's it."

"I hate you!"

"Good, then I'm doing my job."

"I wish you were shot instead of Daddy!"

And the bomb goes boom.

two

. . .

Danielle

"SHE WAS FUCKING SMOKING!" I pace around as Nicole tries to calm me.

"So what? We did far worse than that, remember?"

I glare at her. "That was different!"

I'm not sure why I'm here. Nicole is the absolute worst person to try to get sympathy from for these kinds of things. She was that asshole friend who got me grounded more times than I can count. The bitch who convinced us that we needed to do whatever moronic idea she came up with because she needed accomplices in all her shenanigans. And me, Heather, and Kristin were the dipshits who followed the really bad leader.

It suddenly hits me. I gave birth to a Nicole.

I'm so fucked.

"How? You were the one who got caught smoking outside the *church* parking lot ten minutes before confession," she reminds me.

"Because you made me!"

She bursts out laughing. "Yeah, but you didn't have to smoke it."

"I need new friends."

Nicole shrugs and then gets up from her desk. "Listen, she's been through a lot. Losing your dad blows when you're her age."

My head falls back and I groan. "I know, but she's drinking, smoking, telling me she hates me, and God only knows if she's having sex." Dread fills me. I didn't even think about that and now I imagine starring on 16 and Pregnant. Wouldn't that be the icing on my life-is-shit-cake.

"Oh, she's totally getting laid," Nicole smirks.

"Fuck." I drop my head in my hands.

"Stop," she laughs. "I'm kidding . . . maybe. But look, either way, she's a smart girl. I'll have a talk with her if you want."

I lift my head, eyes narrowed because Nicole isn't going to talk her out of it, she'll encourage the crap. "No."

"I'm not going to make it worse," she defends. "I'm all responsible and shit now. Just let me talk to my hellchild niece and fix her ass. I'll scare her."

It can't get any worse, right? "What made you finally snap out of it?"

She sighs and leans against her large mahogany desk. "I don't know. I think it was you, Kristin, and Heather. Or maybe your parents? It was like I didn't want to disappoint them. Disappointing my mother, on the other hand, was the single joy I had in my life."

I smile, remembering. There were times I thought she was nuts, but most of the time, it was hilarious to see Esther lose her mind. Nicole pushed every button that woman had, and it's clear Ava is the same.

"Well, Ava is definitely on that same path. And I understand she's angry that her father was murdered, I am too, but I don't deserve to be her punching bag. I'm doing the best I can."

Nicole places her hand on my arm. "You're doing great. This is just teenagers being assholes. She's pissed at the world. She loved

Peter and he was angry with her the day he was shot. Imagine that heavy burden she's carrying, Danni."

"He loved her. She knows that."

"Does she? She can't ask him. I'm sure a part of her gets it, but she's pissed off and you're the only person she has left that is pretty much required to love her disrespectful ass."

"Am I though?" I joke.

No amount of attitude would dull the love I feel for my daughter. I just wish she didn't make it so difficult to *like* her.

Nicole shrugs. "My moral compass broke a long time ago, I wouldn't go by me. If my kid ends up being anything like me, I'm selling him to the highest bidder."

She's full of shit. For all the crap she pulls, her heart is ten times too big. She loves the people around her more than any of us deserve. I showed up at her office and she cancelled a client because I was unable to get a grip. That client might have been her husband, but still.

"Well, I have one teenager free of charge," I offer, only partially kidding.

"Yours is defective. If you want someone to take the goods, you need to sell the product better."

"Idiot."

"Whatever." Nicole tilts her head. "But I'll talk to her today. Maybe take her out for dinner, slap her around a bit since no one can call child services on me, and bring her back with a shiny new attitude."

If only it worked that way.

"I appreciate you trying," I say and then look out the window.

Nothing any of us said to Nicole ever changed her ways, so I don't think she'll be able to get Ava to stop her crap either. Then again, no one has ever really been able to resist Nicole, so maybe there's hope after all.

"Look, I can't promise anything, but I understand where Ava is at right now."

My eyes meet hers. "Angry?"

She nods. "When my dad left, I was pissed! I hated him, my mom, the girl who took him from my mom. The fact that he couldn't care less about me made it easy to act like a total jackass. Ava lost her father too, and isn't coping."

I've tried everything to get her to open up and Nicole knows that. I've taken her to counseling and spent time with her one on one. My parents have even tried, and she refuses to give an inch.

At the counselor, she literally sat there refusing to speak. I was the winner of a two-hundred-dollar therapy bill and zero words spoken.

"I'm just at a loss. I feel like I lost both of them the day Peter was murdered."

Nicole takes my hand, "I'll talk to her."

I squeeze. "Thank you."

"You know, Heather might be a good one too. Her parents were killed as well, and maybe she can shed some light on breaking through to Ava."

I nod. "It's been hard for Heather," I say. "She's endured so much loss. I hate to ask her to even touch any of mine."

"You're an idiot."

"Hey!" I protest.

"For real. You think Heather gives a shit? She wants to be there for you, Danni. You've pushed everyone to this outer fringe of friendship the last eighteen months. Kristin barely speaks to you, Heather calls and you don't answer, the only reason you talk to me is because I don't give a shit about boundaries. You tried with me, but I won't let you. I'm not nice like them and won't give you space. I know you're only using it as a big fat excuse to run away and hide."

I get to my feet, ready to fight. "Fuck you!"

"No thanks, I'm a married woman."

All of the anger I had drains as she stands there with a smile, and I burst out laughing. "God, I hate you sometimes."

"I'm not trying to hurt you. You know that right?"

I look at my friend and nod. "I know."

Nicole walks closer. "I can't begin to imagine what you've been through. I lost Callum for a week and I thought I was going to crumble. To know that I would never see him again, would destroy me. So, I won't stand here like an asshole and tell you how to live, but I ask you this, are you living?"

I don't have the answer to that. I wake up, I function, I survive, but I'm angry. I'm angry at the piece of shit who stole away my husband. I'm livid that we don't have answers because the justice system that Peter was a part of continues to fail me. I feel a deep rage at the fact that we're the ones who suffer because of it all.

I lost my husband.

My *children* lost their father.

Our entire lives were altered because of someone else.

Someone who still hasn't been brought to justice for his crime.

If this is living, then no, I'm not.

"I'm doing the best I can," I say.

"Callum said he offered you his brother's old position?" she asks, changing the subject.

Nicole watches me and I stare at her. I know that she'll tell me I should take it. That Parker is old enough now to have his mother return to the workforce in full, and she's right. It's not because of him or Ava, but because I don't know if I'm emotionally stable enough to do the job.

After another beat, Nicole's lip turns into a slow smirk and her eyes roll.

"Don't look at me like that," I warn her.

"Like what?"

"That."

She shrugs. "I'm taking it that you've formed some crappy excuse as to why you're going to turn it down then?"

Nicole knows I once had aspirations. I was building an empire while Ava was in diapers. I was selling a lot of homes, getting contacts everywhere, and preparing to launch my own real estate agency once she was in school. Instead, Peter begged me to slow down because he was on the verge of becoming partner. His case-load was growing, and that meant less time at home. It would've worked out, but Ava became very ill as a baby, and she was in and out of the hospital. Which meant someone had to care for her. In other words, me.

Now I have to take care of Ava, Parker, and myself, without the benefit of a career. "I actually haven't."

"Haven't what?"

"Decided to turn it down," I inform her as I lean against the desk beside her.

Nic smiles. "Really?"

"I figure I suck at everything else in my life, might as well have one thing I can kick ass in. Plus, Ava will be starting college soon, if she's not knocked up or in jail," I sigh. "The life insurance money is going to need to go to that or a car. It makes sense for me to take a better position."

Her head moves up and down slowly. "I'm impressed. I bet a month's worth of blow jobs you wouldn't take it."

"You really didn't have to tell me that."

"It's fine, I'll take my punishment like a champ—in the ass."

"Seriously don't need to hear this."

Nicole laughs. "Callum likes it when—"

"Stop!" I smack her arm. "He's my boss and I seriously don't need the imagery of you and him in my head when I have to convince him to do something in a meeting."

"Well, I'm happy for you." She nudges me.

"Thanks." We sit here for a minute and reflect on how different our lives are. She's married, has a kid, and it's as though we've swapped places. I was married, with kids, happy, and now I'm single and trying to find my place in this world. "All right. I'm going to the office now to tell your husband."

She kisses my cheek and gets up. "Go kick some ass and I'll kick your daughter's tonight."

Here's to hoping she kicks it in the right direction.

"I accept the position."

"Brilliant." Callum smiles. "I thought you might."

"I would like to discuss the ability to work from home one day a week if I have to. If Parker gets sick or . . ."

Callum lifts his hand. "I know where you're going with this, and my lovely wife would make my life quite difficult if I made yours miserable. I do expect you in the office more often than our current arrangement, though. That part I can't negotiate, but I do understand that your situation is unique."

"Of course," I agree. "I know this new position means a greater workload. I'm willing and ready to carry that."

"Wonderful."

The financial increase will make my life a hundred times easier. We've done fine for the last year, but money goes fast when you're spending and bringing very little in. Now, I'll have a steady stream, which will allow me to replenish some of the savings I dipped into.

"All right then, you'll need to hire an assistant to handle the measly tasks that I don't need you working on anymore, and you'll have full authority to replace anyone you don't feel is a good fit for your division."

And just like that, I feel different.

I'm not small time. I'm not building from the ground up. I'm owning this damn mountain, and I plan to make it rise from the earth.

"I'll get right on it. Thank you, Callum."

He stands, extending his hand. "Nonsense. You're the right person for the job."

I shake his hand and get to work.

The team doesn't need to be shaken up at this time, but the fact that I can if I need to speaks volumes. What sucks is that I'm not replacing someone who has been working in the office for months. Flip side, I have no shoes to fill. I can make this position exactly what I want it to be.

A few hours pass. I've talked to our human resources manager, reviewed a dozen applications for assistants, and gave her back my top choices. Overall, I'm doing okay . . . until I check my email.

Holy shit.

What the hell?

In four hours I received over two hundred emails.

I start going through it all when my phone rings.

"Hello?"

"Good afternoon, is this Mrs. Bergen?" the sugary sweet voice asks.

"This is she."

"This is Mrs. Crenshaw from Ava's high school. We were calling because she wasn't in her seventh period, but she wasn't marked absent for the day."

I close my eyes and pinch the bridge of my nose. "That would mean she ditched."

This girl is going to military school at this rate.

Mrs. Crenshaw sighs. "I was afraid that was the case. I know she's been struggling a bit this year, but she's going to have to have disciplinary consequences."

"Good," I say, hoping she cares a little about that. Although, I don't think she cares about anything at this rate. "Just don't suspend her. Give her a month of Saturday detention or extra homework, but giving her time off school seems a little counter-productive, don't you think?"

I never understood that. If you cut class, and then they suspend you, then the student wins. I'm all about making her suffer at this point. She's already lost her phone and going out privileges. There's not much more I can take away, other than my sanity.

"I'll tell the vice principal your concerns."

"Thank you. I plan to deal with her at home as well."

"Good luck," she chuckles softly.

God knows I need it.

three

• • •

Danielle

"YOU DON'T CARE about me anyway!" Ava screams as I take the television out of her room.

"Nope. I sure don't," I agree as I keep walking.

She skipped school, she gets nothing. It's bare necessities for this kid. I tried the civil route. I asked her why, what was going on, if I could help, but she told me to go to hell. So, she's going to find out what hell is like and spend some time there herself.

"I hate you!"

I turn, and nod. "Then I'm doing my job. You're going to learn that life sucks, Ava. Rules, disappointment, and tragedy is a part of what we deal with daily. It's not a free pass to act like this. If you're pissed off because someone killed your father—you should be. You can feel it all, but in a healthy way. Skipping school, drinking, smoking, and whatever else you're doing, aren't the right choices. Make better ones and you can have the privileges back."

Ava probably heard one tenth of that and then tuned me out, but I feel better having said it.

I send Kristin a text.

Me: Good luck when Finn becomes a teenager.

Kristin: Ava being a brat again?

Me: Again? When did she stop?

Kristin: That's why we have two kids. The first one we fuck up and then fix all the mistakes with the second kid. Parker is your do over.

She's so stupid.

Or maybe she's brilliant.

Me: Nicole is on her way to talk to her.

Kristin: You think Nicole is the best one to give her advice? Are you drunk?

Me: Desperate.

At this point, I would take help from anyone. My parents left for a two-month cruise and land tour of Europe. Peter's parents are worthless. When he died, in their eyes, so did we. I'm the girl who got knocked up, forced him to get married, and stole their son. I've always been the anti-Christ, only now they don't have to pretend anymore. And my sister, Amy, moved to Brazil with her new husband. I'm pretty much on my own.

"Mommy?" Parker's sweet voice breaks the silence.

"Hi, buddy." I open my arms and he doesn't hesitate.

Parker climbs up and fits perfectly to my side. "Do you think

Daddy can hear me when I pray?"

I look at him, trying to control my shock. "I sure hope so."

His eyes fill with unshed tears. "I miss him."

"I do too."

"Why did he go to Heaven?" Parker asks.

Because a selfish asshole didn't want to plead guilty to a crime he committed and decided to kill your father for pushing the deal.

I give him the softer version. "Sometimes, the people we love are needed as angels,"

He lays his head on my shoulder and sighs. "I wish God let him stay."

"Me too, Spiderman. Me too."

"Why do you call me that?" he asks with a knowing smile.

I grin back at him. He loves this story and I love to tell it. "Well, when we found out that we were going to have a baby, your dad wanted to name you something super cool and I didn't like the name Peter." We both giggle. "I was joking about all the crazy names that he kept throwing out, like Hulk and Ironman." I widen my eyes. "Trying to make Daddy laugh, I said, sure, why don't we name him Peter Parker."

"And he said Spiderman!"

"Yes, he did." I tickle him. "So, I loved my Peter and I love my Parker."

"I love you, Mommy."

My throat dries and I fight back the tears. "I love you and Ava with my whole heart."

I thank God Parker doesn't remember how hard life was after he was born. All he'll know is that his father loved him. He'll be able to hold that to his chest, where Ava remembers how much Peter and I fought, mostly about the little boy in my arms.

Peter loved him, but finances were tight and I needed to go back to work, but I wanted to give our son the same attention Ava received. With that choice came sacrifices to the life we were living, and I was willing to make them, but Peter wasn't. He wanted the new cars, the addition on the house, and Ava to stay in private school. Coupled with that, and Parker's first year of cleft palate surgeries . . . we almost fell apart.

Parker and I sit like this, and I think about all the things he'll miss having his father around for, and my heart aches again.

I'll be the one to teach him how to throw a ball, which will probably be more like him teaching me. When he starts the gross things, I'll have to find a way to navigate it, not having a clue about boy stuff. The only thing I actually can do better is the girls part. Peter wasn't exactly smooth or romantic, so hopefully Parker will let me guide him there. Lord knows boys are dumb when it comes to women.

A knock on the door breaks the sweet moment I was having with my baby. He jumps up and runs to the door, pulling it open as I stand behind him.

"Aunt Nicole!"

"Parker on the street!"

I roll my eyes. "Stop making fun of his name."

"You picked it," she tosses back.

"And your son's name is better?"

She shrugs. "Colin is a great name."

"Like a colon, full of waste," I smirk.

"Very mature," Nicole deadpans.

"Parker," I say. "Can you go watch tv in your playroom please?"

He nods and runs off. He doesn't normally get to watch a show on the weekdays, but I don't want him anywhere around when his sister starts her tirade.

"Thanks for this," I say to Nicole.

"Don't thank me yet. I have no idea if anything will make a difference," she squeezes my arm and heads into the blast zone.

Nicole is in there what feels like a lifetime. I pace around, check on Parker twice, and then I can't handle the waiting anymore. With my ear pressed to the door, I listen for anything. What I hear, though, is not what I was expecting.

Laughter.

Lots of laughter.

What the hell is so funny? Nicole is supposed to be my backup in taming the beast, not laughing with her.

I stare at the wood, wishing I had x-ray vision because surely my hearing is wrong.

Before I can register what is happening, the door opens and Nicole is standing practically nose to nose with me. "Hi," she smiles.

"Hi, I was just . . ."

"Sure you were," Nic cuts me off and turns back to Ava. "Don't forget what I said, okay?"

"I won't. Thanks Aunt Nic." Ava's lips turn to a smile. Something I haven't seen in months. Something I thought the kid forgot how to do, since it's so rare. But here she is, a small glimpse of the little girl who was once happy.

The girl I miss more than anything, and would move heaven and earth to get back.

———————————

Last night ended with Nicole telling me absolutely nothing of value. Basically, my daughter promised her nothing and I'm screwed. I'm grateful she tried, and at least Nicole was able to drive home the safe sex talk so I'm not a grandma before I'm forty.

Forty.

Just that word sounds like a curse.

I pull out the mirror from my office drawer and look at my face. My dark brown hair is long and probably the only good thing about me right now. Thanks to having a little bit of natural curl, it hangs in perfect coils against my back. My eyes aren't bad either, the blue seems to deter you away from the bags that are now covered with concealer. The rest though . . . ugh. Lines that weren't there weeks ago are now forming, my skin sags a little, and I look tired. Fuck getting old. It sucks.

Honestly, I'll deal with the wrinkles and sagging boobs if I could sneeze without peeing myself. It's ridiculous that I worry so much about coughing, laughing, or anything scaring me because I don't want to wear Depends yet.

"Mrs. Bergen, your ten o'clock interview is here," the receptionist says.

"Send her in, Staci," I instruct.

I had one interview earlier today that will not be getting a call back. I don't know that she could find her way out of a paper bag let alone be my right hand.

When the door opens, I take a step back.

There stands a tall man with dark hair, green eyes, and lashes that any woman would die for. He wears an expensive suit that cuts his body perfectly. His eyes roam my body and I feel naked even though I'm fully dressed.

This is not the new college graduate who is here for an interview.

I clear my throat. "Can I help you?"

"You sure can," his British accent fills the air. My eyes narrow as he steps forward. "You can get out of my office, sweetheart."

"Excuse me?"

"You're in my chair."

Staci looks to me and then shrinks out. "Call security, Staci," I call to her. "I'm sorry, sir, but I'm going to have to ask you to leave."

The man sits in the seat, throwing his leg across his other. "I'm not going anywhere, but you're welcome to call the owner. Tell the daft prick I'm here for my job."

And then it hits me. The eyes are the same color as Callum's. Only he has beautiful, thick dark hair but then the accent . . . I know exactly who this is and why he's here.

Milo Huxley has come for his job—well, my job.

four

. . .

Milo

"YOUR JOB?" she asks, her blue eyes wide.

"I asked to see the Senior Vice President of Acquisitions and Logistics." I look back at the door for her name, but it's missing.

"Well, yes because that's not *your* job since they brought you to see me." she crosses her arms over her ample chest.

I drop my leg and smirk at her. She doesn't seem the least bit bothered by me being here or confused as to who I am. "You know who I am?"

"Yes, Callum spoke of his brother and how he wasn't returning to his position."

I stand, extending my hand. "Milo Huxley, and you are?"

"Danielle Bergen, Senior Vice President of Acquisitions and Logistics."

Cheeky.

She places her hand in mine with a firm handshake. "Well, Danielle, I'll be sure to tell my wanker of a brother he can relieve you of your duty."

"Why don't we call him together?" she suggests.

I like her boldness. A woman who is assertive in the board room is sexy as hell. What's not hot is her ring. Married women are my hard limit. I've done that once and I'd rather not repeat my mistakes. Nothing says good morning like a man with a shotgun.

"Sure thing, sweetheart, let's call Callum and get this mess sorted."

He's clearly going to pick his own flesh and blood over some American. Cal is pragmatic at best. Besides, our Mum will intervene. No one messes with her precious baby, not even my brother. Well, half-brother, but I don't hold it against him that his father was a douche.

I let her lead the way, staring at her arse as she walks in front. Danielle is exactly the kind of woman I'm attracted to. Long legs, light brown hair, deep soulful eyes. I'm a dickhead, but not one that would take another man's wife knowingly. If I was ever stupid enough to marry, I would kill the bastard who touched what was mine. But that doesn't stop me from enjoying the view.

We walk in silence, but I can feel the tension rolling off of her.

"Have you been working in my job for long?" I ask as we make our way through the corridor.

She tries to mask her emotions, but fails miserably. "Long enough."

"Really?" I smile letting her know I don't believe the lie.

She stops. "Listen, I worked hard for this position and I'm not going to let you come in here and take it away from me. Just a fair warning. I don't care who you are, this is *my* job."

I like her. I admire a woman who will fight in business. It's sexy as fuck.

"Noted."

I extend my arm, inviting her to go ahead and knock on the door.

"Yes?" Callum's voice calls through the door.

My brother has no idea I'm here. I figured it would be much more fun to spring it on him. We haven't spoken since he tucked his cock between his legs and ran to America to marry his wife. I sadly missed their wedding while I was with . . . what's her name?

Sally? Samantha? No, Sandra. I was with Sandra in Italy, which I'm sure he'll give me hell for. My mum already gave me an earful too.

The door opens and I wish I was filming this. His face is priceless.

"Hello, brother." I grin as I step forward.

"What are you doing here, Milo?" he asks.

"Well, it seems you gave my job to this beautiful creature here, and I've come to save your arse."

Callum is a shrewd businessman, no doubt, but he has no vision when it comes to property. The reason he did well with his investments in England was because of how I approached each acquisition. I saw what could be and ensured that it became that. No matter what he thinks of me personally, there's no way he can deny that I was good at my job.

Until I lost my head and told him to fuck off.

"Save me?" he laughs. "Do I look like I'm struggling?"

His accent sure seems to be. "Well, I see you're returning to your American roots." I smirk, knowing it'll piss him off.

He gets to his feet. "Would you excuse us, Danielle?"

She studies him for a moment and then her eyes meet mine. I wink, because I'm an arrogant man, and I catch the narrowing of her eyes.

"Of course. I'll be in my office."

Not for long sweetheart.

She leaves and the air in the room thickens. My brother and I have always had a tricky relationship. He's nearly six years older than I am, and hated that Mum loved me more. Even if that wasn't the case. My mother was harder on me, always comparing me to her precious Callum. Reminding me that I was the fuck-up son, even if looking at Callum was difficult for her at times.

Callum's father was American and they met when she was on holiday in Florida. Their relationship was brief, but ended up with her pregnant. He sent a check monthly as payment for her pain.

My dad came around when Cal was no more than two, raised him like his own, and Callum took his name when they married.

But Callum has always hated me for being a real Huxley.

I've also done my part to further wedge the knife.

"So, you can fire her now or she can be my assistant if you'd rather," I suggest, plopping on the couch in his office. "Either one is acceptable."

"Can I now?"

"I'm sure she's done a fine job, but let's be honest . . . I'm your brother."

"Yes," Callum agrees as he comes around his desk. "You are. My selfish, irresponsible, worthless brother who continues to act like everyone in this world owes him something."

I shake my head. "Do I have my job back or not?"

Callum sits, his chin resting on his hand. "Not."

I rocket upright. "Excuse me?"

"You heard me."

"I came to America for you!"

He laughs. "We've been here almost two years, Milo. You quit a year ago when I said I was going to move here permanently. If I recall correctly, you told me to." He looks off like he's trying to remember. "Oh, yes, rot in my stupid fucking company with my stupid fucking wife."

I don't recall that, but I don't deny it either. "I was drunk."

"You're always drunk."

I roll my eyes. "I worked hard for you. I built this company with my blood, sweat, and tears, and then you run off to another country without so much as a, hey, Milo, I want you to run the London office and I'll run the American one. No, instead, you give it to our numpty cousin Edward! Let's keep the facts straight on why that happened."

He decided, not me.

"If that's how you remember it, you're wrong. You disappeared, like you always do, for whatever model you're chasing, leaving *this company* to deal with your absence! Regardless, you don't get to march back here now and demand your job back."

"You can't tell me she's doing a better job than I would do."

Callum huffs like the prick he is. "She's doing more than you ever did. She shows up, for one."

"I always showed up," I say. "When it was actually important!"

He laughs. "Where were you for my wedding? Or have you met your nephew? Hell, do you even know my wife's name?"

I try to recall. Is it Natalie? Nancy? No, that's not it. I'm not good with names.

"Nicole!" I shout as though I just won a game show question.

He doesn't look impressed. "You took off. I replaced you."

"Just like your father, I see." As soon as the words leave my mouth, I wish I could put them back in. Callum doesn't need to say anything because his eyes show his hurt. "Fuck, Cal, I'm sorry. That was out of line. I'm . . . a twat."

I realize that my happiness has come at a cost for him, but I'm ready now. I *need* my job back. Being rude to my brother probably isn't the best idea.

"Yeah, you are," he agrees. "Where have you been the last year?"

"I've been living."

I refuse to show my weakness to anyone, let alone him. I never do. My life has been vastly different than my brother's. When Callum had doors open to him, they closed for me because I didn't have to work hard enough for things. My mum forced Callum to become a man, where I was sheltered because she was afraid to "lose me too". I wanted to live. I had dreams of being on my own, but Mummy had other ideas. Instead of letting me live, I was forced into a cage. My brother may have looked at me like a spoiled, bratty, and entitled prick, but I was secretly jealous of him.

He shakes his head. "Well I've been running a business. I've been raising a family. I've been behaving like a fucking grown up, where you are. . . the same as always."

That one stings a little.

"I'm here now. I'm asking you to give me another chance."

Callum starts to pace the room. "I can't do this again, Milo."

"Do what?"

"This!" He yells with his hands raised in the air. "Where I bail you out time and time again. It's always the same story, just a different setting. I'm not going to fire Danielle because you decided you finally wanted to come get your job back. If it was that important to you, you would've come with me from the start. Instead, you ran off, like you always do, and left me in a bind."

If everything was as simple as Callum believed it was, we would have no problems in the world. He doesn't see what it cost me, for him to leave. We lost our father when I was sixteen. Callum was more than just a brother to me, and it was so easy for him to leave London, for a fucking girl.

"So, you're going to just toss me out? Homeless, without a job, in another country?"

"You want a job?"

"Are you daft? Of course I want my job."

He eyes me carefully. "In the acquisitions department?"

He really is slow. "Are you toying with me?"

"No, not at all." Callum moves toward me, and I suddenly feel like I'm being set up. "You're reinstated, Milo," he claps me on the shoulder. "You're going to be Danielle's assistant."

five

. . .

Danielle

"MY ASSISTANT?" I ask.

"I know it's not ideal, but I give him three days—tops. He'll never last. My brother is . . . well, Milo."

Great, so basically, I've adopted a grown man-child. *Ugh*. This is not how I planned to start my new career at Dovetail. I wanted to prove myself, not babysit the owner's brother.

Not to mention that I clearly suck at parenting, if we take my daughter into account.

"Callum, I'm not sure this is going to be a good idea," I say with a sigh.

"This isn't to punish you, if that's what you think."

"No," I say quickly. "I don't, I just . . ."

"I hoped you'd rise to the challenge." He smiles.

My eyes meet his and I straighten in my chair. I know what he's doing, and unfortunately, it's working. I don't back down. I tackle things head on, especially in business. My life might be in the shitter, but here, I can command what I want.

"I can, but this isn't really a challenge, this is personal," I clarify.

He nods. "It is, but I'm offering you a chance to put my spoiled brother in his place. To make him your bitch." He grins.

"You want me to make his life hell?" I ask.

"As much as you can."

Well, that I can do, but it still feels . . . wrong.

"He's your brother, though."

My sister is the world's biggest pain in the ass, but she's my sister. It's true what they say about siblings—I can pick on them but no one else better.

"Yes, but he's always been in charge. It'll be good for him to see what ground level work is."

I can't actually say no. The reality is that Callum is my boss, and I just got this position. Do I like being in the middle of some family feud? Nope, but I like money. I like working, and promotions, and the company car, and access to the vacation homes that the company owns. So, I'm going to suck this up, and do my best to get Milo to quit so I can get a real assistant.

"Okay, if you really want me to do this, you're the boss."

Callum nods as I get to my feet. "Thank you."

"No problem."

What I really want to say is: I hate this.

I walk down the hall, praying that Milo already quit, but no such luck. He's sitting there in my office with a notepad.

Great.

He continues sitting and I take a minute to compose myself. If even half the stories about Milo are true, I'm in deep shit. He's the male version of Nicole, but she controls herself when it comes to work. According to some of the office fodder, he does not.

"Okay, so you're my new assistant it seems," I say from behind my desk.

"That I am, even though I did your job for . . . oh, seven years." He gives a fake smile. "But my brother has once again underestimated me. I wouldn't suggest you do the same, sweetheart."

"Danielle or Mrs. Bergen."

"Come again?"

"Don't call me sweetheart. I'm your boss," I say. If I don't put my foot down and squash this now, it'll get worse. I need an assistant, and if that's his job title, he's going to start acting the part.

"Oh." He gives a mischievous smile. "I see, you're the boss and I'm the employee. I like it."

I would like if his voice didn't make me want to sigh and ask him to say other things so I can hear him talk.

Why is an accent like catnip to women?

I shake the thought from my head. "Yes, so, I'd like to have you start working on a few projects we have coming up."

"You're serious?" Milo asks.

"Why wouldn't I be?"

"You're going to have me do menial tasks?"

"As opposed to . . ."

He bursts out laughing and slaps his leg. "Okay, I get it. Lesson learned. I'll be a good boy from now on."

I have no idea what the hell he's talking about. "Since Dovetail is now a US based company, you'll need to fill out a bunch of forms and go down to personnel. I'll have some things on your desk for when you get back."

Milo's face falls when he realizes I'm not kidding. However, he gets to his feet and heads to the door.

"Milo," I call his attention.

His eyes meet mine and I can feel the anger roll off him. Instead of backing off, I further assert myself as the alpha in our new relationship. "Be sure to close the door on your way out. I have a lot of work to do."

"This is going to be fun for both of us." He grins and heads out the door, closing it behind him.

After a second, I release a heavy breath and close my eyes. "Yeah, loads of fun."

I pour a glass of wine, chug it, and refill it again. After the day I had, I should grab a straw and drink from the bottle, but I'll keep it classy for now.

It's now nine. Parker is asleep, and Ava is giving me the silent treatment, which is like a gift from God. I'd rather have peace and quiet than her yelling right now.

I turn the television on and shove another piece of pizza in my mouth. Calories don't count on days like this. Tomorrow, I'll spend an hour at the gym to make up for my meltdown today.

I'm flipping through the channels when someone knocks on my door.

What in the hell?

I open the door and see Richard Schilling, Peter's partner at the firm standing before me.

"Danielle." He smiles.

"Richard, is everything okay?" I ask, looking at what I'm wearing, wishing I didn't look like a hot mess.

"Yes, sorry I didn't call first, but I saw the lights on and thought this would be better in person."

I haven't seen Richard in months. When my husband was killed, I found that everyone wanted to help. They'd come by with food, mow the yard, fix the shutter that fell, or offer to take Parker to Cub Scouts because . . . I lost that person. Then, they gradually stopped calling or coming over. Their lives had gone on with their own families, and we'd been forgotten.

I get it.

I don't begrudge them, because when our neighbor passed away, it was the same thing. I would bring casseroles, sew a costume, or anything to help, but it became an afterthought as time passed.

"Yeah, of course," I say pulling the door open. "Come in."

He enters, and I can imagine his thoughts about the house. It's a mess, but I don't give a shit. I'm a mess. My kids are a mess. It's only fitting the house be in disarray as well. I'm doing the best I can and fuck anyone who judges me.

"Would you like something to drink?" I ask.

"No, no, thank you. How are you doing?"

I shrug. "I'm making it work."

A few months ago, I decided to stop telling everyone what they wanted to hear about how we're doing. The truth is ugly, but it's real. No one is doing great after they lose their husband like I did. Yes, you find a "new normal" but there's a void that will never be filled. That's reality, and I don't give a shit if it makes me look weak. I'm holding my family together with tape and chewing gum right now.

"Lisa sends her best," he tacks on.

"Tell her we said hello as well."

I've known Richard a long time. He's a ruthless lawyer who always had big plans for his life. With Peter by his side, they were an unstoppable team. Right now, he looks like he'd rather be in court trying to defend a killer than here. He shifts his weight back and forth while gripping his neck.

"Richard," I say after a few moments of awkward silence. "What's going on?"

He looks at me and I see him slip into lawyer mode. As sad as it sounds, I've missed that face. Peter would do the same, and it's been a while since I've seen it.

"We got the trial date set."

"Oh," I say, taken back a bit. It was postponed twice and I pushed it so far to the back of my mind, I almost forgot. "When?"

"In two weeks."

"Soon," I note.

My chest is tight when I think about all of this being brought back to the front. The trial is supposed to be a form of closure, but I'm going to have to fight through pain to get there.

"We've petitioned the court to be released from his defense, but then he contested."

My head jerks back. "What? You mean you're going to defend the man who killed Peter?"

Richard walks toward the couch and taps the wood table. "The judge will side with us considering the circumstances."

"I don't understand," I say quickly. "How the hell is this even possible?" My voice is on the edge of frantic. None of this makes any sense.

"Peter's killer was my client, not his. He was on retainer and Peter was helping out when I was already tied up in another trial. So, there's a lot of legal crap, but we have to petition the court to be released from being his attorney."

I release a heavy breath and tears fill my vision. "But that could get denied, right?"

"Well— yes, but it won't, Danni."

How does he know that? "Why would he even want you to be his attorney? That seems so stupid."

"It is," Richard says. "Which is why we're not worried about it. The issue is that whatever he said is bound by attorney-client privilege. I can't . . . tell you more . . . but there's a reason he wants me to stay on. It could jeopardize his case and if he keeps me on, I can't testify."

"So, I could have to go to that courtroom and see you sitting next to the man who shot and killed my husband, your partner and best friend, in cold blood?"

"Danielle," he touches my arm. "No judge will do this. They won't . . . we . . . we're doing what we can to make sure it doesn't happen."

I start to move around, needing to work off some of my excess feelings. This can't be real. If this is even a possibility, I'll never be able to handle it. If Richard didn't think there was some real chance, he'd never tell me. A heavy sense of betrayal fills me.

"This! This is why he's dead! Because you help *criminals*. People who are murderers, rapists, pedophiles and God only knows what because," I put my fingers up and air quote, "this is where the money is."

"I'm not trying to upset you, I just wanted to give you all the info."

This is unreal. "So what happens if the judge makes you do it?"

"That's highly unlikely," he says as soon as I finish.

"But it's *possible*, isn't it?"

"Sure, it's possible, but not probable. Please, calm down."

"Then why tell me?" I toss back.

He runs his hand through his hair. "Because if it does happen, I don't want you blindsided."

I can't even imagine what would happen if that had been the case. I try to calm myself, but my imagination runs wild. I envision Richard sitting beside my husband's murderer, finding a way to get him off on some bullshit technicality, because he's that good. It would be horrible to see someone, my daughter's godfather, defend her father's killer.

"If this happens . . ."

"It won't," Richard tries to reassure me. "Right now, we need to go before the judge because the client is appealing. Like I said, I know things that I'm sure my client wants protected."

"Murderer," I correct.

Richard looks at me with confusion.

"When you call someone a client, or the suspect, you humanize him. He's not a human to me. He's a monster. We're not just guessing this guy did it, Richard. He walked into your law firm, saw my husband at his desk, shot him, and walked out. It was on camera. We saw his face. He's not a client, he's a murderer. Calling him anything less than that is an insult to me, my husband, and our children."

I'm not a heartless person. I've tried my entire life to see the good in others and be forgiving. There are some things that no one can forgive.

"I'm sorry, Danni, I really am. This is . . . murky water for the firm."

Once again, I'm reminded of the things I hated about Peter's job. In my world, there's a right and wrong. Those who do wrong should be punished, but Peter's job was to take the facts and create illusions and holes in the case.

I can't even count how many times he and Heather went to war at a dinner or cookout.

"I guess for you it is." I rub my forehead. "I'm not sure what to say at this point."

"I promise, none of us want to defend him. No one in my office is willing to fight for him, but we're not the ones who get to make the call. If the judge believes we run the risk of a mistrial in his other case, we could be forced to stay on as his council, I just don't think we hit that point where that's possible."

I know he feels it won't happen, and I can only hope a judge has mercy, but I've seen stranger shit happen in court.

We don't know what the outcome will be, but the trial will happen soon, that much is true. I'll have to face him again, hear details, and find a way through a new round of grief. As if this last one hasn't been brutal enough.

six

Danielle

"SO, IS HE HOT IN PERSON?" Kristin asks as our kids play in backyard.

"Is who hot?"

She rolls her eyes. "Umm, your new assistant."

"Why are you asking me this?"

"Because you're avoiding talking about it." She looks at me over her wine glass.

"I am not."

Okay, I am a little, because there's nothing to say. He's Callum's brother, my assistant, and . . . I'm in mourning. Guys aren't hot to me right now.

The only thing I find *hot* right now is a bubble bath with wine and candles where no children pop their heads in to ask if they can have milk. Or a night without Ava and Parker fighting, that would be hot as hell. But my assistant?

Sure, he's good looking, has thick arms, and a voice that's silky and smooth, but he's not hot. He's a guy. One that I've heard is a player with entitlement issues. No thank you, I already have a sixteen-year-old.

"If you're not avoiding it, then spill. Is he hot or not?"

I huff. Lying to Kristin is foreign to me. I don't know that I've ever felt like I needed to, but I don't want to talk about this. "Can we change the subject? The way he looks is irrelevant."

"After you tell me if he's hot." She raises her brows in a challenge.

"What does it matter? He's Nicole's brother-in-law, my employee, and was a pain in the ass for the whole two hours I dealt with him."

Kristin puts her wine glass down and leans forward. "Not the question I asked, Danni. I asked if he was good looking, which by the way your cheeks have turned bright red, the answer is yes."

"You're a dick."

She leans back with a smirk. "You just hate that I'm right. I've seen pictures, we all know he's freaking ridiculously sexy."

Kristin is my person. She's the one who I would bury a body for, not that I wouldn't for Nicole and Heather, but Kristin gets me on a whole other level. We were pregnant at the same time, we were each other's maid of honor because my sister is a complete ass, and we know pretty much everything about one another.

There's nothing in this world I wouldn't do for her.

However, right now I'd like to slap her.

She takes a drink and stares at me. When I don't answer, she continues on. "So much so that I'm shocked Nicole didn't swindle Callum into some three-way with Milo. Could you imagine her with the two of them?"

"Oh my God!" I groan, trying to cover my ears. "Please stop talking. Callum is my boss and Milo is my . . . assistant . . . until he quits. I don't need visions of them in bed with Nicole."

Kristin giggles. "Fine, fine, so tell me about him."

I have no idea why she's pushing me. "Is Noah coming home soon?"

"Why?" she asks.

Her boyfriend is doing reshoots this week for the movie he just finished. He's been very in demand since his last movie won a ton of awards. It's great to see him happy and able to be more selective about what roles he takes. Noah is truly a wonderful man. He takes care of Kristin in a way she's never had before. Her ex-husband is the shit on my shoes, but Noah showed a love worthy of her.

He also distracts her from meddling in my life.

"Just asking when you'll be too busy to care about dumb crap again and focus on what matters."

"You're not dumb."

"I didn't say I was dumb," I correct.

Kristin touches my hand. "As much as you think this is about Milo and his hotness, it's not."

I look at her with confusion.

She sighs and continues. "This is about you getting back out in the world. Seeing things again without tunnel vision."

Here we go.

"I am out in the world, Kris. I needed money, so I got a job. A good one too. I have my family, friends, and I don't sit around crying. Am I sad? Yes, I'm sad. I miss him, but I'm out there living, doing everything I can."

"I'm not judging you. I'm just saying that talking about your feelings goes a long way."

I appreciate where she's going with this. I really do, but talking about my hot British assistant doesn't check any mourning boxes in my world. It's inviting problems where I definitely don't need them.

My husband could be an asshole, but he was a good man. He loved me and the kids, provided for us, and while we almost ended our marriage, it wasn't like Peter was abusive. He didn't cheat. He loved his job and didn't know how to balance it with life.

I place my hand over hers. "I know in your ever-romantic heart you're somehow trying to push me to think about a man again, but I'm not there yet."

"I'm just saying open your heart a little."

"Like you did with Noah?" I remind her.

Kristin fought that off for a long time. She had walls that were forged in steel, Noah had the fortitude to keep pushing until he broke through.

"And who was it that told me I should let myself feel again? Who said I deserved to be happy even if I wasn't even divorced yet?" she asks.

"It's different."

Kristin gives a small smile. "Yes, it is, and yet it's not. I'll stop now," she promises. "But promise me that you won't close yourself off to anything. Not Milo, because from the stories we've heard, he's a freaking idiot, but. . . don't say never to another man."

I'm not closed off, I just have no desire to feel for a man right now. I have this anger that sits inside of me, wanting to know *why*, though I may never know the answer.

Of all my friends, Kristin understands more than the others. She saw me when I was on the ground, unable to stand. She heard me scream, cry, throw things, and then gathered me in her arms and held me.

I wasn't a good mother those days. I know this, and I've pushed myself to atone for it. Hell, I still am.

"I need to focus on Ava and Parker," I remind her. "I wasn't exactly mother of the year after Peter's death."

"Stop it. You were doing everything you could to survive."

"I wasn't there for them when they needed me." I think about how I should've done more, but I couldn't see past my grief. I let my mother and friends be there as I wallowed in my pain. The guilt still eats at me.

"Mommy!" Parker runs over. I turn my head and wipe the tear that was falling. "Aubrey told me we were getting married! Is that true?"

Kristin and I burst out laughing. "You're way too young to get married," I tell him.

Aubrey comes over with her hands on her hips. "Parker, we *have* to get married!"

"I don't want to," he tells her.

"Aubrey," Kristin slips into her motherly voice. "You need to stop this. You've told four boys this week the same thing."

Aubrey shakes her head. "Because *Margaret*," she sneers. "Took the other boys, so I'm taking the ones that are left."

"You only get one, honey," I tell her. "You can't collect them."

"Oh." Her face falls. "Then I want Noah."

Kristin has her hands full with that one.

We both giggle a little and I sit back, ready to watch Kristin explain. As funny as it is, at least the girl didn't pick her father. Scott is the last man I'd hope Aubrey would try to find in her life.

Kristin looks to me for help, but I raise my hands. "Why don't we have lunch?" she changes gear. "Chicken nuggets and ice cream?"

"Yay!" Both kids yell and I laugh. Leave it to Kristin to feed the kids chicken nuggets and ice cream at eleven in the morning to avoid a conversation with her daughter.

"Well, that's one way to handle it," I smile as the kids run inside.

"You have no idea what else I would've offered if it got her off the subject," she says.

We spend the next hour getting the kids settled, and then Nicole and Heather arrive. Colin was down for his morning nap and Heather worked the night shift, so they couldn't come for our impromptu barbeque.

Normally, we'd have our traditional one in a few months where I hosted it and all the families were here for hours. It was Peter's favorite thing to do.

Last year there was no way I could do it. My heart wasn't there, but my best friends came over anyway.

This year, I still refused and they decided we'd make it for us women on a different month and start a new tradition. So, this is our first cookout without husbands. It's a time where we can drink, enjoy each other, and catch up. Even though we all live in Tampa, since they're all either married or in serious relationships, we don't see each other like we did before.

Heather and Eli travel so much between his career and the music tour. They're also still in that newlywed type stage where they can't get enough of each other. Kristin and Noah aren't married, but live together in the house they bought, and he's bouncing between Hollywood and Tampa, so when he's here, Kristin doesn't exist. Nicole . . . forget it, she's a new mother and wife who's still running her business empire. It's a shock any of us see her.

"Where's the booze?" Nicole calls out from the backyard.

"I'll grab the sangria!" Heather replies.

Ava has little kid duty. Since she's grounded, this is part of her punishment. She sits in the yard with her ridiculously large sunglasses on as the kids run around her. I hope she hates every moment of this.

"I'm so glad Colin is off the tit," Nicole blurts out.

"That's a conversation starter I never thought I'd hear," Heather says before tipping her glass back.

"What? I can drink again, eat what I want and not worry about him having gas or shitting because broccoli is also a laxative to babies. I'm just saying it's nice to have my boobs be for play again and not food."

My friends are fucking wackos.

"Are they super sensitive?" Kristin encourages.

"Yes!" Nicole smiles. "Like, orgasm from barely touching them. Callum is totally enjoying it."

"Another image of my boss I wish I never had," I grumble.

There are no boundaries with the four of us, and never were. I'm the baby of the bunch and they taught me everything I needed to know about puberty. Nicole has always been a nutjob and never had a problem telling—or showing—all her new bits.

"Oh, please, he rode me so hard last night that I saw stars." She waggles her brows. "Like, hot, sweaty, dirty fucking that left my legs like jelly."

"I'm so happy for you," I toss back.

Nicole leans back, takes a drink, and continues on as though I didn't say a word. "I think Callum was working *extra* hard since he was so pissed that Milo is back. He kept walking around the apartment going on and on about his arsehole brother. I hear he's actually your new assistant?"

"Yeah, I swear, my relationships sometimes feel like I'm a psychological experiment you're all studying to see how long someone has before they snap."

She laughs. "Don't worry, Danni, we have a pool going that it's by the end of the week."

"That he quits?"

Nicole smirks. "Or you kill him."

Wonderful.

"God forbid you be helpful and tell me what you know about him so I can actually do my job and not suck." I raise my brow.

"I don't know much," she admits. "Callum bitches about him and how hard he had it in comparison to Milo. Callum was always bouncing between the states and London, never really enjoying his childhood thanks to his parent's custody agreement. Milo was a pampered, spoiled rich kid. I've met him once before now, and I like him, but . . . what do I know?"

"Nothing," Heather answers and laughs. "Sorry, it was too easy."

"Bitch."

I roll my eyes as they start to bicker. This is who we are and always will be. We're the friends that can call each other names, tell it like it is, and still love one another. I never have to worry that they'll think less of me because it's impossible. There comes a point in time when my best friends became my family. My sister Amy wasn't here every other day to check on me, they were.

They set up a schedule, cooked, cleaned, and made sure my kids were fed.

My mother came a few times, but it was Heather, Kristin, and Nicole who kept my life from completely crumbling.

Kristin slaps them both. "Do I need to separate you two?"

"No, Mom." Heather pretends to look ashamed.

"Well, Monday will be the test," I muse. I hoped that this would be a new start to my new life. With a promotion, new ideas, and a chance to establish myself as a businesswoman, I finally had a goal. Now, I'm not so sure.

Nicole scoffs. "Please, you'll do fine."

The other two nod their heads in agreement. "Seriously, you raised toddlers. There's no way Milo can be worse."

I look at my daughter who was a dream as a child. Now, not so much. "Yeah, it can always be worse. They become teenagers."

seven

. . .

Danielle

"CAN you contact the surveyor and see if he's done yet?" I ask Milo.

"Of course, Mrs. Bergen. Anything else you need at the moment?" his voice is a tiny bit higher as he tries to sound helpful.

"That's all," I say without looking up.

It's been three days.

Three days and he's no closer to quitting than the day he started.

The worst part is I can't even complain. He's doing everything I ask, with a smile, and actually has been helpful. Since he literally did my job, he knows things I don't. At one point he caught something I overlooked, and instead of being a dick like I would've expected, he pointed it out.

He's up to something. I can feel it in my bones. He's building a false trust and I'm not buying it.

I lean back in my chair and look out the window. "What game are you playing?" I ask aloud.

He and Callum aren't speaking. They barely acknowledge each other, and the tension is thick. Yet when Callum sees me, he's all smiles. Clearly there's no love lost between those two.

No matter what's going on between the brothers, Milo hasn't wasted any time making friends in the office. He's flirtatious, smart mouthed, and egotistical. Yet I can't seem to get Staci to stay at her desk for more than thirty minutes without coming to "check" on him. She said it's her job to make sure everyone feels comfortable in the office.

I have a feeling I'll be interviewing for a new receptionist once he leaves.

My email dings and I spin back around, needing to focus on what I can control—my job.

The email, though, is from Nicole with the subject line: Favor?

This can't be good.

I open it up and sure enough, I was right.

D-

I need you to make sure Callum isn't late tonight. My mother is keeping Colin overnight and I plan to have some really kinky sex. You know, think sex swing, lube, and props. Maybe a good spanking, too.

Hope that made you uncomfortable.

Love,
    N

For her birthday, I'm buying her three visits to a therapist.

Milo knocks a moment later and then enters. I try to cover the blush that must be on my face because I can feel the heat. Nicole is always good for making me feel mortified.

"You all right?" he asks.

Yup. Just trying to shove the mental image of Nicole and Callum out of my head.

"I'm fine. What's up?"

He shifts his weight. "You received another call."

"Yes?"

"A Richard Schilling called, wanted to let you know that," Milo looks at the paper. "The trial will begin tomorrow." His brow raises.

"I hoped this wouldn't happen," I mutter aloud.

I'm not ready for this. I don't want to sit in that courtroom, but I don't think I can stay away either. A part of me needs to hear it all, be involved so I have some answers. I remember Peter telling me that a trial is like a show, to believe none of what you hear and only half of what you see.

This is going to be the ultimate shitshow.

"Have you gotten yourself in a bit of a jam?" Milo asks leaning against the doorjamb.

"What?" I jerk my head back.

"I just love a bit of a bad girl." He winks. "You were hoping it wouldn't happen so it must be something good—or bad. Especially since you have to go to trial. Tsk tsk."

I tilt my head. "I bet you do," I taunt him back. "I'm a really *bad* girl. I'm worried I might actually end up completely broken by the end of this."

Milo moves closer as though I'm giving him some juicy gossip. He sits, puts his head on his chin. "Do tell," he smirks.

I lean in, playing it up since he has no clue what I'm about to hit him with. I drop my voice real low and keep my face void of emotion. "Do you promise not to judge me?"

"Sweetheart, I would never."

I let his term of endearment go this time. "A few months ago, something happened."

"Yes?"

"It was . . ." I look away as though I'm embarrassed.

From the corner of my eye, I catch the grin that spreads across his face. Dumbass thinks he's got me where he wants me. "Does my brother know?" I nod. "Then it can't be that bad or he would've terminated your employment."

This is the most fun I've had in a long time. I turn my head back to him. "He couldn't fire me for this. It wouldn't be good for Callum if he did."

His eyes go wide. "Does it involve my brother? Did he break the law as well?"

"No," I whisper.

"You're stalling. It must be downright scandalous. Did they use the cuffs on you?"

"I wasn't involved like that . . ."

Milo scoots forward. "Then out with it, what naughty thing have you done, Danielle?"

I let out a heavy sigh and look to the ceiling. "You have it all wrong," I tell him.

"Let Milo know your dirty little secret," he urges.

What a tool.

"Fine," I sigh. "It's a trial for the man who killed my husband sixteen months ago."

Milo's face falls and I watch the emotions roll through his deep green eyes. "Excuse me?"

I lean back in my chair and continue to swirl the pen, needing some sort of anchor. "Get back to work, Milo."

"No, you said your husband was killed?"

"Yes, now get back to work."

"When?" he asks.

"A while ago, out!" I point to the door.

"You were toying with me?" he asks with a mix of awe and indignation.

"I sure was, and you were eating it up. I swear, I'm not going to ask you again," I warn.

He gets to his feet but doesn't leave. I have the worst assistant in the world. "You made me think it was you who were on trial!"

I wish it was me because my husband would be alive.

Loss isn't something I truly understood before his death. I thought the people who were sad for years after a tragedy should get on with their life and heal by moving on. I judged those who would say the things I now felt because I couldn't grasp the amount of pain they were in. To want to die because you lost someone was once insane to me, but when I was in that sea of despair, I got it. I felt the hurt in my bones and I would've given anything to make it stop.

"No one said that. You assumed it and I was playing along."

Milo shakes his head with a grin. "Bravo. You were quite believable. You said the trial is for a man who killed your husband?"

No such luck on him overlooking that bit of news. "Yes," I say, feeling the dread of the million questions that will follow.

"I'm sorry," Milo says. "My father was killed. Did you know that?"

"No," I say softly. Callum may be part of our little crazy family, but I don't know much about him. He and Nicole were a whirl-wind. We met him, spent very little time with him, mostly because she kept him a secret, and then they were married. It was crazy, but when it comes to Nicole, we expect it.

Even working at Dovetail for over a year now, I still don't know *him*. I know what he's like as a businessman, and I respect him. But personally, I have no clue about his family or past.

Milo's face morphs to anger. "I was sixteen and he was in a car accident where the other driver was absolutely pissed. That cow walked away without a scratch and I lost my father."

Now it's my turn to apologize. "I'm sorry, Milo."

He shakes his head. "It's life. We don't get to decide, do we? We make the best of it."

"I guess you're right."

"Of course I am," he laughs. "I'm wrong, but so very right."

And back to the Milo I expect.

I roll my eyes. "Go back to work. I think there's some filing to be done."

Instead of huffing, like I would do if I was a senior executive at this company before and someone told me to file, he snaps tall and gives me a salute. "Yes, Ma'am."

"You know." I place my hand on the desk. "You don't have to continue working here. I can't imagine you're happy."

"And let my brother win?"

"Is that what this is about?"

Milo moves toward the door and stops. "Callum has won everything. Since we were just tots, he always won. He got to come to America for holiday each year. He attended the best schools, was loved by my father as his own, and was Mum's favorite, even if I always tried to convince myself I was. Nothing I did was good enough because Callum always did it better, and did everything he could to show everyone my insignificance. His arrogance disgusts me, and he believes I'm weak. He's wrong. No one should underestimate my strength."

Without another word, Milo walks out the door.

His words bounce around in my head, and my hopes of him quitting are gone. He's not going anywhere, and I'm going to need to up my game.

eight

. . .

Milo

STUBBORNNESS IS a trait I wish I didn't possess, as I'm sure Mum would agree. Trouble finds me because I refuse to give in. There's no quitting in my world. I fight. I conquer. I take no bloody prisoners.

At least until I lose interest.

I could do Danielle's job with my eyes closed. Even without knowing American real estate the way she does. Instead, I'm stuck doing the most ridiculous tasks and waiting for my opportunity to pounce.

I would quit, but that would be exactly what they want.

Instead, I'm driving to Danielle's house because she forgot a file at the office.

A fucking file.

One she probably doesn't even need since she's not working on this deal, but as her assistant, it is my duty to assist.

Idiot brother of mine.

The GPS tells me to stop here and I stare at the home that matches the address she gave me. It's a nice neighbourhood, I guess. Not exactly like the trendy area I'm staying in, but she was married so I can see the appeal.

I grab the file and walk toward the door. The weeds are over-grown in the garden, and the yard is atrocious. I remember then that her husband was killed, and see my Mum for a moment.

Danielle, however, is not my sweet, loving Mum. She's the woman who stole my job.

As I lift my hand to knock on the door, it swings open.

"Well, hello there." The smaller version of Danielle says. "And who might you be?"

She runs her tongue along the bottom of her lip and I swear she's coming onto me. "I'm Milo," I say hesitantly. "You are?"

"I'm Ava." Her eyes roam my body.

"Yes, well, I'm here to drop off something for your mother, I presume?"

I don't know if Danielle has kids or how many. I don't really care to ask. The more I know, the more I'll probably feel bad when I destroy her and take back what's rightfully mine. Or I could not be a fool and get all the information possible in case I can use it later.

Such a tricky situation this is.

"Yup." She grins. "Are you my new daddy?"

"Are you mad?"

"Does that mean crazy about you?"

Jesus. Danielle has her hands full. "No, it means just crazy. Is your mother home?"

She shakes her head. "Nope. It's just us."

Wonderful, I think to myself.

"I love your accent," Ava says stepping forward.

Dear Lord, this girl is positively mad. "Would you give this to her?"

"Want to come in? You can wait here, we could . . . talk."

"Yes, because that sounds like a fab idea," I roll my eyes. "You're quite the little trouble maker, aren't you?"

Ava shrugs, moving closer again while I step back. This is not going well. All I need is her mother to think I'm coming onto her child.

"I have daddy issues," she says.

I jerk back at her comment. What a strange thing to say. Then again, she has lost her father, which would make sense as to why she's acting out.

And then I see it. She's me.

"How old are you, Ava?"

"Sixteen."

Her father died at the same age mine did. I was so angry at the world when I lost him. The cow who drank too much and got behind the wheel. She stole someone I loved and I wanted everyone to pay for it.

It seems Ava is dealing with the same.

Daddy issues indeed.

And Danielle has no idea what else might be in store.

"Well, it was a pleasure meeting you," I say as I take a step back.

"Don't go," she says quickly. "My mother . . . she'll want you to stay. You know how she is. Hates leaving me all by myself. I'm sure she'd be fine with her very good-looking assistant watching me until she gets back."

I'm many things but a fool is not one.

"You're a minor," I remind her. "And while I appreciate the compliment, there's no way I would ever take you up on that. You're a beautiful little girl, but I'm a grown man."

"I'm not a little girl! You don't even know me."

That's where she's wrong. "I know more than you think. You lost your father, and you're trying so hard to figure out how not to feel all your anger. Am I getting warmer?"

She's trying to come up with a retort but falls short. "Whatever."

Despite her attitude, I can see in her eyes that I struck a nerve. "Take it from me, you should be careful who you say things like that to," I tell her. "I may be a gentleman, but another man might not be."

"Thanks for the unwanted advice."

As much as I hate to admit it, I kind of like her. She reminds me so much of myself I can't help but think she's fantastic . . . since I am and all.

"You're quite welcome." I smile as if she actually meant it and wasn't being a sarcastic prick.

A car turns into the drive and Danielle emerges, opens the back door, and helps a younger child out.

She approaches with a disapproving look. "Ava, you know you're not supposed to open the door."

Ava shakes her head, accompanied by an eye roll. "He was hot and I wanted to meet your new boyfriend."

"Boyfriend?" the boy asks.

"He's not my boyfriend," Danielle tells him. "He works for Mommy."

The small boy walks over with his hand extended. "I'm Parker Bergen."

"Milo Huxley," I say as I give him a nice strong shake. "Quite a grip you have there, Parker."

"Dad said a man is measured by his handshake," he tells me.

I smile. "Your dad was right."

I fight back the feelings that start to make their way up around my heart. I will not care that she's a widow with two kids. My job was taken by her, which means she's enemy number one. First rule of war is not to have any empathy for the other side.

"Go inside, Parker. I'm going to talk to Milo for a minute about boring work things."

He nods. "Nice to meet you. I like your accent. It's like Thor's!"

I laugh. "Thor wishes he was as bloody cool as I am. I'm more Loki than Thor anyway."

"So, you're a bad guy?" he asks.

I decide that yes, I'm most definitely the villain that you can't help but love. I tell Parker, "I think Loki is misunderstood and has a do-good brother that makes him crazy, don't you agree?"

Parker purses his lips as he ponders what I said. "I think Loki makes bad choices."

He would be right again, but since I'm drawing parallels to my own sibling's life, I feel the need to defend him. "But if Odin didn't have favorites, Loki wouldn't need to prove his worth."

"Well, maybe if Loki didn't do bad things, he could be the hero," Parker disagrees.

"How old are you?"

He smiles. "Six."

Why am I arguing with a child?

"Talk to me when you're nine."

He laughs.

"All right then, that's enough super hero analysis," Danielle says as she puts her hand on the lad's shoulder.

Parker looks up with sad eyes and then sighs. "Okay, Mom."

"Go on inside now," she reminds him.

"Bye, Milo!"

"Bye, Parker."

"Sorry about him. He's really into superheroes and watches them non-stop, reads the comics, and it's just . . . his whole life. Plus, the kid is a damn genius, so when he finds something, he fixates. Three years ago, it was trains. I swear I knew more about engines and all the different models than I could've ever wanted to know, but Parker loved them. So, he'd spend hours educating me and Peter on all the working parts. It was impressive . . . *annnd* I have no idea why I'm rambling on like this."

Because she's falling apart at the seams. "I'm a superhero buff myself. It was nice to meet another person that can keep up. Even more impressive that he's just a young boy."

"Anyway, thanks for dropping this off," she says. "I appreciate it."

I didn't have much of a choice, did I? "I'm here to make your job easier," I reply.

"Sure you are," she laughs.

"Have I been less than helpful?" I question.

She sighs. "Let's not play games, Milo. You're not happy about being my assistant, just the same as I really didn't want you to be. As you can see, my hands are full, and I would rather us both lay our cards on the table and be real with each other. I don't have the time or inclination to lie to you."

Interesting. Time to test that theory.

"If I asked whether or not you planned to step down, you'd say?"

"Not on your life."

I grin. She's feisty and I like it.

"Understood," I reply.

"I need to get inside," she explains. "Thanks again for dropping off the file."

I dip my head and wait for her to go inside. I am a gentleman after all.

I get in my car, then sit there pondering when to make my next move.

Women like Danielle are my weakness. I love when there are no games or ulterior motives. Honesty is the best policy and all. It's going to be sad when she finds herself as my assistant in a few months, because if she doesn't step down, I'm going to have to take her out.

nine

. . .

Danielle

TODAY IS a day I wish I could ignore. My mind is scattered, I can't focus, and each time I close my eyes, I see Peter's face.

Not the smiling one in the picture that sits on my desk.

Not the man who that morning was laughing and tossing kisses my way.

Instead, I see him as he was at the morgue. Cold, unmoving, and gone.

"Are you hearing a word I'm saying?" Milo asks, snapping his fingers.

"What?"

"Clearly not," he huffs.

"Sorry, I'm . . . my mind is elsewhere."

Like on the trial that I'm supposed to be at in an hour. I'm not technically supposed to be here. Callum instructed me to take the week off and focus on the kids, work from home, but I sat there, staring at the wall, and cried.

I made him promise not to tell Nicole it was starting. I don't want to hear shit from my friends. They have no clue what this feels like. The helplessness that's eating me alive. I don't want to hear the testimony. I don't want to see his face and watch him draw air when Peter isn't.

"Very professional," Milo mutters. "Were we going to work today or would you prefer to stop now?"

Fuck him.

"I'm doing my best!" I snap. "I'm here, which is more than I can say about you the last year or so." I get to my feet, perhaps a bit angrier at him than the situation calls for. "I'm your boss, remember that. You don't get to be an asshole to me!"

Milo stands with his hands out in front of him. "Okay? I was being sarcastic. But since you brought it up, I was trying to piece my damn life together. My brother ripped the company I helped build from my hands, moved across the ocean—for a girl I might add—and didn't bother to consider me at all. So, yes, you're my boss now. How is that for doing your best?"

My heart is racing and I feel as though I'm being ripped in half. All this time I've been holding myself together and right now, I don't think I can anymore. I'm battling wars everywhere and winning none.

This isn't about him. It's about me and how he thinks he can just steamroll over me. It's about how none of this should even *be* my problem.

"So that entitles you to be a dick?" I scream.

"I'm sorry, but I'm failing to see how calling you professional is being a dick."

"Because you didn't mean it!" I continue to yell as Milo stands there with his arms crossed. "You think I'm stupid, huh? Do you think I don't see that you want to destroy me? Well, guess what? I'm already at the bottom so the only way is up."

"Are you on drugs?" Milo asks in his thick accent. "Maybe you should take them if you're not." He laughs. "I have no idea what you're so upset about."

"Everything! You! You being here! My lunatic teenage daughter who is making my life a living hell! And this whole situation—your brother wants to teach you a lesson, and I'm stuck dealing with it." I look in Milo's deep green eyes, furious that this has gone so wrong. "None of this was how it was supposed to go. My life was perfect." I say as my lip begins to tremble. "I should be at home, raising my kids with my *husband!*"

When I say the last word, a sob rips from my chest and I begin to cry.

Although, it's not that silent tear kind of cry. It's the loud, obnoxious, snot streaming kind of cry.

Milo's arms wrap around me and he holds me to his chest. I grip his lapels and clench, losing control.

"I can't!" I shake, but Milo tightens his hold. "I can't go today. I'm not strong enough."

"Today?" he asks.

"The trial," I barely get out before the next round of hysteria breaks free.

Milo guides me to the couch and sits me down, and then presses my head to his chest. I don't think, I take the comfort he offers. I'm too broken to care who is helping. I'm too far out in the sea of grief to swim back to shore.

I lost everything and now I have to feel it all over again.

I want to kill that man myself.

I want his family to know the agony he inflicted on mine.

I want Peter to walk through the door again, but I know that will never, ever happen.

I rub my face against Milo's chest and the scent of his woodsy cologne fills me. Then it hits me. I'm . . . sobbing . . . on Milo.

My assistant who wants my job.

The pain in my ass who's planning to get me kicked out of this office.

"Oh God!" I lift my head, covering my face with my hands. "I'm so sorry."

"Not another word," he commands. "Is your husband's trial today?"

I nod, a new wave of embarrassment hitting me. "Look, I don't know what just happened. I lost it." I wipe under my eyes and release a heavy breath.

"You've been holding that in a while, I presume?"

"I guess so."

Milo nods slowly. "I had the best assistant when we were in London. She was smart, funny, put me in my place on more than one occasion. She was there when my dog died, and she was of great comfort. Anyway, her job was so much more than just assisting me in work."

I look to him, wondering what the hell he's talking about. "Not sure where you're going with this . . ."

"I'm not either," he admits.

"Glad we cleared that up," I say attempting to joke.

Milo doesn't laugh though. "My point is . . . that while I'm stuck in this position, I'm here to help."

"Help?"

"Yes."

I study him warily. "Help how?"

He huffs. "I don't know, but I'm trying to be nice."

And he is being nice. "I appreciate that," I say.

"Are you better now?" Milo's emerald eyes watch me as though I'm a wounded animal. Which, maybe I am. Peter's death had me at extremes. I was either a broken dove who couldn't fly or I was a tiger, ripping people's throats out. I've not found the middle, and it's wearing on me.

"I think I'm going to be." I place my hand on his arm. "Thank you."

"Happy to help."

"You know, you make a great assistant," I tease.

I wait for the indignation and disgust, but instead, he looks at me with a mix of awe and wonder. Something, I don't know what, is different right now. He seems a little kinder, non-threatening, which is a bad thing. It's scary to be honest.

"Why are you here today?" A deep voice breaks the moment.

"Callum," I say, getting to my feet.

He looks at Milo and then me with a wry smile. "You're off for the day, Danielle. I implicitly told you to be with your family. It's where you *need* to be."

"You didn't tell Nicole, right?"

"No, I hoped you would by now." He sighs, placing his hands in his pockets. "I realize this is a bizarre situation, but she loves you and wants to be there for you."

"I know, but I'm not ready."

Callum's eyes fill with empathy. "I understand, just know we're all here to help."

Milo clears his throat. "I hate to break up the party, but someone should do some work in this place."

"Are you implying Danielle doesn't?" Callum challenges him.

I wait, my heart pounding in my chest. Here's a chance for Milo to sell me out or tell him about the screw up I had with the survey. His eyes meet mine and then move back to his brother.

"No," Milo says with conviction. "You found a great replacement for me, brother."

Callum's eyes blink in surprise. "Well, that was very grown up of you."

I see Milo's hand open and close, but he doesn't reply.

Now it's my turn to do for him what he did for me. "You know, Callum, Milo has been a real asset." I turn to look at him with a smile. "He found an error on the survey, fixed it, and it saved the company a bit of money we'd have lost had it gone through."

Callum shakes his head and pushes off the doorframe. "So, he did his job? Great news. I guess there's a first for everything."

I want to defend him, but Milo grips my wrist. "It's fine, he made up his mind about me a long time ago."

"Some patterns are hard to break," Callum rebukes and then walks out the door.

I think back to the conversation he had with Parker about superheroes and brothers.

"Maybe you're more like Thor than you think," I say as he turns.

"Don't paint me as the hero."

"You were a few minutes ago. You could've told Callum everything, made me look stupid. You could've told him I had a freak out where I was sobbing, but you didn't."

"How do you know I wasn't playing the game we've been set up to play?" Milo asks.

I realize I don't, but something in my gut says he's not.

Milo has no reason to be nice to me. He's a rich, arrogant, egomaniac who has lived a life I can only dream of, but only a fool wouldn't see his motives. He's desperate for his brother's affections. The man he looked up to, wanted to be like, but has never been good enough in his eyes.

Just like Thor and Loki.

"I guess we'll find out. But maybe you're not the bad guy, Milo. Maybe you're looking for something."

He leans in close, his eyes trained on mine. "Don't try to see something that's not there. You'll only end up disappointed, just like everyone else. Now, grab your handbag, we have a trial to get to."

ten

. . .

Danielle

"ARE YOU READY?" Milo asks as we sit outside the courthouse.

"No."

Is anyone ever ready to deal with something painful? That question always baffles me. When the doctor would tell the kids that they were getting a shot, he'd ask, "are you ready?" It was a stupid question. Of course they're not ready. They knew it was going to hurt like a bitch.

Just like this will.

However, I'm not four years old. I'm an adult, and I have to take the pain.

"Okay, then," he says as he opens the door. I watch him walk around, opening mine, with his hand out. "Let's go."

And face the man who destroyed my entire world.

Not wanting to seem like more of a hot mess, I place my hand in his, and exit the car.

Thankfully, since our exchange in the office, he's been totally silent. I've been so lost in my thoughts. I sent a text to Richard but got no response. I'm not sure how I'll handle it if the judge didn't recuse him from defense.

Milo keeps his hand on the small of my back as we go through security. As crazy as it is, I'm glad he's here. I don't know him well and that could be the reason why it's comforting. There's no expectations that I need to keep it together or fall apart. I can feel whatever it is I feel and he's still going to show up for work.

My stomach starts to churn as we stand before the doors. "I can't do this," I whisper.

"You can."

"No." I shake my head quickly. "I can't. How do I not scream? Cry? Flip tables over when he walks in? How?"

Milo takes my face in his hands and releases a heavy breath through his nose. "You should do those things."

"What?" I screech and grab his wrists, pulling them off. "What kind of advice is that?"

He shrugs. "It would make the evening news. Maybe you could even go viral," Milo smirks. "Think of the footage. Crazy lady in Tampa climbs over pews to attack the suspect, only to be carried out in cuffs. It would be rather fitting, don't you think?"

"Ass." I can't stop myself from laughing though.

"I bet Ava would love that."

I cover my hand over my mouth to stop the giggling. "Yeah, she'd love her friends posting it and embarrassing her."

"See, two birds with one stone."

"Okay, so I should go in there, make a scene, and become internet famous?" I ask.

Milo taps his finger on his chin. "I would be chuffed. With you in jail, I'm the next logical choice to get my job back."

I roll my eyes with a grin. "Well, anything to make life easier for you."

I release a deep breath and push the door open. My eyes stay down as I make my way to the first row and take a seat. Milo sits beside me, completely casual and unaffected. I, on the other hand, feel like I'm going to crawl out of my skin. I look around, taking a moment to see the room. I've been here a few times, but it's as if I'm seeing it with new eyes.

The light oak wood covers the room with maroon accents. The judge's seat is set high, showing his authority over the proceedings. We're sitting on the right side of the courtroom, so I can sit behind the prosecution.

I don't see anyone from Peter's office and try not to let my worry set in because there's no one yet on the defense side.

A hand touches my shoulder, and I jump. "Mrs. Bergen?"

"Yes."

"I'm Rachel Harlow, the prosecutor on your husband's trial," she smiles. "Sorry to startle you, I wanted to introduce myself."

I look at the woman no older than twenty-nine years old with questions swirling. "I don't understand, where is Joshua? I thought the district attorney was prosecuting."

She does the contrite lawyer look that is a mask to cover her disappointment. Peter invented that look. "He's overseeing it, but considering the facts of the case, we're very confident. There's another associate counsel with me, so please don't worry."

"Not a chance of that, Ms. Harlow. How many murder cases have you tried?" I ask.

Rachel bristles. "This is my first, but I'm well-prepared."

Peter always said no one is prepared for a murder trial. While I appreciate her confidence, it doesn't do anything for my nerves. She could be young, hungry, and ready to make her mark, but I would've preferred it not be my husband's trial.

She's young, and I remember all too well Richard and Peter thinking they were hot shit when they definitely weren't.

"I just was expecting Josh, that's all." I give her a soft smile. "Who is representing the defense?"

I know most of the law firms because they were Peter's competition. He made it a point to watch other trials to see who was good and who sucked. Knowledge fueled his fire, and nothing burned his inferno more than another worthy lawyer.

I say a prayer over and over to not be Schilling, Bergen & Mitchell. I'll walk out, and Milo won't be able to stop me.

"I believe it was changed late last week," she says as she opens her file, scanning the paper.

It doesn't comfort me that she doesn't even know who she's going to be opposing in the trial.

"Danielle," a deep voice says from behind.

"Richard, are you?"

"No," he says immediately. "We're not defending him. I wanted to let you know earlier this week, but I was in trial."

I guess calling me was too much trouble . . .

"Richard," Ms. Harlow says tersely.

"Rachel." No love lost there, it seems. "Are you prepared to win?"

"I'm always prepared."

"Yes, but that doesn't mean you have the best record. I assumed that Joshua would be . . ."

"He's not. I understand you both know Joshua and he has an impressive record, but let me be frank, I'm just as good. I know the ins and outs. I'm well aware of the evidence, witnesses, and all the inner workings of this case. You can be assured that this case is my top priority. I knew Peter as well," she looks at me with kind eyes. "We may not have been on the same team, but he was one of us. I don't take this lightly."

"Thank you," I say while squeezing my hands tight.

The nausea I was battling grows stronger when she walks to her table. I sit here, singing some random song in my head to keep myself from passing out.

Then, the side door opens.

My head feels light and my hands are numb. Everything is hazy as he walks into the room. His hair is cut shorter than his mug shot, and he shaved. He's wearing a suit that is a little too big on him, either he's lost weight or it's borrowed.

I knew this moment would be hard, but I wasn't even close to prepared.

Tears form and I gasp when his eyes meet mine.

"You can do this," Milo's deep voice says against my ears. "Don't show weakness."

I turn toward him, letting Milo see the pain that's filling me. I can't hide it, but I cannot let the killer see.

Of all the people in the world, Milo is the second worst to see this side of me. He wants to take from me as well. He plans to strip me of something I love and want.

However, right now, I don't see that in him.

"How?" I whisper the word.

Milo's eyes lock on mine. "You control it. You don't show him you're gutted. You show him he didn't break you."

I close my eyes, harnessing any strength left inside of me.

I'm not broken, I'm just in pain.

I think about Ava and Parker. How strong they are and the way they got through it.

A hand rests on my shoulders, and I quickly turn to find my three best friends sitting in the row behind me.

"What?" I ask. "How?"

I never told them. I knew what would happen if I did. They'd take off work, sit next to me, and be . . . well, them. My friends do too much for me as it is. I've relied on them for the last almost two years, and I didn't want to burden them further.

"You didn't think we'd let you do this alone, did you?" Kristin asks.

"But you have work," I look at them. "All of you have other things. I didn't want . . ."

"No one in this tribe walks alone," Nicole tells me. "You were stupid to think we wouldn't find out."

Heather's eyes are filled with love and a twinge of frustration. "I'm on the witness list. I was just waiting for you to tell us you needed us." She looks to Milo and then back. "But I'm glad you had someone, even if it wasn't us."

It's not like that. Milo isn't my someone, he's my assistant who took it upon himself to be here. Probably to get dirt to use on me later.

"Milo, didn't—"

"It's fine," Heather cuts me off. "We were glad to see you weren't alone. Truly."

"Now I get it," Milo says softly so only I can hear.

"Get what?"

His grin grows wide. "Why my brother moved to America."

The judge walks in and I don't have time to reply.

"Please rise," the bailiff calls and we get to our feet. "The honorable Judge Evan Hellingsman presiding."

And so it begins.

eleven

. . .

Milo

I DON'T KNOW why I'm sitting here, wanting to comfort her.

It's unlike me in every way.

Danielle has a life that I want no part of. She's a widow, with kids, and it's clear what type of life she wants to live. She wants the husband to adore her, raise children as a unit—well, that's not me.

I'm reckless in every facet of my life. I like adventure, sex, and having zero responsibilities. My family likes to say I'm immature, while I would rather say I'm stubborn and smart. Why tie myself down when I was meant to soar?

Stupid really, if you think about it. I would be doing whoever was daft enough to love me a disservice.

Danielle starts to fidget with her hands, and I cover them with my own.

She looks up, and I squeeze a little. "Are you all right?"

It's clear she's not, but she nods anyway.

I move my hand back to my lap, pretending I don't feel a protective urge when it comes to her. She joked about assaulting the bastard sitting on the other side of this railing, but it was me who had to grip the seat to stop myself from doing just that. The opening arguments were hard to listen to. They described Peter sitting in his office at his desk, how he was facing the photos that lined his desk with his family before him. The picture was clear, I would've thought I was there, watching this man walk in, raise his gun, and ending Peter's life. When I saw her tears, I almost went into a fit of rage. It's ridiculous that a woman I barely know makes me lose control.

But here I am, sitting beside her, wanting to find a way to ease any of her pain.

"Okay, I'd like to call a recess for the day. Trial will resume tomorrow at nine," the judge says and bangs the gavel.

Danielle shifts to face the three women, including my sister-in-law, behind her. They start to chat, and I sit here, berating myself for thinking any of this was brilliant. I should've stayed at the office and worked on outdoing Danielle. I shouldn't be in a courtroom with her.

I shouldn't be doing a lot of things that I can't seem to stop myself from doing.

"Ready?" Danielle asks.

"Yes, of course." I get to my feet and follow her out.

Immediately, the brunette hooks her arm with Danielle's and makes her way forward. Nicole and another blonde are at the end. I start to move down the aisle, but someone grips my forearm.

"Can I help you?" I ask Nicole.

"What's your game?"

"Game?"

The blonde huffs and crosses her arm. "Whatever you're doing, don't," she warns.

"I haven't the faintest idea what you're talking about," I say.

Nicole takes a step close, and though she's much smaller than me, she's quite scary at the moment. "She's like a sister to me. She's family."

"Well, dear sister-in-law, we are as well," I point out.

"But I like her."

"I'm wounded." I clutch my chest.

"Yes, you will be," she threatens. "Heather is a cop and knows all the best places to bury a body."

I look over to the blonde who just nods with a smile. "Understood," I say.

"Good." Nicole smiles and hooks her arm with mine. "Now that we've got that settled, tell me all the dirt on Callum that I can use against him later."

I laugh hard. "I might just love you."

She looks up with a grin. "I don't doubt you will."

Seems my brother has beat me in yet another aspect of life. He's found a woman who is clearly amazing.

Nicole and I exit past where Danielle stands, her brunette friend comforting her. I try to imagine how today must've felt for her, but I can't.

This man knew her husband on some level. He was aware that Peter had a wife and family, but because he was facing a possibility of jail time and couldn't handle his rage, he killed the person who was defending his worthless life.

He's a pitiful soul.

"Thanks for being here," Danielle says to her friends.

"Of course we're here, dumbass."

Danielle's lip starts to tremble and a tear falls. "I didn't want to do this. I didn't know if I could do it, so if I didn't tell you, it wasn't real."

Nicole releases my arm and rushes to her. "We get it, but you never have to hide with us. If you couldn't do it, we would've stayed at your house and watched movies."

Fucking hell. Who has friends like this? Not me, that's for damn sure. My mates were more worried about beer and sex than even asking how I was after my father died. Callum was at university and thought I needed to step up more.

No one understood how it felt or cared for that matter. I was filled with rage at the incident. I wanted justice, answers, for him to come back.

I needed someone to give a damn, but they didn't. So I got angrier, drank more, and gave the world the middle finger.

I turned out just fine if you ask me.

"I'm so sorry. I love you guys," Danielle cries harder.

Women.

"I don't know about all of you," I say, breaking their tearful moment. "But I think we could all do well with a pint or two?" No one answers. In fact, they stand there as if I'm speaking another language. "You know, we should get pissed?" I clarify.

Nicole shakes her head. "He means beer and drunk."

"You don't have to stay." Danielle comes close to me. "I appreciate that you came at all, Milo. I really do, but I can't imagine you would want to stick around."

Here's the out every man waits for.

She's gift wrapped it.

And I'm going to return it—like a fool.

"My treat." I wink. "I insist."

Danielle places her hand on my arm, pushing me further back from her friends.

"If this is some . . ."

"It's not." I cut her off before she can say game or whatever other word she might come up with. "Let me do this," I implore her.

"Why?"

That is the million-dollar question.

Because I like her.

Because she's strong, resilient, and I see my life in hers.

Which is a very bad thing.

twelve

. . .

Danielle

WHY CAN'T I stop looking his way? Was Ava right when she said he was "sex on a stick hot"? I don't think he's ugly by any means, but . . . it's been a long time since I looked at a man like that.

Is it his personality that people are drawn to? My friends sure were laughing at his jokes, smiling with him, and having a good time last night. Not to mention the waitress who practically fell in his lap towards the end.

They know he's trying to take my job. I know this as well, but here I am, staring at him, trying to figure out what the hell is wrong with me.

"Can I help you?" Milo asks as he catches me.

"I'm fine."

"You're staring," he calls me out.

"I'm just trying to figure out something," I confess.

"Is it why I'm so deliciously sexy?"

I laugh. "No."

"Are you sure?"

"Positive. Your mouth totally ruined that."

Once again, I really look at him, trying to see him through a single girl's eyes. His scruff is a few days old, giving him a gruffer look than when he's clean shaven. He definitely works out by the way his shirts fit, unless he buys them too small to look bigger. Heather's ex-husband Matt did that, and we would all make fun of him for it too. I don't think Milo would stoop to that level, but I wouldn't put it past him either.

"You think the accent is sexy then?"

I sigh. "Why do you think it has anything to do with what you look like?"

"Because those blue eyes are roaming all over my body."

Busted.

"Fine," I acquiesce. "I was staring because everyone thinks you're hot, but I wasn't sure. I was trying to understand what all the hype is about."

His jaw falls open as if what I said is completely insane. "I'm sorry, you're what?"

"I'm trying to understand the hype," I say unapologetically. "I was just putting the pieces together."

"On whether or not I'm?"

"Hot."

Milo stares at me, his green eyes darkening. "And?"

"And what?"

He groans, running his hand down his face. "And what have you concluded?"

He's really not going to like this, but I've already inserted my foot in my mouth enough, might as well swallow it now.

"I'm still not sure."

"Unbelievable. I'm offended," he huffs.

Shit.

I'm his boss and I basically told him I was checking him out. *Way to go, Danielle.* Why don't you just slap yourself with a sexual harassment suit while you're at it. I need to fix this.

"I'm sorry, that was out of line. As your boss, I shouldn't have said that."

He scoffs. "I'm not offended because you're my boss!"

"I just know I have a position of power over you. There's the whole "me too" movement and I wasn't trying to make you think . . ."

"That you're bloody insane? I already do thanks to this. How do you not know if you find me sexually attractive?"

"Okay," I say slowly. "I can see that this is a touchy subject for you. I don't want you to think that since I'm your boss, I was trying to take advantage of that."

Milo's brows raise and he stops speaking.

Well, if I didn't screw myself the first time, I sure did now, pointing out my major professionalism fail.

"Milo?" I finally say after a few minutes of awkward silence.

"I've been told by many that I'm irresistible."

"And humble?"

"No, never that, but I can't believe you're questioning whether or not I'm attractive."

I shrug. "Do you consider yourself hot?"

"Damn right I do," he stands, pulling his jacket off.

"Okay, keep your clothes on!"

"I'm merely showing you what you need to see," he says while unbuttoning his shirt.

"Milo!" I laugh.

He sits back down, still not happy. "I have never had a woman be unsure if I'm good looking. What is wrong with you?"

"Me?"

"Yes, you!"

This wasn't going the way I'd hoped. "Maybe it's you," I point out. "Do you think I'm attractive?"

"Yes," he answers without a pause.

"Oh. Well. Okay. Thank you?"

He thinks I'm attractive. I don't know how I feel about that, but I'm all warm on the inside. It's been a long time since a man has said that to me. Even my husband was never overly affectionate. I know he loved me, but I wondered if he thought I aged well or if I was still beautiful to him.

Our lives were crazy and we didn't make time for those things.

"You're welcome. Did you seriously doubt that?" he asks.

"Doesn't every woman?"

"Yes, and you're all fucking bonkers!"

I don't really like his tone, but I'm going to let it go since I'm sure I broke about ten company rules in this conversation.

"Okay, so tell me," he says with frustration in his voice. "What has you so mystified?"

There's no way out of this. I'm going to have to be honest.

I lean back and cross my arms. "What it is about you that people like? I think you're a nice guy, despite trying to act otherwise, but my friends and daughter seem to think you're some kind of catch."

Milo's eyes go wide. "I think it's rather obvious."

Of course he would say that. He's in love with himself. "It's definitely not your personality."

"I'm a catch, Danielle. I'm rich, sexy, fantastic in bed, and I—"

"Have a very modest opinion of yourself," I finish his sentence.

Milo puts the folder to the side and shakes his head. "You're missing the bigger picture."

"Enlighten me, then."

I can't wait to hear this. Here I was, thinking about the nice things he did yesterday and he's about to remind me why he's the ass Callum says he is.

"Apart from the obvious, I'm exactly what women want. I don't play games or make you believe I want something I don't."

"Women don't want that!"

"Maybe not American women."

Idiot.

"Because your wife tells you . . . oh, that's right, you don't have one of those?"

Milo glares at me. "By choice, sweetheart. I don't want a wife or love or anything to do with that rubbish. I'm quite happy with my life."

"That's what they all say."

I believe that despite Milo's proclamations, in the core of each human is a desire to be loved above all else. It's why we seek companionship as soon as we start to detach from our parents. I wanted, more than anything, to be loved so deeply that it gave me life.

Then I realized that shit only exists in stories. I got a husband who loved me, and kids, the house, and then I remembered that being loved is only part of a bigger picture.

We also needed to work, take care of things, and ride out the rough patches of living together in tandem. And then it ended abruptly in the most painful way possible.

However, I would do it all over again because in those few moments when I was Peter's entire existence, they carried me through the hard times.

Milo rises, lifting the folder he placed down. "I mean what I say. I've seen the downside of marriage, and I want no part of it. However, when I find that girl who knocks me on my arse and makes it unbearable to be away from her, she'll know I chose her. I chose to love her against my will to be single. That's the girl I'm looking for, but I don't think she exists."

I rest my arms on the desk and grin. "I can't wait to see her knock you on your arse." I use his word because British words are so much cooler than American ones.

He chuckles. "I can't either."

I see it in his eyes. Right now, he's no more immune to love than the rest of us. He's just gotten good at pretending.

"You're not going!" I yell at Ava as she's throwing her shoes on.

"You can't make me stay home. I'll get a ride to the courthouse on my own then!"

I move closer, gripping her arm. "Goddamn it! You can't sit through it. You can't!"

She can't see the photos of her father lying in his blood. I know she thinks she's old enough to tackle the world, but she has no idea. Court isn't fun. It's hell and it's sucking the life out of me.

I refused to go today. I had to meet with an inspector and I didn't think it was a good idea to reschedule. Of course, Milo brought up the fact that I have him as my extremely overqualified assistant and I was making excuses, but . . . he can suck it.

Now I'm arguing because Ava thinks she has a right to be there.

"Don't tell me what I can't do, Mother! I'm a lot stronger than you think. I'm not a child."

"That's exactly what you are," I say as I slump down on the couch. "You are a child, Ava. You're my child and listening to that . . . it's not what your father would've wanted."

"I need to know," she admits.

How do I keep her from this? Is trying to protect her even the right thing? I look to the ceiling, praying for some help here.

When no one answers, I decide to dig deeper to see what the real reason she wants to be there is.

"What do you think you're going to hear that's going to help you?" I ask.

She moves towards me. "I don't know, but at least I can see the man who took him from us. Parker will never know Daddy. I want the man responsible to see my face."

I realize how much she's like her father right now. Peter had the same fire inside of him. He wanted answers, the truth, and to fight the injustices in the world. I wanted to be happy. Ignorance was bliss for me.

"Do you think he really cares?" I toss back. "Because I can promise you, he doesn't. Seeing your face isn't going to suddenly make him ashamed of what he did to us. It won't make things right. It won't bring Daddy back. It will do nothing to him and everything to you."

She sits on the couch beside me. "I'm not a little girl anymore, Mom."

Oh, how wrong she is. At sixteen, she's nowhere close to knowing the hard realities that adulthood offers. I would give anything to be young and dumb again. It was so much easier.

I also understand the want she has on some level. She lost her father and this is something that might help bring her closure.

"I know you're not," I say. "I can't let you go to the trial, but if you agree to not fight me on this, then you can come to the reading of the verdict. I want you to skip the gruesome parts, but I think you should be there for the closing arguments."

Ava leaps toward me, wrapping her arms around my shoulder. "Thank you, thank you, thank you. I won't fight you."

I return her hug, trying to remember the last time she embraced me. We've been on opposing sides of everything for so long.

She releases too soon, and I go to say something, but the doorbell rings.

"I got it!" she yells and rushes over, pulling the door open before I can get to my feet. "Well, if it isn't double-oh-sexy," she twirls her hair.

"Jailbait," the British accent I spent a good part of my day sparing with replies. "You need a proper spanking."

"Want to give it to me?" she asks.

Oh, dear God. Milo's jaw goes slack even though he walked right into that one.

"Go to your room, Ava," I order and she frowns.

"But he's so pretty."

"Go." I point.

"At least your daughter has eyes that work," he replies.

"Yes, my sixteen-year-old thinks you're pretty, you should relish in that."

Milo ignores me and pulls a folder out. "The city is being run by a bunch of pricks who sent this back. You're getting a lot of pushback from the existing neighborhood."

It blows my mind how much people will resist change. This project is to clean up a deteriorating apartment building and revitalize the area. We plan to put a park in for the kids, new basketball hoops because the old ones are broken, and little stores to help with jobs. All of these things are good, but you'd think we're chopping down a forest to put in a parking lot.

It's crazy.

It's also making me look like a fool to Callum. I pushed him on this land. I practically sold him on the idea of how wonderful it would be. Now, he's fielding all kinds of letters, complaints, and issues with the permits.

"I'm going to have to come up with an idea."

"I should say so," Milo agrees with condescending smugness.

Then I remember he works for me. "Well, assistant, since you're my bitch and all, I think you could really shine in this area."

"Your bitch?"

"That's what Callum called you." I grin. "I think it's time we put that woman magnet personality and good looks to the test."

This is going to be so much fun.

thirteen

. . .

Danielle

"I'LL GET IT!" Parker yells as the doorbell rings.

"Shit!" I grumble as Ava stands in front of me with a makeup brush.

"Mouth, Mother."

"Yeah, like you don't say shit when I'm not around?"

"Oh, I say a lot that you wouldn't be happy with," Ava informs me.

"Why did I even ask," I mutter.

"Mom!" Parker yells. "Milo is here!"

I look at Ava who is smiling at me. "Why are you looking at me like that?"

"Nothing."

"Are we done yet? I don't trust Milo out there with Parker."

Ava rolls her eyes. "Parker can handle him. He'll talk him to sleep. No one can be mean to that kid, he's the best."

I laugh because she's not wrong. Ava may be a raging bitch to me, but when it comes to her brother, she's completely different. She's always been protective towards him. Now that her father's not here, she sometimes seems to think she's another parent instead of a sister, but he loves her and doesn't mind. Parker is the one thing Ava cares about more than anything.

I'm grateful for that much at least.

"You're right." I fidget in my seat, hating this dress. I feel like no matter which way I move, something is falling out that shouldn't.

"Stop moving or your face isn't going to be perfect for your date."

"It is not a date," I correct.

This is a business meeting-slash-coercion mission thanks to my assistant. After another three days of following up with the city only to be ignored, Milo asked me to let him off his leash. He explained that he has a connection—that he made in less than a month of living here—in the inspector's office.

Last night, I got a call that everything was set. I needed to be dressed to the nines because we had a dinner with the inspector and his girlfriend.

Milo begged me to trust him and let him work his angle since we tried mine and have come up short.

Trusting him is a stretch, but I'm tired of being dicked around by this guy and if Milo has the in, I'm willing to take it. However, this is *not* a date.

"Whatever. You're dressed up, have sexy underwear on, and you're wearing fuck me shoes, it's a date."

"Ava Kristin Bergen," I hiss. "Don't use that word around me, and these shoes are the ones you made me wear."

"Because they're hot, Mom. You need to look hot if you're going to follow Milo's plan. Now, stop moving so I can fix your face."

Fix my face? "What the hell is wrong with my face?"

Her upper lip rises and she shrugs. "I guess nothing's wrong with it if you plucked your eyebrows more often and maybe put some makeup on."

"Gee, thanks."

"I'm just saying, Mom. You're getting older and it's going to be harder to attract a man if you don't put a little effort in."

I slap her leg. "I'm not old. And I don't want a man."

I'm fine being alone. I have my kids, my job, and my friends. There's nothing a guy is going to bring to my life other than a headache . . . and maybe an orgasm, but I can make that happen on my own.

"Sure, you're almost forty."

"Yeah, almost, but not yet."

Ava rolls her eyes. "Well, when I'm done with you, you'll look twenty and hopefully you won't look frumpy."

Peter and I used to joke about what we'd do if something happened to one of us, and I always said I would never remarry. Maybe it was because we never wanted to get married in the first place. We loved each other, but we had goals bigger than a wedding ring. I wanted to build an empire in real estate and he was going to be partner.

Then, I got pregnant and we had to alter that. Well, I did.

I look at my daughter, the child we didn't plan for who brought me down this road, and touch her hand. "I know you and I have had our differences, but I want you to know how much I love you, Ava. Thank you for helping me tonight."

Ava sighs and for a moment, the walls she's built around herself come down. "I love you too, Mom. But if you don't shut up and let me concentrate, you're going to have contour on the wrong part of your face."

And then they're back up.

"How did you learn all this anyway?" I ask.

"YouTube."

Great. Now I'm really scared.

I sit in silence as Ava continues to grab things, paint my face, and hmm and haw at her work. I have no idea what I look like, but she's pleased.

"Done," she announces.

I stand up, and she moves quickly in front of me. "Ava, move."

"No! You can't look. You have to trust me."

Yeah, that's a problem. I don't trust her. This is the ultimate way she could serve revenge for her grounding.

"Nope, move."

"Mom! Please!" she begs. "I promise, you look gorgeous. Just walk out there, and see what Milo and Parker think. If you don't look hot, he won't take you and you know that Parker will say something."

She's right there. Parker still has that childlike honesty that every woman hates. He likes to poke my side and ask why it jiggles. Or when he touches the lines around my eyes and asks why they crinkle like Grandma's.

Everyone should have kids, they're great for self-esteem. Said no one ever.

"Fine, but if I do this and I look like the bride of Chuckie or something, you're grounded for an extra month, got it?"

She nods. "Yup. And if you look gorgeous, I get my phone back tomorrow?"

Now it's my turn to laugh. "Not on your life, but nice try."

I release a nervous sigh and start to walk, but these shoes are impossible. Peter bought me a pair of Christian Louboutins for our ten-year anniversary. He said I never would've bought them myself, so he took care of it. I wore them once, thought my feet were broken, and never wore them again. Plus, I look like a baby giraffe finding its legs when I walk.

Nicole looks like a runway model. I look like a moron.

However, they matched the barely-there dress I'm wearing perfectly.

I'm going to get fired when Callum hears about the fool I'm about to make of myself. There's not a doubt in my mind. I let Milo rope me into tonight and I'm going to end up paying for it.

I stumble trying to get out of the bathroom, but Ava grabs my elbow. "Really, Mom?"

"Listen, the best-case scenario tonight is that I don't break an ankle."

She huffs as she walks to her room mumbling. "No hope."

I get downstairs and stop at the bottom step. I feel ridiculous in this outfit. God only knows what my face looks like, and I can't walk.

Disaster waiting to happen is what this is.

"Batman or Superman?" Parker asks.

"Are you sure you want to debate this?"

"Are *you*?"

Parker is very passionate about this topic. I hope Milo knows what he's getting into here.

"There is no discussion. It's Superman. Batman isn't even a real superhero."

He's about to get schooled. "He's an even bigger one than Superman!" Parker yells and I can picture his little face filled with all the fury he can muster. "He has to figure out how to do it without any alien help. He's better because he's smart. That's a superpower. And he doesn't worry about kryptonite because he's human, like we are."

"He's not faster than Superman or stronger," Milo goads him.

"He's better because he could be me or you."

"Well, definitely you, but I'm not nearly as smart as Bruce Wayne," Milo tells him casually.

I smile, knowing how much Parker has missed this with his father. They went and saw each movie, read comic books and debated the way things should go, and Parker loved that time with Peter.

My head rests against the wall, willing away the tears that threaten to form because as sad as I am, I'm more so for my kids.

"You can be my Alfred. You have a cool accent and I think you'd do the job," Parker offers and I laugh.

"All right," I say walking out into the living room, keeping my eyes on Parker. "I think it's time for you to go to bed, buddy."

"Whoa!" Parker says. "You sound like my mom, but you don't look like her."

"Is it bad?" I ask with fear.

I don't make any eye contact with Milo. I'm not ready to see his reaction to whatever I look like. It's not like I go to work looking like I rolled out of bed, but I was a housewife for sixteen years. I don't know what's trendy. My insecurity is at a ten out of ten and if Milo looks at me with disappointment in his eyes, I might lose it.

Which is insane because he works for me and hates me.

Parker smiles at me and puts my nerves at ease. "You look pretty."

"Well, I'm glad you think so." I tap his nose. "Ava is upstairs. Go get ready for bed and she'll tuck you in, okay?"

"Okay, Mom." Parker walks back to Milo. "Have her home by ten, okay?"

Milo laughs and ruffles his hair. "I'll do my best."

"Bed," I order.

Parker runs off, leaving Milo and I alone. I look at the floor and Milo's feet enter my view.

"Well." He clears his throat. "Are you ready to see my charm, as you so call it, in action?"

I laugh at his ridiculousness and do my best to settle the butterflies wreaking havoc in my belly. There's no denying how unbelievable Milo looks right now. He's wearing a black suit that's cut to fit him perfectly. His shoulders are square and his normally light brown hair looks a little darker. The stubble that was on his face is now thicker and more of a beard than before. I'm not sure if it's the suit or the way he's wearing it, but Milo is most definitely sexy.

"Are you all right?" he asks as I stand there staring at him.

"Me? I'm . . . yeah. I'm great. Ready to get this dinner over with already," I say nervously as I tuck my hair behind my ear.

He takes a step closer and I remind myself I'm his boss and this is not a date. This is dinner with a purpose.

"This will work brilliantly. My plan is foolproof."

"I'm giving you a shot at this, Milo. You've got one opportunity to make it work."

He takes a step closer, and my stomach drops. He even smells fantastic.

Jesus Christ, Danielle, stop it. Focus. Work date with your subordinate.

"I'm fully aware of the terms," he smirks. "Remember I once had an assistant, and part of being a good boss is knowing when someone can do something for you."

"Right. And your job is what now?"

Milo's hand lifts, grazes my cheek and then drops. "Making your life easier."

I shake my head and focus on putting my nerves to the back of my mind. I have to pretend that I don't care one tiny bit about how good he looks or smells. I have to remember that it doesn't matter what Milo thinks of how I look or this dress or the fact that he hasn't made a single comment. I'm not a woman and he's not a man. This is war and we're dressed for battle.

I have to lie like my life depends on it.

"I like your suit, by the way," I say as I grab my purse off the side table.

He tucks his hands in his pockets and rocks on his heels. "Glad you approve."

I wait for him to say something about what I'm wearing, but he doesn't.

I square my shoulders and shake my head, the strands tickling my bare back. "Let's see if your talk is as good as your walk."

Milo's eyes drift to my chest and then back up. "I'm going to rather enjoy myself. I hope you're ready, Ms. Bergen."

Maybe he's not as uninterested as I thought.

"This was your brilliant plan?" I ask Milo as I pull my dress a little lower, only to have the back drop lower which means the top of my butt is showing. I can't win with this damn dress.

We're standing in the club, waiting to see if the girlfriend of the city inspector shows up. Apparently, Milo didn't actually have a dinner *planned*. No, he just found out where the guy would be and plans to crash his date. So, we're at the country club that Nicole hates more than life itself because this is where he frequents.

I had to come here a few times with Peter and once with Nicole. This place is where the rich, snobby self-proclaimed society hang out.

A girl passes by, gives me a smirk and I remind myself never to let Ava help me pick out a dress again. She vetoed everything I came out wearing until this one. She demanded I not take it off and that I let her use her "mad skills" on my face. Tonight has been like living in an alternate reality.

"Stop squirming," he tells me.

"I feel ridiculous. What if he doesn't even come here?"

"Just relax, he'll be here."

That's not why I feel ridiculous. It's because I look like a very expensive hooker. Not to mention this is some *I Love Lucy* type scheme he's concocted. I'm not sure if I'm Ricky or Ethel in this role.

"Milo, I think this is a mistake."

"What is? This is exactly what we need to do. Don't get your knickers in a twist."

"Okay?" I snort laugh at his choice of words. "They're panties, but sure."

He looks at me with one eyebrow raised. "Knickers is much more dignified."

"Nothing about this is dignified."

"Trust me, this is all going according to plan. I have everything the way I need it to secure the permits he's been dragging his feet on."

Everything the way he needs what? That makes no sense. All the plan consists of is a possible "friend" from the gym is going to be having dinner with Darren, the inspector. What kind of plan is that exactly?

"You needed me to look like *this*?" I hiss.

In the car he informed me that my role was to help entertain his friend while he worked his magic. If that didn't work, he wanted me to look alluring and help him find a way to manipulate the inspector. Little does he know I have zero plans of either of those. I'm the boss and I'm going to get shit done the right way. I just needed him to set up the meet.

"You do look rather delicious," he grins, eyeing me up and down. This is the first time he's said anything about what I look like. Not that I haven't caught him looking. In the car, when I sat down, the dress barely covers . . . anything . . . and I saw his eyes flash and he shifted in his seat. Then, when he helped me out of the car, Milo did his best to keep his eyes on his feet when I know he had a view of my boobs. And a few moments ago, I saw his eyes go from my feet to my waist before he cleared his throat and looked away, but still not a word.

"You think?" I ask and twirl around.

I'm toying with him a little. It's only fair since he's made it his mission to catch me looking at him.

"Yes, the back on that dress is divine."

"There is no back," I remind him.

"I'm aware, and it's definitely working for you." Milo wiggles his brows.

And by the looks of the man who stopped with a grin, he agrees as well.

Milo steps closer, putting his arm around my back, fingers grazing the skin on my back and making me shiver.

"Cold?" he asks.

"A little."

I'm full of shit. It's never cold in Tampa. It borders on hotter than hell and roasting in a fire pit.

"I would offer you my jacket, but then we'd be covering your back and that's what our secret weapon is," he mutters conspiratorially.

"What?"

"Your dress, Danielle. It's going to knock him on his arse."

He's insane. I can't do this. "This is such a bad idea," I tell him. "You know what? I changed my mind on this plan. We'll get the permits because we have the paperwork in order, not because we flirted with him at the club. I'm a grown ass woman with a good head on my shoulders." I step out of his hold, but he grips my wrist to stop me.

Being that I don't normally wear four-inch heels, I teeter and almost fall.

Milo's arms wrap around my waist, holding me steady. "Look." His front is to my back, and I fight from closing my eyes and leaning back. His lips graze my ear as he whispers. "You are all those things. You're more than that, but this is our chance to play him. It's time to show him who you are, but it requires a little finesse. Do you see that man?"

I nod.

"Good. He's here and ready to find out exactly who is in charge at Dovetail."

Thankfully, that snaps me out of it enough to see the inspector who's been dicking us around standing right there.

The bottom line is that I need to get this done and we have an opportunity to do that. I can walk out this door with my dignity or I can walk out after doing what I need to do to get my job done.

Milo's fingers slide against my bare arm and take my hand, and I move with him.

"Kandi, darling," Milo's accent is much thicker than it was a few seconds ago. "I didn't know you frequented this club."

How does he lie so effortlessly?

"Milo." She grins back. "Have you met my fiancé Darren?"

"Darren Wakefield," Milo says with his hand extended. "I didn't know you were Kandi's main squeeze. I believe you know Danielle Bergen."

Milo Huxley, I need to keep my eye on you.

He makes it look like he was genuinely surprised. It was effortless for him and a little scary to me how the words came out like second nature.

"Yes, how are you?" I ask.

Darren smiles warmly, then he shakes my hand. "Danielle, what a pleasant surprise. It's great to see you outside the confines of work."

Liar. He's shitting himself right now.

"It's a pleasure to see you here too, Darren."

Darren tugs Kandi to his side and Milo places his hand on the small of my back. This time, I'm able to suppress the shiver that his touch brings.

"I didn't know you were a member of the club," Darren says to Milo.

"Oh, I'm not. My snob of a brother is. I'm here for the first time. I wanted to see what all the fuss was about."

Kandi runs her finger down Darren's chest, her eyes on Milo all the while. "Why don't we grab a table since we're all friends? We could grab a few drinks."

"We'd love to," I say quickly before Darren can object. "I'm going to powder my nose."

"I'll come with," Kandi says.

"I'll never understand why girls can't pee alone," Darren laughs.

My eyes are on Milo and I mouth to him, behave.

He winks and I shake my head with a smile.

Like that will ever happen.

fourteen

. . .

Danielle

KANDI and I stand in the mirror, fixing our hair and lipstick. She's extremely pretty. Her long blonde hair sits in those perfect curls that I can never get my hair to do. She has crystal blue eyes, and her boobs are definitely man-made. Darren looks to be about fifty and his receding hairline isn't helping him look any younger. But I don't think she's with him for his looks.

I finish fixing my red lipstick, once again wanting to ground my daughter for making me look this way, and turn towards her.

"Where did you meet Milo?" I ask.

Why did I ask her that? I wanted to ask how she met Darren, not Milo. That was what I had meant to say.

"We met at the gym." She smiles. "He said you're his boss?"

"I am."

"God, how do you stand it?"

"Stand what?" I question.

She laughs and tilts her head. "Looking at him all day. I would never get any work done."

Oh, great, another groupie.

I won't tell her that today, I do find his good looks a little distracting. But even still, he's so arrogant, cocky, full of himself, and . . . Milo. Sure, he's nice, caring, funny, and seems to go out of his way sometimes for people. Yeah, he's smart, and Parker came running when he came to the door, but that's because he *is* a child.

Instead I ask, "Aren't you engaged?"

She laughs, leaning against the counter. "I can still browse the market without buying the produce, honey. Besides," she says looking down at my hand. "You're on a date with him and you have a special ring on your finger."

I glance at my wedding ring and cover it. "Well, I guess not everything is as it seems."

"How so?"

There's no reason I need to tell her anything, other than to shut her up. We're nothing alike in this moment. I'm not flirting with men at the gym when I have a fiancé. I'm not even flirting with anyone and I'm technically single. But I can't put her in her place because this is Milo's big plan, and if I screw it up, then I'll never hear the end of it.

"My husband died almost two years ago," I say. "I just haven't taken it off yet." My words may be strong, but my voice definitely isn't.

"Oh," Kandi touches my arm. "I'm so sorry. I didn't mean . . ."

"No, it's okay," I reassure her quickly. "We should probably get back to the guys."

She nods. "Can I ask you something?"

"Sure."

"Are you . . . you know . . . *with* Milo then?"

I'm not sure what Milo has told her and I'm not good at this kind of thing. So, I do what I can do . . . deflect. "If you want to know, you'd have to ask him. I'm not at liberty to say one way or another."

I'm hoping she has no idea what that means because I don't myself, and I said it.

"Oh, because I think he's incredible."

"How long have you known him?" I ask.

"Just a few days," she smiles. "But . . . when he talks, I swear, I could just die."

Instead of making the gagging noise I want to, I nod. "Well, don't go and do a thing like that."

Save us all and just kill me, it would make this whole thing easier.

"So, if you guys aren't a thing, do you mind if I . . . make a move?"

Now I'm confused. If she's engaged to Darren, how the hell is she going to make a move when she's got a big ass rock on her hand.

"But you're engaged you said?" I say it as a question because . . . huh?

She giggles obnoxiously. "Of course I am, but what Darren doesn't know won't hurt him."

That's a real solid foundation you're building there, Kandi. This conversation is starting to weigh on me. To make it end, I grab my bag, "Milo will probably be looking for us. We should get going."

"Yes, we definitely don't want to keep Milo waiting," she sighs and then walks out with me behind her.

I hate her, I've decided. Why does she care so much about him? Because he's good looking? That's dumb. She's known him a few days and suddenly she's all over him? Does she know about his father? About how hard it was on him when his brother moved here? Nope, that would be me. I doubt she even knows his last name, but she's sure excited to drop her drawers and let him in.

"There you are." Milo's smile is wide as I approach—without falling I might add. "When you were in the loo, Darren was telling me about his affection for cars."

"Oh, Darren could talk cars all day," Kandi smiles. "I have other things I'd rather do with my time."

I've always been envious of women who were forward. Nicole, for example, is someone I've been jealous of. She's confident, sexy, doesn't give a damn what others think, and goes after what she wants. Kandi reminds me a little of her, only she's gross. Because she seems to want Milo.

Why that bothers me is not a point I'm willing to think about right now.

She's not even trying to hide her flirting. Right in front of everyone, she's hanging on her fiancé, but staring at Milo.

"Should we get a table?" I ask.

"Danielle, I didn't realize you were such a fox." Darren's eyes linger just a bit too long.

Are they swingers or something? Maybe this is an agreement they have, an open relationship. But no thanks. This is the most bizarre encounter I've ever had. Now I wonder what exactly Milo told Kandi in their gym sessions about whatever fake relationship he and I have.

"Thanks, I think."

Milo wraps his arm around my back, his fingers digging into my hip. "We're lucky men, aren't we? To have such spectacular women on our arms? And don't let Danielle's beauty fool you. She's bloody brilliant too. You'd be wise to listen to her ideas." He gives the man a pointed look.

When Darren starts talking to Kandi, I lean in and tell Milo, "Way to lay it on thick. Think he got your meaning?"

His hand slides around to my belly and he turns me so we're almost chest to chest. "Darren is the kind of man who likes to feel important. Butter him up and make him think you're his friend, and he'll show you how important he is by doing you a big favor."

I press my hand to his chest, to anyone else, we look like a couple, being affectionate. "If this doesn't work, this entire miserable night is for nothing."

"I certainly wouldn't call tonight miserable. And if this doesn't work, I'll quit."

I look up to see if he's lying, but his eyes are unwavering. "You're that sure?"

He nods, bringing his hand up my bare back and my stomach

drops. "There's only one thing I'm unsure of about tonight, but it's not him."

There's another meaning behind his words, but I don't trust myself to question it. I'm the world's worst flirt. I have no idea if that's even what he's doing or if I'm imagining it.

"What are you unsure of?" I ask.

His fingers ride along my spine and I swear my knees are going to give out. Milo's arm goes around me when I buckle a little. "Nothing anymore," he grins at me and now I know. He's flirting. He's really flirting, and he's very good at it.

"Well," I clear my throat and take a step back. "Happy you're all . . . knowing and whatever."

"Milo and Danielle," Darren calls. "Let's have a few drinks."

He moves so his hand can touch my skin again. "Yes, let's do that."

The walk over to the table feels like miles. Each step my heart races faster, knowing I have to now pretend I'm his date or it could be because he realizes I'm not as unaffected as I thought.

When did this change?

When did I suddenly look at Milo and not want to knee him in the balls, but instead, see if his beard scratches when we kiss?

"What would you like to drink?"

"Water please," I say to the waiter, wanting to stay sober. No way am I going to follow in my two dumbass friends' footsteps and drink. Kristin and Heather both own the t-shirts on that. I'll stick with sober and fully in control.

"We see who is the sensible one out of this lot," Milo jokes and then his hand is behind my chair.

The rest order drinks and I sit back as the men discuss cars.

I start to sing "Ninety-nine Bottles of Beer on the Wall" to keep myself from going crazy. When I get to sixty-two, Kandi takes matters into her own hands.

"Milo," she purrs. "Darren hates to dance and I love this song, would you mind dancing with me?"

"If that's all right with your fiancé?" he asks looking at Darren.

"I don't mind at all."

He gets to his feet with a smile. "Then I would love to."

Well, don't ask me, Milo. I'm totally not fine with it, but whatever. You do you, I'll be here with my water not hoping Miss Skinnyass falls and busts her ass.

I should've ordered vodka.

Now I'm forced to sit here, watching them walk to the dance floor. His hand doesn't touch her, but it's close, and I seethe.

Then, she stops, turns, and her wrists rest on his shoulders. Milo's hands are on her waist, and I have to grip the seat to not make a scene.

I don't like him touching her.

I don't like that I don't like him touching her.

I shouldn't give a shit if his hands are on Kandi or any other woman for that matter, but here I am, staring at them, seething.

"She's beautiful, isn't she?" Darren asks, pulling my gaze away from Milo.

"Yes, you're a lucky man."

"I agree. She keeps me young."

Oh honey, that ship is long gone, just like your hairline.

"That's great," I say.

"Yes," he agrees, looking back at them dancing. "It really is."

"You're lucky to have someone who makes you happy."

I don't want to think about Peter, but I do. I remember dancing with him in the living room, smiling, laughing, and being silly.

"I was sorry to hear about your husband," Darren says. "I didn't know him, but I remember the news of his murder."

I always wondered why people apologize. Darren didn't kill Peter, so why is he sorry? It never was something I cared about until it happened to me. My heart was broken after his death, but I found myself having to comfort others. They didn't know what to say, and I would do what I could to help them help me.

Losing someone unexpectedly is impossible to explain. There was no deterioration or something that we could cling to like the way he fought or how prepared we were.

He went to work one day and never came home.

"I appreciate the condolences," I tell Darren.

He pauses again. His eyes keep finding Milo and Kandi, which makes me wonder if he's actually as comfortable as Milo seems to think.

I watch them on the floor, my own jealousy tingling in my gut, and I push it aside. Milo is my employee. He can dance with whoever the hell he wants. At least that's what I'm telling myself. I do a pretty good job at it until I see him smile down at her, her fingers playing with the back of his neck, and something inside of me aches.

"I know what this is," he says before sipping his drink.

"What, what is?" I lean back and regret it as my dress shifts again. Seriously, I'm going to burn it when I get home and dance around the flames.

Darren places his glass on the table, spinning it as he talks. "You're here to get me to sign the papers."

"I promise that's not why I'm here."

It's really not. I'm here because my assistant is an idiot and I let him talk me into trusting him.

"I'm not trying to be difficult," he says.

Now it's my turn to push. "Then why the hold up?"

"There's complications with the paperwork," Darren informs me.

He's full of crap. That paperwork was gone over multiple times, everything is in order, but as much as Milo might know guys like him, I do as well. I know him, or guys like him, in the business world. He likes to feel important, needed, and have women at his mercy.

I'm the wrong girl though.

"I'm not sure how that's possible," I push back. "Why don't you tell me what the issues are so we can resolve them."

"There was another company that requested permits, and I think the wires are crossed."

Such a liar. I thoroughly researched this property before we purchased it. There were no permits filed since the previous owners basically let the complex crumble. It was a shithole. Each day this property sits untouched, we're losing money.

This is a power play.

"Even if that's the case, I don't see why that would tie up our permits. You know that we're the owners."

Darren appears to mull over what I said. I don't know if he thinks I'm stupid or going to play his game, but I came to win tonight and he's not getting out of this one.

He shrugs. "I'll look it over again on Monday."

I bet he won't.

"You two look cozy," Milo says before I can respond to Darren.

"Not half as much as you two did," I fire back.

His eyes widen, grin grows, and I realize I just gave myself up, letting him see I was paying attention. "You noticed, did you?"

"No, actually, I was too busy having a stimulating conversation with Darren."

Milo takes his seat with a cocky smirk.

Jerk.

"Well then, why not let us all in on what you were discussing."

For the next few minutes, things vary from tense to even more tense as Milo commands the conversation. He informs Darren of his errors, but always manages to pull back before going over the line. His tone is firm, powerful, and I'd be full of shit if I wasn't completely turned on by it.

This is the man that's been hiding underneath being my lackey. His strength is intoxicating. The way he plays Darren like an instrument, bending each note until it plays the way he wants it.

Has he been doing this with me the entire time?

I can't help but wonder because he's good at it.

Now I decide to unleash my own power and go in for the kill.

"Aren't you getting tired of all this back and forth, Darren? And it's not going to stop until we get our permits. I'm sure you have much bigger things to worry about with your wedding coming up. You know, booking the venue, planning the honey-moon . . . negotiating an ironclad pre-nup."

Kandi giggles. "We won't be doing a pre-nup, silly."

Darren clears his throat. "Actually . . . I uh . . . I think we may want to discuss that."

Kandi's drink sloshes on the table as she puts it down with a thud. "Are you kidding me, Darren?"

"Like I said, you've got a lot on your plate," I say. "So why don't I come by on Monday to pick up the signed paperwork and schedule the walk-through inspection so we can get our permits? Then we'll be out of your hair for good."

Milo's arm rests behind me and his fingers graze my bare shoulder. "We both know the excuse of the paperwork is a load of bollocks. So, what time on Monday works best for you?"

After a long grumbly sigh, he says, "Ten o'clock. And don't be late or you'll miss your appointment, and I don't know when I'll be available next."

fifteen

. . .

Milo

"OH MY GOD!" Danielle says, grabbing my leg as we sit in the car. "We did it! We got him to stop his crap."

I'm not celebrating until I have that permit in my hand, but I'm not going to ruin her mood yet. She's looking at me as though we're a winning team, and I quite like it.

"You're welcome."

Tonight *was* a success, but Darren is still a pompous arsehole. We'll have to find out if we actually get what we need come Monday.

That doesn't mean I won't bask in her praise a bit.

She rolls her eyes. "Please, you didn't do this on your own. I started the conversation while you were dancing with the blonde bimbo and flirting with her, and I totally closed it at the end. This was not a solo mission, buddy."

The pads of my fingers slide against her creamy skin and I watch her eyes shift away from jealousy and into desire. All night she's been doing this dance. If my attention was on Kandi, Danielle's body became stiff and anger almost radiated from her. I'm going to see if I was right about her dislike for her.

"I'm sensing a bit of jealousy regarding Kandi," I say as I start the engine, loving the fact that we have total privacy in the car. She can't run, can't avoid this conversation, and I plan to use the upper hand right now.

"I was not jealous."

Lies.

"Then why call her a bimbo? She's perfectly nice, engaged, and you don't know her. I think you're jealous."

"You don't know what you're talking about," Danielle huffs and looks out the window.

"Really? Because if you've changed your mind about finding me desirable, I wouldn't blame you."

Her head turns quickly as she glares at me. "I don't."

"So, you wouldn't care if I said Kandi and I are going for a nightcap after I drop you off?"

"Nope. She's probably not in the mood anymore though. She seemed a little pissed off when we left."

"I can get anyone in the mood. So, you're perfectly fine if I sleep with her?"

She pauses just a heartbeat and then spits the word. "Yup."

Oh, I don't believe that for a single second.

"And you think that would be a good idea?" I continue to irritate her.

"What do I care? I'm your boss, not your babysitter. You want to sleep with the whore from the gym, have at it. I can't stop you."

"She's a whore, is she? I didn't know you knew each other."

What Danielle doesn't know is that I didn't even see Kandi's face all night. I danced with her, wishing it was Danielle. I had to stop myself from tossing Kandi out of my arms, and taking Danielle to the dance floor, just to feel her skin.

It was bad enough that I couldn't seem to control my hands from finding subtle ways to touch her all night.

She glares at me. "I know girls like her. She's engaged and she couldn't keep her hands off you. If she wasn't touching you, she was making bedroom eyes at you." Her voice goes a few octaves higher. "Oh, Milo, you're so funny. Oh, Milo, I just love to dance. Would you like to touch my body? Don't worry, Milo, I'll be back because I want you to say dirty British words to me. Giggle. Snort. Giggle."

I laugh at her impression of Kandi. "Definitely not bothered at all by her I see."

"Gross. Get some dignity, lady," Danielle continues. "She knew you were there with me and it was like I was invisible. Rude much?"

"But you're not jealous, right?"

Danielle points her finger at me as her anger grows. "You're an idiot. I'm not jealous, I feel sorry for her."

"Well, then." I shrug. "Since you're perfectly okay with me sleeping with her, could you send her a text letting her know I'll meet her at my flat?"

Her jaw drops and she twists away from me. "I'm not your assistant, do it your damn self."

There's hurt in her voice, and that lets me know everything I suspected. Somewhere in the past few weeks, things have changed. I don't look at her as the woman who stole my job. I see a strong woman who lost her husband in a dreadful way. She's sexy, smart, resourceful, and I look forward to seeing her, even if it means I take orders from her.

This is going to be an issue between us if we continue to ignore it. I'm not known for being a patient man, so right now, we're going to get to the bottom of it.

I make the turn onto her street, and park in her driveway. She makes a move to exit the car, but I grip her wrist. "What if I told you I didn't want you to message her anyway?" I challenge her. "What if I said I don't want to meet her, touch her, see her again?"

"Why wouldn't you? You're single, she's . . . not, but clearly that doesn't faze her."

"Because." I pause waiting for her to look at me.

"Because?"

"I don't want her. Not even a little bit."

Danielle's eyes widen a little and her breath hitches. "You don't?"

"No."

"Oh."

I smile at her innocence. "There's someone else I want, Danielle."

She shifts, facing me in that fucking dress. Every inch of her is perfect, and this dress left me dying to see it on the floor. I've always found her beautiful, but tonight, she's stunning. I almost lost my mind when I saw her walk out. I couldn't move, think, talk, and I was never more grateful than I was earlier when Parker had her attention.

I was standing there like a bloody fool with my mouth open.

Now, I'm clearly not thinking as all I want to do is take her face in my hands and kiss her until we can't breathe.

"Who do you want?" she asks.

"You."

Danielle's eyes widen and her breathing hitches as I admit to her what I tried desperately to avoid.

"Milo," she breathes my name.

"Tell me you weren't jealous," I demand.

"I . . . I . . . I'm not going to do this with you," she tucks her hair behind her ear and looks away.

"Do what?"

"This! You work for me."

"And?"

"And I can't complicate things."

Not a good enough answer.

"I'm not asking about any of that," I inform her.

Are there countless reasons to walk away? Yes. But right now, I want her to admit she feels what I do.

"Just . . ."

"Tell me you weren't jealous. Tell me you don't feel differently about me and this conversation is over. Don't fucking lie to me, though."

I want her. Every fucked up part of me wants her. I don't care about the fact that she's holding my job. I want to kiss her, get this out of our systems and go back to focusing on what is important —getting my job back. Not spending my days asking Mum to find my old comic books for Parker, or worrying about her husband's trial.

So, we need to set this aside and go back to the way things were. If she says she doesn't feel the same about all of this, I'll walk away. If I'm wrong, we'll never speak of it again.

However, I know I'm not. I saw it tonight, clear as day. Desire was in every touch we shared.

"It's too confusing. I don't know what I'm feeling," Danielle admits as though she's confessing to some mortal sin.

I always liked the phrase less talk and more action. I pride myself that I've lived by that motto.

Doing what I've wanted to do all night, I tenderly take her face in my hands. My thumb brushes against her cheek, and she grips my wrists. "What do you feel now?"

Her eyes meet mine. "You."

"And what about now?" I ask as I move my face closer to hers.

"Scared."

"I won't hurt you," I promise.

The last thing I want to do with her is cause her more pain than she's already endured.

Her eyes close for a moment and then her lids slowly lift, revealing her beautiful blue eyes. "What are we doing?"

"What do you want me to do?"

She drops her gaze to my lips and I don't need her to answer because I already know.

I inch closer, waiting for her to snap out of it and push me away. "Do you want me to kiss you?" I ask as our lips are so close I can feel her breath.

sixteen

. . .

Danielle

WHAT DID HE ASK?

Were we even talking? I can't remember because all I feel right now is Milo. He's everywhere and I can't think straight.

"Danielle," he mutters. "What do you want?"

I want him.

I want . . . I want . . . I want to know if this is real or not.

I want to remember what it feels like to be kissed, wanted . . . touched.

And I want it to be him that shows me.

But there's a part of me that isn't sure if it's the right thing or not. I worry this will only complicate things.

I open my eyes, looking for answers in his stare, wanting to know if I'm overthinking this or if maybe he's kidding. I see the confliction, longing, and hope swirling around, but there's a softness on the edge of it all.

"I'm scared," I admit again.

He closes his eyes, pressing his forehead to mine, and I move my fingers down his arm. Life is short. I've seen it first-hand. I've loved and lost, but somehow, I survived the hurt. I don't know what this is or why I feel it, but I do.

Maybe it's the way he looks at me sometimes. Maybe it's how he treats my kids. Maybe it's the way when I was falling apart, he held me together. Whatever the reason is, I like him. I feel something and tonight it's impossible to deny.

"I'm a fool," he says quietly.

No. He's not. I am. I'm the fool who wants him but is too afraid. I bring my hands back to his wrist and say the words that have been on the tip of my tongue.

"Kiss me."

Milo's head snaps up. "What?"

"Kiss me," I say again. "Kiss me before I change my—"

And he does. His lips press against mine and I freeze. Milo's mouth is firm but not rough as he holds my head steady. I don't move. I can't because his lips are touching mine. My head starts to spin and I try to focus on the feeling of it, but I'm thrown.

He pulls back. "If you want me to kiss you, you better kiss me back, get out of your head."

"I-I was just shocked," I try to explain.

"Kiss me like you want me. Unless you're too afraid, and would prefer I kiss someone else?"

He wants me to kiss him? Oh, I'll kiss him.

"Shut up," my voice is hard. I don't want to think about him kissing anyone else.

"Make me."

"Fuck you!"

"If you're offering . . ." Milo tosses back. "Or you can prove that you're not afraid and show me you know what you're doing."

"You want me to kiss you?"

His nose brushes mine. "Yes."

"Fine."

Asshole. I'll show you what kissing me is like.

I grab his face and lean over the console. I kiss him hard, unyielding, and with everything I have. He's just as rough with me and suddenly I'm back in my seat again with him holding me. I push against his lips as he leans harder against me. His tongue slides across my lips but I don't let him in.

Milo lets out a low groan that boarders on a growl when he tries again. That's right, buddy. I'm not meek or mild. I can blow your fucking mind.

Finally, I open my lips just enough and when our tongues touch, I'm gone. No longer do I have any control of this kiss. Milo has seized it from me or maybe I've given it to him. Either way, I couldn't care less. His hands tangle in my hair, holding me to his mouth as I grip the collar of his shirt.

I've been kissed, but never like this. Never have I felt weightless and yet aware at the same time. No one has ever made my head swim or heart race like this. I crave more. This is a kiss that women dream of.

The movie scene is set, lights are dim, and all anyone can focus on is us.

I move my hands to his neck, holding on because I might float away.

Milo devours my mouth, and I couldn't fight him if I tried.

With each brush of our tongues I melt deeper into his arms. Even in the car where there's no space, I can't get close enough to him.

Suddenly, there's a knock on the window and I shove him off me.

Oh my God.

I struggle to catch my breath. The windows are completely covered and the heat inside the car is stifling.

Another knock. "Umm Mom?" Ava's voice is full of amusement. "Are you and Milo okay?"

"Shit," I mutter.

"Do you guys want to explain why the car is foggy?" she asks while cupping her hands to the window trying to see in.

"What the hell am I going to say?" I ask him.

"That you're an adult and for her to mind her business. Or that you and I were snogging and you like me."

"What the hell is snogging?"

"It's kissing, Mom. You know, like in Harry Potter . . ." Ava explains. "Seriously, Mom I know you're in there. I can hear you."

Damn it. I can't believe I got so carried away. I shift my dress so its back in the right place and she knocks on the window again, which causes me to jump.

"Jesus!"

Instead of Milo trying to fix his shirt, hair, or anything else that got messed up, he leans over me, pressing the window down.

"Can we help you?"

Ava grins and looks at me. "Thought it wasn't a date? And your lipstick is totally ruined."

When I was a teenager, I never got caught making out with my boyfriend. As a grown adult, I get busted by my teenager. Oh, the irony.

"Go inside," I say.

"Your hair is all jacked up."

"Enough," I give her my best mom voice. "Inside."

She laughs. "This is great." Then the child does something I might actually beat her for. She grabs her phone, takes a photo, and then runs inside. "Hashtag, busted!"

"Ava! Get back here!" I yell as she closes the door. "Oh my God! What was I thinking? What the hell was I thinking?"

I lean back and tears begin to form. I'm so stupid. I shouldn't have kissed him. I'm an idiot. Milo works for me and he's trying to take my damn job. Seeing him any other way is stupid. This could be what he wants.

"Danielle," he says my name, but I can't look at him. "It's fine."

"No, it's not fine. I have to go. I never should've been here with you. I'm a total idiot. Why did I kiss you? Why did I let myself think this . . .?" I trail off and get out of the car. My heart is racing as the consequences of my error catch up to me. I kissed him. In front of my house where my freaking daughter saw.

Clearly, I wasn't thinking. I was being so selfish and I didn't take any of the reality like my kids, my job, my life into account. I just wanted his stupid, perfect lips.

The cool night air hits me and I start to walk, but these fucking shoes hate me and I sink into the grass, and fall.

As if this night could get any worse.

"Really?" I say looking toward the sky. "Really?"

I start to get back up, but Milo's hands are already on my waist helping me.

"Stop," I say pushing him away. "I don't need help. I'm fine and you need to go."

"Are you serious right now?"

"Do I look like I'm joking?"

I get to my feet, slip the stupid shoes off and trudge barefoot toward my door. I can't believe I let myself slip like this. I was so caught up in being conflicted that I let my stupid emotions get the better of me. I wanted him so much. I wanted to be wanted more than anything and for all I know this was a game to get me to let him in.

How easily I caved.

"What the hell is going on?" Milo asks as he grabs my arm, stopping me from climbing the steps to my house.

"Nothing."

"Nothing?"

I try to pull my arm back, but he won't let go. "This was a mistake."

"A mistake?" he asks.

"What are you, a parrot? Yes. This. Whatever that was." I point with my shoes to the car. "Can't and won't ever happen. I don't know what this is that you're doing, but I'm not playing around. I have other people to think about and I can't lose my job because you're getting me to . . . whatever your plan is . . . won't work."

His hand drops. "You think that's what I was doing? Playing some silly game with you?"

My chest tightens when I see the hurt flash in his eyes. "Yes! I know what you want and the fact that you could play on my emotions to get me to be so dumb is low. I need to go inside."

Pulling away, I suddenly feel stupider than I did before. I'm emotional and a sense of guilt is hanging over me.

I know Peter's gone. I know I'm single, but all I could think about when Milo was touching me was how much better his lips felt.

How Peter was never possessive.

How Peter didn't kiss me that way.

How Milo was different and I liked it.

God, I'm a horrible person.

"Do you really think I'm pretending? Did you not sense the way I wanted you all night and even the days leading up to it? Do you think I make it a point to support people I barely know the way I've tried to do with you? If this was a game, as you so say, why would I help you? Wouldn't I let you fall and laugh at the outcome?"

"I don't know what to think, but I'm not a child who can go around making out with employees!"

He laughs. "Please, that was hardly making out. We're grown-ups, blowing off steam and clearly you're attracted to me, not that I blame you."

"You arrogant asshole. You were coming onto me all night."

"Was I? I was rather busy with Kandi if you recall."

"Wow, I was right about you. We're all pawns in your little chess game. Here I thought you were a good man, my bad. Won't make that mistake again. You've told me all along who you are. I should've listened the first time. You're exactly what your family says."

Milo takes a step closer, his back is straight. I can sense the pain my words just brought him. It was a low blow, but he's not exactly fighting fair either.

"I'm not this man, Danielle. Make no mistake, I'm not the good guy you want, but I'm not the villain either. I'm not playing a game to take your job. I kissed you because I wanted you, but clearly I had an error in judgement as you pointed out."

Milo's hurt is gone and has been replaced with anger and disappointment.

"I didn't—"

"You don't have to say anything else. I think you've made yourself rather clear on your feelings about me. I'm sorry you feel that kissing me was such a mistake. I'll ensure you don't make the same one twice. Besides, it was just a kiss. It means nothing in the grand scheme of things, does it? Not like we're ever going to be more once things shake out the way I plan. Goodnight, Danielle."

I stand there, watching him walk away, wanting to say so much, but I don't. If we end things like this, there will be no confusion. He shouldn't care what I think at this point. He's already made it clear that he has no desire for any relationship. Whatever this is, it's insignificant to him. I can't be that to anyone. If I give the little piece of my heart that's left and he breaks it, then what?

I have to think about my kids, their future, and the fact that I need my position.

He reaches his car and our eyes lock. Then he shakes his head and gets inside. When Milo's car backs up and I can no longer see the tail lights, a tear falls.

I'm only fooling myself if I think I don't care about what just happened. The remaining piece of my heart is already hurting.

"Good morning, Mrs. Bergen. I have your call sheet along with some files you need to review. Would you like me to leave them here?" Milo asks.

I've been dreading this moment. To the point that I almost called out sick today. That's how much the idea of seeing him after Saturday night upset me.

All day Sunday, I thought about calling him. He did nothing wrong and I treated him as though he had. I asked him to kiss me and then pushed him away. Now, I need to apologize and find a way for us to work together.

"Milo," I say his name and he looks at me with a hardness I haven't seen before.

"Was there anything else you needed?"

"I think we should talk."

He huffs. "There's no need. I have nothing to say."

"Well, I do," I counter.

Milo stands against the door with his arms crossed. "Does it pertain to business?"

"Yes. Come in and take a seat."

I can see how much he hates this right now. My being his boss and since he's so adamant about not talking about anything personal, this is torture for him.

"Did we get the approval from Darren yet?" I ask. Darren called to explain there was an emergency and he couldn't meet. Now we're back to waiting again.

"No."

"Have you reached out to the city to follow up?"

"Yes."

Great, we're on one-word answers. Time to step it up. "All right, how did the call go?"

Milo smirks. "Fine."

My anger starts to boil. "What did he say?"

"Nothing."

I might kill him. "Are you serious? You're really going to act like this?"

"I'm going to be having a long lunch with the owner of Dove-tail today to discuss my future with the company."

Oh. "Okay then. So you mean to tell me you're going to have lunch with your brother?" I'm stunned. I don't know what to say. I knew he was upset with what happened, but Milo has never treated me so coldly.

"Yes."

Seriously, I hate him right now.

"Are we not going to talk about the other night?"

Milo looks up from the papers on his lap, his expression stone faced. I'm not going to give in. He's acting like a child, and I'm trying to be an adult here. It doesn't have to be this way.

I wait.

And wait.

And Milo doesn't move.

With each second that passes, I think of a different way to make his life miserable.

"Stop already!" I crack.

"Stop what?"

"This! This whole 'I don't care' attitude and one-word answers with me. I'm sorry I freaked out okay? I'm still trying to get my shit together and I got scared. I never wanted to hurt your feelings, Milo. Never. You've been great and you make me feel things that scare me. I'm trying here, please talk to me. I don't . . . I want . . . I can't get hurt again."

Milo gets to his feet. "Scared?"

Ugh. Another one-word reply.

He moves toward me, around the desk, and stands in front of me. My head tilts back to see him.

"Scared of what?" Milo asks as he leans down. His hands rest on both sides of my chair and now we're nose to nose.

My pulse spikes at his closeness. Why does my traitorous body care about him? I try to slow my breathing, but even I can hear how labored it is.

"I don't want to feel these things again," I whisper. "I don't want to blur the lines."

"I think it might be too late, don't you? Don't you think the lines were crossed when my tongue was in your mouth?"

Why does the thought of that make my stomach clench?

"No," I shake my head.

"Do you really think I'm going to use you to get this job back?"

I want to say no, but the truth is, I'm not sure. None of this makes much sense to me. Milo has already told me the kind of man he is, but he also has always been honest. He explained that he doesn't play games, so why am I now not going to take him at his word?

"I won't lie to you. I don't know what to think."

His face is close, lips right in front of me, and my throat goes dry. "Don't think. Feel, sweetheart."

I lean in a little closer without giving myself permission to do so. The scent of his cologne, the confidence that he exudes, and the richness in his voice is like a drug. You can't have just one hit, you want to relapse over and over.

"We can't," I whisper.

"Oh, but we can, and you want to, don't you?"

Yes. I want him to kiss me again.

He tilts his head a little more and right before our lips touch, a noise breaks the moment.

"Am I . . . interrupting something?" Callum's voice fills the room. "I can come back if you two were busy."

Please let this not be happening. I close my eyes and feel the burn on my cheeks.

"Perfect timing as always, brother," Milo laughs as he releases my chair.

"I was checking if we were still on for lunch? Hello, Danielle," Callum smirks at me.

Now I've been caught in a compromising position with Milo by both my kid and my boss.

"Callum, I was . . ."

"Yes?"

"I was just . . ."

"She was about to kiss me, but you ruined it," Milo finishes.

Seriously, I want to crawl under my desk and never come out. I don't know that I've ever been this mortified in my life.

"I was not!" I declare. Maybe I was, but there's no way I'm admitting it.

Milo shakes his head. "Right, we were checking each other's breathing in case I needed CPR. Better?"

I drop my face in my hands. "Yeah, great."

Callum laughs. "I'm not touching this with a ten-foot pole. I'll be in my office when you're ready, Milo."

I slowly lift my face, praying Callum left.

"Well, that was rather embarrassing." Milo grins.

My stomach roils as I let the mortification take me under. This man makes me crazy and drives me to do stupid things. I need to keep my distance.

"Did you know he was going to show up?"

Milo looks at me with a confusion. "How would I know when Callum is going to magically appear?"

"I don't know, but . . . ugh! This couldn't be any worse."

He walks toward the door, looks back at me with a grin, and says, "Don't worry, I won't tell him about our little kiss the other night. I wouldn't want you to have any issues with human resources."

Fuck my life.

seventeen

. . .

Milo

MY BROTHER BORES ME. There's no other way to describe it. He's always been a bit stuffy, but now he's truly . . . drab.

Every rule he follows.

Every part of his life has been analyzed and combed through to find the right choice that will yield him the proper results. The only impulsive decision he's ever made was marrying Nicole.

I have to give him credit, she's definitely the best choice he's made. The fact he had to move across the Atlantic, however, is what brought our relationship to this point. Had he stayed in London, this luncheon wouldn't be necessary.

"You wanted to talk?" Callum asks as he cuts his steak.

"Not exactly, but you asked if we could have this little conversation, so I'm assuming it's about my position in the company." I grab the glass of scotch and take a sip while I wait.

"Are you leaving?" he finally asks.

"To go . . .?"

Callum places the fork and knife down, pats his mouth with the napkin, and then shrugs.

I don't know what that means, so I stay quiet and wait. Does he think I'm quitting? Does he want to go to another restaurant? Really the options are endless.

"You're going to make me say it?" Callum finally asks.

"Clearly I don't have the faintest idea what you're talking about, so yes."

"To London, Milo. Are you leaving to go back home? Because we both know this little charade isn't going to last much longer. In fact, I'm rather surprised you've endured it for this amount of time. We both know you're unhappy."

This is again where I find my brother to be dim. He thinks he knows everything about me, but never bothers to actually ask.

I lean back in my chair. "How wonderful that you're a mind reader now, Cal. I didn't know you had so many talents."

"You can't tell me being her assistant is what you want."

"Piss off. You don't know what I want. Or you don't care because you're a bastard who doesn't give a toss about anyone else."

Callum laughs. "You think I enjoy the calls from Mum about her little baby not having his job back?"

"Maybe she thinks you're a prat."

I'm sure that's not true. Not her perfect Callum who does everything right. She loves to point out all my faults and remind me of how I continue to disappoint her. I'm tired of trying to find the sun in Callum's shadow. It's exhausting and humiliating.

"Maybe she thinks you're never going to change."

"Then she's right. I'm the same irresponsible man I was all those years ago, right? Same old Milo, different country."

He shakes his head. "I thought you had changed these last few weeks. Seeing you with Danielle, being a team player and all. I guess I was wrong."

"Again, you make assumptions. Have I caused a single problem since I've been back?"

"No."

"Have I asked you to reinstate me as an executive?"

"No, and why is that, Milo?"

Because that would mean Danielle would lose her job.

That reason alone should have me running for the next flight to London.

What in the bloody hell is wrong with me? I came here to get my job back and destroy the bastard who took it from me. I wanted revenge of the mightiest kind. My goals were clear, my plan was foolproof, and then I met her.

I found out that she was not so easy to take down, and I saw what it would cost her. Turns out that she's not a bastard at all. She's actually quite perfect.

"Because I'm a fool," I say to Callum.

"Ah." He smirks. "I guess I don't have to ask why, since when I walked in you were about to kiss her."

"I'd rather not talk about it," I say through gritted teeth.

Callum rests his arms on the table. "Did I ever tell you the story about when Dad met Mum?"

My face falls because the last thing I want is a trip down memory lane. "Really? No, and I don't care to know either."

He continues on as though my answer is irrelevant. "Mum and I have a different version of the story, even though the outcome was the same. What Mum doesn't know is that I used to listen to his phone calls. He knew my biological father, and I suspect that he was placed in our lives for a reason. You know my father was a ruthless business man who thrived on making others cower to him. I think he wanted the same for Mum, but we know there's not much that will make that woman roll over."

"Is there a point here, Callum?"

I don't care about this. Dad is gone and however they met has no bearing on my life.

"Don't be a tosser." He glares. "I'm telling you that Dad didn't meet Mum and just fall in love. Sometimes you find yourself together and you choose to feel or not. You're not a heartless bastard, Milo, but you sure are daft."

"How do you figure?"

Callum throws his napkin on the table. "I'm not going to point it out to you. I think you bloody know what has you so pissed off right now."

"Yeah, you," I toss back.

"I know," Callum laughs and stands. "I'm the villain as always. It has nothing to do with your feelings towards Danielle. Suddenly it's all me who is making your life difficult. Am I right?"

He can fuck off. I don't need this. I don't feel anything but the desire to punch him in his mouth. Danielle has made it clear what she thinks of me, and she's right. I'm a selfish bastard who's unfit for a relationship.

I'm the guy who will hurt her because I don't know any other way.

I will fail her, because my history says that it's inevitable.

In no way am I deserving of her and pursuing her will only end one way—disaster.

I get to my feet and toss money on the table. "No, you're just the wanker who needs to mind his fucking business."

"And here I thought we were going to have a nice lunch."

Now it's my turn to laugh. "I guess we both know better than to try again."

I start to walk out the door, not wanting to deal with his shit for a minute longer, but he grabs my arm as I get outside.

"I'll keep trying. I want you to know that. Not because of Mum or any of that, but because you have a family who gives a damn about you, regardless of what you think. You have a nephew who should know his uncle, and Nicole apparently likes you, although once she gets to know you, she might change her mind. Also, you have a brother who is tired of not having his brother around. I'm not giving up on you, no matter how hard you push me away."

He claps me on the arm, and heads to his car as I stand there without the ability to speak.

In all my life, Callum has never shown me that he cared. He's always been too driven to deal with my shit. I'm not sure how I feel about this.

Callum drives away, and I'm like a statue, still trying to process what just happened.

eighteen

...

Danielle

"AND DID you knowingly enter Mr. Bergen's office with the gun?" The prosecutor asks as my hands begin to shake.

"Well, I knowingly had the gun, but I wasn't looking for him specifically," the man who killed Peter replies.

I'm amazed at how calm and collected he is. As if this is a day like any other. Not a single ounce of remorse on his face.

I didn't plan to be here. After that first day in court, I've found every excuse to miss it. Yet somehow, I'm sitting here, listening and wishing I had stayed away. I needed to leave the office after what happened with Milo. I grabbed my purse and headed to my favorite little food stand by the beach. I sat there, watching the waves lap the shore, wondering how the hell I got here.

Sure, life is crazy. I get that. But this is beyond crazy. This is out of control.

I thought about my kids, my friends, and my family. Before I knew it, I was done eating and instead of heading back to the office, it was as if someone else was driving my car, bringing me to the courthouse.

I don't know why I felt compelled to be here. Maybe it was because my last thoughts while watching the ocean were about

Peter. Maybe it was the guilt of almost kissing Milo again. There was a niggling feeling inside of me that there was something important happening, and I was right. Adam McClellan wasn't supposed to take the stand today, but I'm sitting here, watching it happen.

"And was your intention to use the gun?" she asks.

"I didn't go there to kill him if that's what you're asking."

"Then what was your motive?"

He looks at me for a moment and I swear my heart stops. I'm not sitting up front this time. I'm in the back, trying to hide behind anyone I can. However, he zeroes right in on me.

"Mr. McClellan." She steps in front of him, breaking the eye contact. "Did you have a motive when you went to Mr. Bergen's office?"

"I was just going to scare them a bit."

"With a loaded gun?"

He shrugs. "Yeah."

"And then what happened?" she pushes him.

I can't listen to this, not without someone beside me.

I reach my hand out, wishing Milo was here to hold it.

Funny that my mind goes to him. He's what has me so torn up inside. I shouldn't think about him the way I do. I shouldn't want to be around him all the damn time. I definitely shouldn't be sitting in my husband's trial, thinking about Milo, but I am.

My chest aches and I realize that I have to get out of here. This is wrong and I'm even more of a mess than I realized. I slide over towards the end of the bench, but when I get to the edge, Milo walks in.

His eyes find mine and he levels me with one look. He watches me as he sits beside me. "Were you leaving?" he asks in a hushed tone.

"Why are you here? How did you find me?"

Why did you magically appear when I wished you would? Is what I want to say.

He moves in close and my heart races. "I called your phone, couldn't find you, so I opened your Find My Phone app, and figured it out."

Now my assistant is Sherlock Holmes. Just what I need.

"Great." My voice is laced with sarcasm.

Milo confuses me, takes my emotions and puts them in a blender and sets it on high. I don't know whether I want to lean on him for support or run screaming.

Adam takes a few seconds, his eyes find mine again in the crowd and I could vomit. Everything inside of me feels cold and dead. He doesn't get to look at me. He shouldn't be allowed to sit there looking so smug.

"I walked into his office. He was sitting there . . ."

I cover my ears with my hands. This is too much. I should have known better than to stay here.

Milo glances at the stand, seeing who is there and then turns back to me. He pulls my hands down, and he speaks softly, lips brushing my ear. "There's nothing he can say that you haven't already pictured in your mind."

Adam's angry voice replaces the gentle one of Milo's. "I asked him to call my lawyer, but he wouldn't. I told him I wasn't playing around, and he told me to calm down."

I look at Milo. "Isn't it better to live with the lie?" I whisper.

Milo takes my hand again. "Never."

I've gone through a million scenarios in my mind on how Peter was killed. They played out like a movie before me. Each scene more graphic and horrendous than the last. Did he beg for his life? Was it fast? Did Peter save another lawyer by sacrificing himself?

More than anything, I want to know if Peter thought of me and the kids. Was there a moment when our faces were in his mind, and he felt our love?

I hope so.

I hope, more than anything, in his final breath he knew how

much he meant to me. How his love and determination kept our family together.

Milo is right, though. I'll never know what Peter was thinking. I'll never get those answers, but I can get these.

"Mr. McClellan, how did the gun go off?"

I grip Milo's hand tighter, feeling as though it's the only thing holding me to this world right now. I feel weightless, dizzy, and unsteady. However, I can't take my eyes off of what's unfolding now.

"I don't know," he replies.

"You don't know?"

"I was holding it, and then it . . . went off."

The prosecutor doesn't waste a second. "Did you fire the weapon?"

"No. Like I said, it was an accident. The gun went off on its own."

The defense is lying. I've seen this done before and I pray to God it doesn't work. If they can plant a seed of doubt that the murder was accidental, this man could walk away with a slap on the wrists. There are no witnesses to the actual shooting of the gun, just the video showing him walking in and out of the office. No one actually saw Adam kill Peter.

The prosecutor takes a slow walk in front of the jury.

"You mean to tell me that you went to the office with a loaded gun, and Mr. Bergen ends up shot, but you never meant to harm him?"

"That's correct."

"You had no intention of using the gun? Yet you put a full chamber of bullets in it?"

Adam drops his head. "No, I wanted to talk to *my* lawyer. I wasn't even there to see Peter."

My fingers squeeze harder and Milo does the same in return.

"With a loaded gun?"

Slowly, Adam raises his gaze, I watch as he attempts to look contrite. "Yeah, but it wasn't supposed to be loaded. I thought it was empty."

"So you mean to tell me that it misfired multiple times? Because he was shot multiple times—shots that took him away from his wife and children forever."

"Like I said, I was an accident. And I'm sorry for his family and all, but there's a chance he abused his wife and kids – that's what I heard anyway. So if that's the case, maybe it's not the worst thing that could have happened."

And I lose it.

I'm out of my seat, unable to control my emotions a minute longer.

"Liar!" I scream out. "You stole him from us and you have no remorse! How dare you!"

"Order!" The judge calls.

I continue to yell, but I don't know what I'm saying. Just anger and devastation come out from my lips. That bastard killed my husband in cold blood and now he's trying to tarnish his memory.

Milo's arms are around my waist, pulling me out of the courtroom while the judge bangs his gavel and yells for order over and over.

My heart is pounding so hard in my chest I worry I'll bruise. I hate him. I hate that I'm so weak and I came here anyway.

When the door closes, I collapse in Milo's arms. He holds me to his chest as I fall to pieces. I cling to him, trying to bury my face because no one should see me.

"It's all right, Danielle," Milo tells me as I sob. "You're all right now."

I'm not all right. I'm a crazy person who lost it in the courtroom. No one will remember Peter's smile. They'll see his psycho widow screaming at a man on trial. I did this. I know better, but I couldn't stop myself.

Anger replaces my shame and I suddenly don't want comfort.

"No, it's not!" I push back out of his arms. "I just delivered the defense a small victory. I did that. I gave them something."

"You gave them nothing."

"I did!" I tell him. "I fucking know better. I need to leave. I knew I couldn't handle this. I can't handle anything because everything I touch falls apart."

Milo grips my arms, stopping me from walking away. "You're being too hard on yourself."

"Did you miss that scene in there, Milo? Did you close your eyes and miss the lunatic that went crazy in there?"

"You don't see how magnificent you are. You're handling the weight of the world and you don't give yourself any credit, do you?"

I've done nothing but fuck things up left and right.

"Please," I scoff. "I don't deserve credit for anything. Don't you get it? I destroyed everything!"

He's not hearing what I say, though. He takes two strides forward and pulls me in his arms.

I may be falling apart, but he's holding me together. Milo leans his forehead against mine. "You don't see yourself."

I wish that were true. But I saw everything I just did, and none of it I like. "You only see what you want," I say.

Milo lifts his head, wiping the tear that's slowly falling, leaving little black rivers against my skin. "I see you. I wish I didn't sometimes. You can continue to push back, and that's fine, but I've been dealing with people doing it to me my entire life, Danielle. I've gotten bloody good at fighting back and I'll fight for you."

I'm not pushing him away. I'm breaking apart. There's a difference. All my fight is gone. Watching that was too much. "You don't want me, I'm damaged."

"And I'm not?"

"Not in the same way, Milo."

He rubs my cheek with his thumb. "All of us are imperfect. All of us have flaws. All of us are undeserving of something, but that doesn't mean we don't want more."

Another tear falls as I look at him. "Why are you here? Why did you come for me?"

"Because I needed to see you."

The walls that are usually around him are down. There's a vulnerability in his eyes. Something I saw the other night, and it shakes me. I don't know if it's because I'm emotionally raw or because of what he's shown me the last few weeks, but I lift my hand to touch his face. "What's happening with us?"

Milo brings his lips to my forehead and places a soft kiss there. "I don't know, but I'm not sure I'm strong enough to stay away from you."

I look up at him, realizing that even during this nightmare of a trial, I wanted him. I wished he would be here so I could lean on him. He's been there for me in a way I didn't expect, and I find myself craving him.

"I'm not either," I admit.

Slowly, Milo brings his lips to mine. Softly he kisses me, and for one second, I don't feel like I'm a mess. I feel safe, and that's a very bad thing to feel in his arms.

nineteen

. . .

Danielle

"SO YOU BURST out screaming at the defendant?" Heather asks while pouring a glass of wine.

"Yup."

"Not your finest moment, huh?" Kristin giggles as she tucks her legs under her butt.

I roll my eyes. "Obviously not."

"Well, I can't say I blame you, Danni. You've been holding in a lot of crap and trying to pretend life is great," Heather's voice is full of compassion.

I don't know what else to say at this point. If I cry too much, I feel like a burden. If I don't break down, I'm too strong. There's no right way to handle things.

"I'm not pretending anything. I'm dealing with my life the best I can. Am I a little overwhelmed? Yeah. I mean, my teenager is a freaking lunatic, Parker asked about his father again, I'm working full time and trying to pay bills, and I'm going to be fucking forty in three months." I pull my hair up into a pony tail. "Oh, I also kissed Milo," I blurt out.

Might as well get this over with.

Both of them sit their glasses on the table and then look at each other with their jaws hanging open. "This just got interesting." Heather says.

"Yes, because me screaming like a maniac in court wasn't ridiculous enough?"

Kristin shrugs. "She means the good shit."

"I know what she means," I huff.

Nicole opens the door and then knocks. "Hey, sorry I'm late. I couldn't get Colin to sleep and God knows I'd get a hundred phone calls if I tried to leave him with his—" She stops talking, taking in the room. "—what the hell is going on here?"

"Danielle kissed Milo."

She smirks at me. "Oh, I know all about that. Callum caught them in her office. Naughty girl. I hope you have some dirty desk sex while you're at it."

I drop my head in my hands. "I can't with you people."

Nicole laughs. "Did you think he wasn't going to tell me? He said it was super uncomfortable to watch. That you were all panting and shit and Milo was super anxious through lunch. It seems you like a little British action too. Oh!" she yells and claps her hands. "We'll be legit sisters!"

Kristin bursts out laughing. "All of our dreams right there. Being sisters with the nutcase of the group."

"Please," Nicole huffs. "You wish you had me as a sister."

Heather giggles. "We wish we could erase the years you thought you were our sister."

My friends are absolutely insane. There's never been a doubt about this, but I'm not marrying anyone. Hell, Milo and I kissed—twice. That's it.

"I think everyone needs to simmer down a bit. It was a mistake, okay? I'm clearly having a midlife crisis of sorts and this is just me . . . not handling it well."

"Or you're finally getting a second chance at things," Kristin suggests.

"The fairy tale mentality is gone for me, Kris."

"Right, because when I was considering going for Noah you were so pessimistic?"

She was a totally different story. Her husband spent years making her small and insignificant. He shit on her and she deserved to be happy again. I wasn't miserable in my marriage when Peter was killed.

"It's different and you know it. How can any of you even think this is a good, juicy story? My husband . . ."

"Don't even," Nicole cuts in. "Your husband was not our favorite person and you know it. Peter got better the last two years, but let's be real, even *you* fucking hated his ass for a long time. You almost divorced him how many times? Don't use Peter as your get out of love card."

"Really, Nic?" Heather playfully slaps her arm.

"I didn't think lying to each other is the way we do things in this group."

Nicole looks at me and waits for me to say something. No, she's right, in this group we don't hold back and we don't lie to each other. We're honest no matter what and after our feelings are hurt and we act like the bitches we are, we hug it out and move on. Nicole never liked Peter.

Kristin does what she does best and tries to smooth it over. "You know that I loved Peter like a brother, right?"

I nod.

"Okay, then hear me with an open heart. Loving someone in the past doesn't mean you don't deserve love in the future, Danni. Maybe this thing will have been a make-out session. Maybe you'll kiss him again and then walk away. But what if it's not? What if he's more? What if Milo is your next real love, but you weren't brave enough to see?"

I try to hear what she's saying. Somewhere inside of me, I want to be at peace with it. Peter wouldn't want me to spend my life alone. He wouldn't want our kids to not have a man to look up to and even love his children. That's not how we felt about things. I don't know that Milo would ever be his choice.

Or if he's mine.

"Can we not talk about this?"

"Nope." They all answer in unison.

Saw that one coming.

"Here's the thing, we kissed two times. Two. That's it. Milo has pretty much told me in no uncertain terms that he's not a relationship guy. His own brother doesn't think that highly of him."

Nicole raises her hand. "In Milo's defense, Callum can be a little judgmental. He didn't exactly see the jewel I am until I pretty much forced him."

"Yes, you're a fucking diamond," Heather laughs. "Or maybe cubic zirconia . . ."

"And fuck you, I'm every stone there is because we're all perfect. However, we're not talking about me, here. We're talking about Danielle and her disaster of a love life."

"How noble of you to allow me to have the floor," I roll my eyes.

"You're welcome. Please, continue," Nicole instructs.

I ignore her theatrics because, it's how she always is. Heather and Kristin are watching me and I throw my hands up with a huff. "I'm just saying that you're all acting like Milo is *the* guy. He's just *a* guy."

I don't know how to make it any clearer for them.

Sure, I like Milo. I won't deny that or the fact that I think about him all the goddamn time. And yes, he's been there for me in ways that have surprised me. Which is probably why I feel this warmth towards him.

And I'm not too proud to admit that he's shown me this sweet side to him that he keeps hidden so well, one that I want to see more of.

Or that he kisses really freaking good.

It doesn't matter that I get nervous when he comes around or that the sound of his voice does things to me. None of that is relevant because Milo and I are nothing. I'm his boss and he's my assistant.

That's it.

I'm not going to keep picturing his perfect green eyes, the scruff on his face, or how much I love being wrapped in his arms.

Nope. I'm done with that. I'm a strong woman and I can control my thoughts and feelings.

It's not a big deal that all I want is to be in his arms some days. It's only because he smells so good and I like cologne. Not that he's strong, confident, makes me feel like I matter when he wraps me tight.

Nope.

None of that is the reason.

"Hello!" Kristin waves her hand in front of my face. "Did you hear a word we said?"

Shit. I wasn't even aware they were talking. I rack my brain to see if somewhere I was able to pick up on something. The word "hope" stands out so I try that.

"Yeah, you said . . . to hope or maybe . . ." It's clear they're not buying that.

"Oh, I know that face," Heather giggles. "That's the she's-got-it-bad look. You know, when you can't focus on the world around you because some guy is taking up all your headspace?"

"Yup," Nicole tosses a kernel of popcorn at me.

Kristin shrugs. "I've seen it before, too."

"You guys suck!"

"Tell me that you feel nothing for Milo," Kristin demands. "And don't you dare try to lie."

"I . . . I feel . . . I can't say it."

Heather gets up, sits beside me, and takes my hand. "You are allowed to feel again. You're allowed to have another chance at love. You're allowed to date, have sex, make bad choices because you're a smart woman. Losing Peter was horrible, and I was really happy when you guys found a way through the shit you were going through. When he was killed, I mourned with you and for you, but that doesn't mean the rest of your life is over. Not by a long shot."

I nod. "It just feels so soon."

She smiles. "Look at all of us, my friend. I was married. Kristin was married and fell in love with Noah before her divorce was final, and did you judge her?"

"Of course not," I say quickly. "That was different, and we know it. Scott deserved to be shot, Peter didn't."

Kristin snorts. "Ain't that the truth."

"Preach!" Nicole lifts her hands up.

"Still," Heather says softly. "We all had to go through losing our first love, the guy we were meant to be with forever and learn to let that go. Nicole is the only one who didn't marry hers, but she still lived a spinster life with threesomes until Callum came around."

"God, I miss double penetration," Nicole sighs before drinking her wine.

Heather and Kristin shake their heads. "Point is," Heather huffs. "We all found a love greater than we knew before. I'm not saying Milo will or won't be, but the fact that you're this conflicted tells me he's special, Danni. I would trust that gut feeling because if you lose him, how much will that hurt?"

I don't answer right away because the pain I feel in my chest is growing. I don't want to lose him, I just don't know if I'm ready to open myself to love again.

"If I never have him, it won't hurt at all."

"True," Kristin says. "But can you sit here now, think of him with another woman, and not want to claw that bitch's eyes out?"

I think back to Kandi and shake my head. "No."

"Then there's your answer."

Nicole smiles. "Yup. Fuck his brains out and fall in love. It's really the only answer to your problems."

We all start to laugh and my friends do what they do best . . . drive me nuts and force me to recount every detail of the two kisses we shared.

"Look at how brilliant I am," Milo says as he enters my office with papers.

He has a huge smile and is strutting like a peacock would preen. It's cute . . . dammit. Not cute. No, annoying, dumb, or any other negative adjective because that's what Milo is. Under no circumstances is he cute, amazing, wonderful, a great kisser, has a great ass, oh, and that accent . . .

Damn it.

There I go again.

I clear my throat as he grins at me. "What did you do that has you so happy? Get a puppy? Roast a child over an open fire?"

"Funny. Tell me first, sweetheart. Tell me that I'm the most brilliant man in the world."

I lean back in my chair, waiting for hell to freeze over.

"Not going to happen," I laugh. "I make it a point not to lie if I can avoid it."

"This will change your mind." Milo places the paper in front of me with Darren's signature.

"You got the permit?"

"We damn sure got the permit."

"It's signed?"

He smirks. "Signed, sealed, and delivered, baby."

"You're sure? You didn't forge it or something?"

He shakes his head. "Absolutely not. We've had our walk-through inspection and are fully permitted to build. It's one hundred percent done."

I get to my feet, taking the papers in my hand and read them aloud. "Darren Wakefield approves the plans to have Dovetail

Enterprises break ground and then it's signed," my voice gets higher as I continue.

We did it.

We really did.

That crazy ass scheme of his worked and we got the permits.

"See?"

"Milo!" I yell and rush toward him. "I can't believe this!"

He catches me in his arms and twirls me around. It's been hell with this freaking permit, but we did it.

"Believe it, sweetheart. Now, say the words . . ."

Darren continued his games after the inspection, holding us in limbo for the last few days, but we got it. Callum is going to be so relieved and I might actually get to keep my job. All because of Milo and his crazy plan that actually panned out.

"You really came through for me, Milo," I smile at him as he sets me down. "You're amazing and brilliant and whatever else you want to hear."

"No, you are." Milo winks at me and I suddenly realize how inappropriate that was.

After my wine-fest with my friends, I made a promise that until Milo and I talked, I would not allow myself the opportunity to cross any lines. I'm not a sleep-around girl. I don't do one-night things. I need stability, rules, definitions in relationships, and someone I can count on.

That talk taught me that I can't function in disfunction.

Milo is the epitome of that. He's reckless, spontaneous, lives his life without rules and that works for him, but that will never be how I operate.

I take a step back, but he follows me.

"I appreciate all your help getting this done for the *team*. We needed this win, and you brought it home for Dovetail," I say, trying to slip back into boss and employee mode.

"I don't give a fuck about Dovetail."

My heart begins to race as Milo takes another step closer. He's stalking me, and I'm trapped with nowhere to go.

"Okay, well, whatever your motives were, thank you."

"I did it for you," he says as his body is almost touching mine.

I can't think when he's this close and says things like that. It makes it too hard to remember that we can't go there.

"Don't say that." I turn my head to the side.

"It's the truth."

Our eyes meet and I want so badly for this to be another time in my life. One where I wasn't worried about everything and all my stupid rules. I would let him whisk me away to the kind of world he lives in. Why can't I have what I want? Will I ever allow myself a chance to live and not be worried about everyone else? No. I won't. So all the other questions . . .

My heart races as I answer myself and tell him, "It doesn't matter."

"The fuck it does matter. I did it for you. I didn't do it for Callum or this silly job he's trying to teach me a lesson with. I don't give a damn about any of it."

"Why?"

"Why do you think, Danielle?"

I try to move out of his grasp but he cages me in. "I don't know what to think. It doesn't make sense."

"I know."

My chest rises and falls as my breathing becomes labored. "What are you saying?"

"I'm saying that I have feelings for you. That no matter how many times I tell myself you're off limits, I find myself wanting to touch you." He lifts his hand slowly, pushing the strand of hair that fell in my eye.

"We're not kissing again," I say. "Not until we talk about all of this and come up with some plan."

Milo grins, his lips brush against my ear and I shiver. "Who said anything about kissing?"

twenty

. . .

Milo

I'M A BASTARD.

I'm a selfish bastard but I can't seem to fucking care.

Her lips part and desire swims in her blue eyes as she tries to fight it. Watching her like this is reason enough to keep going.

"I'm saying we can't kiss," her voice is soft and there's no conviction in her words. Her body moves toward me, even though there's very little space left to go, and I know she wants to kiss me.

I glide my finger down her neck, loving the silky feel of her skin. She's absolutely breathtaking right now.

All day I watched her walk around in her pencil skirt with her white blouse that I could see through with the right light. I thought about tearing it open, watching the buttons fall around us as I sunk my cock in her. Each time she sighed, I imagined her lying beneath me as I dragged different sounds from those plump lips.

If she keeps breathing like this, forcing her breasts to rise and fall, I might just act on that little fantasy.

"Then what can we do?" I question.

Her eyes close as I continue to lightly touch her. I'm going to push her as far as I can. She's not fooling me here, and I'm tired of watching her have this war in her mind. When she's unguarded, she acts, and that is a sight to behold.

"We can't . . . we can't . . . kiss because . . . God," she mutters. "I can't think with you touching me."

I love that I fluster her so easily.

She takes her bottom lip between her teeth and I'm rock fucking hard. I want her so badly it hurts. I need to touch her. I can't wait another moment and I don't give a shit about her rules regarding us.

There are no fucking rules.

The attraction between us in undeniable and my feelings for her are more than I ever wanted to allow.

Danielle is the first woman that makes me want *more* in my life. I don't care about the cars, money, job, or any of that. I want to be someone worthy of her. Someone she can rely on and it's driving me mad.

I think about caring for her.

I see things and think of Parker and his love of comics.

My mind wanders all the bloody time to thoughts about how to make her smile again, because the sight of it makes my heart swell. Like a fucking fool.

However, right now, all I'm thinking about is touching every inch of her before I lose control.

"Can I do this?" I ask as I reach the top of her chest. My fingers graze her breast and she lets out a soft moan.

"Milo."

"What about this?" My touch drops lower and I skim across where her nipple hides in her bra. "Do you want me to stop?"

"No, but we should," she admits.

"Says who, darling?"

I move my other hand up her back, fastening her to me and her fingers grip my arm. We breathe each other in and I pause.

Her eyes open. The lust and passion are unbridled. That look is enough to bring a man to his knees.

I know what she said, but I can't stop myself. I have to kiss her. I pull her even tighter and bring my lips to hers—even knowing she might pull away.

Instead, her eyes close, her fingers move up my arms to the back of my neck as she lifts on her toes and she kisses me.

God, does she ever.

Gone is the woman who thinks she has any control. Just like the kiss in the car, Danielle is almost wild. Her hands grip the top of my head, holding me to her as if I was going anywhere. My feet move forward, needing the leverage, but we hit the desk.

My hand hooks under her thigh, lifting her and pushing everything on the desk out of the way. I hear the clanging of things going to the floor, but neither one of us separate to assess the damage.

I've always wanted to do that.

I kiss her hard, resting my weight on the cold wood desk. Another file goes flying, slapping the ground and she moves herself more center.

Her eyes are filled with heat, burning for more. I stand in front of her, laid out before me. My imagination did her no justice.

She's a fucking Goddess.

Her hair is spilled around her, her lips slightly swollen from the kiss, and instead of pushing me away, she smiles at me.

"I'm not stopping if you don't, understand?" I ask as I climb on top of her.

"Milo," she says my name with confliction.

My thumb brushes across her lips and she parts them so I rub along the opening. "Do you want this?"

Her eyes fill with so many emotions I can't keep track. I see the fear, but then it shifts to desire. She's in her head again and I'm going to pull her out if it's the last thing I do.

My mouth replaces my finger on her lip and her leg curls up, hooking around my calf. *Yeah, she wants this.*

Her hands travel down my back and I slide my tongue in her mouth, loving the taste of her.

I kiss her hard, enjoying how much she meets my power. Danielle isn't timid with me, and I fucking love it. I climb on top of the desk, letting my weight settle with her. "God," she moans again.

"You're so fucking beautiful," I tell her.

"More. I want more, Milo."

I'm happy to oblige.

I do what I thought about the entire day and sit up on my knees, looking at that shirt and tearing it open. Her eyes widen, but before she can react, I hook my finger in the middle of her bra and pull it lower, letting her perfect breasts spill out.

"So fucking perfect," I praise her again.

My mouth waters as I lean down and take her nipple in my mouth. I suck, lick, and flick it with my tongue as she arches her back off the desk.

"Oh my God. Oh fuck," Danielle pants.

I need to taste her. All of her. I slide my hand to her legs as I continue to suck her tits. As I make my way back up, I pull her skirt along with it.

When I find what's underneath, it's my turn to be shocked.

"Commando?"

She smirks. "Surprised?"

"Very."

Her cheeks turn the loveliest shade of pink and I decide I want to see if they can get redder.

I get off the desk and her eyes widen. I spread her legs as I get on my knees. "I'm going to enjoy this. Lie down."

"Milo." She starts to protests. I'm not having any of that. I inch her a little further and flatten my tongue, tasting her.

I watch her head fall back as I do it again and instead of trying to push me away, her fingers are holding me close.

I'm not sure how long I eat her out, but I could die a happy man right here between her legs. I lick, suck, twirl around, plunging my tongue in her pussy and then back to work on her clit.

"Oh, yes. Oh, Milo. Right. Yes. Oh! Fuck." She starts to mutter nonsense and single words as I work her over. "Going. To. Yes!"

As she falls back on the desk, unable to hold her weight anymore, I sink two fingers in her heat and I swear I could blow my load just from fingering her.

"Milo!" Danielle screams as she comes—hard.

I continue to draw out any little bit of pleasure I can, and then she sits up. "I need you."

"You need what, sweetheart?"

"You."

"Me to what?" I want to hear it.

"I want you to fuck me."

"I would very much like to as well." I smile.

She sits up and then Danielle's hand is on my belt, undoing it before she repays the favor to my shirt. She rips it apart. Her lips are on my chest as she continues to fumble with my pants. Then, her hand dips down, wrapping around my cock.

Then, she says the words every man dreams of hearing when a woman grabs his dick for the first time. "Holy shit."

I smile, moving my mouth to her ear. "And I know how to use it."

I pull my wallet out, fumbling for the condom and then let my trousers pool on the floor.

"I want to make you feel good."

"You do."

Her voice is husky when she says, "I think you know what I mean."

Well, I have a few ideas . . .

Then she leans forward, her lips enclose around my cock and I groan, nearly buckling to the floor. "Danielle." Her name is like a prayer because she is most definitely heaven sent.

She drops to her knees in front of me, her eyes meeting mine as I hold onto the desk to keep upright.

"Does it feel good?" she asks.

"Fucking hell it's better than good."

She smiles, runs her tongue from root to tip and then takes me deep. "Jesus Christ," I start to sweat as her mouth glides up and down. While I've enjoyed my share of blowjobs, nothing compares to this.

She continues to milk me and as much I would love to continue this, if I don't get inside of her in a few seconds, I might fucking die. "I need to fuck you. Right now."

I pull her up, locking my mouth on hers and devouring her. Our tongues duel and we maneuver her back on the desk. This is far from proper, her dress around her hips, my pants around my ankles, both of us with torn shirts, but there's nothing proper about fucking your boss.

I tear the condom open, rolling it down as she stares at me. "Last chance. I'm going to ruin you for any other man."

She hooks her hand around my neck, pulling me close. "Do your best."

Challenge accepted.

I grip her hips and push inside.

Both of us hold onto each other as I rock back and forth. I take her hands, pinning them above her head as we continue to fuck.

Every sound she makes takes me closer.

"You feel so good," I tell her.

"Please don't stop," Danielle begs. "Please. Never stop."

If I could stay inside her forever, I would. The feel of her around me is better than I ever could've envisioned. We fit together perfectly.

Her hands slide up my chest and I hold her head to keep her

from banging it on the desk, both of us staring into each other's eyes.

It becomes overwhelming. The feelings I have in this moment. Danielle's hand touches my cheek. I tilt my head and it's all too much, I explode.

"Fuck!" I call out as I come harder than I knew possible.

And I realize almost instantly, it's not her who is ruined, it's me.

twenty-one

. . .

Danielle

OH MY GOD.

I had hot, sweaty, and incredible desk sex with Milo.

I lie here, with him still inside me, trying not to freak out. It was like I was completely taken over by this horny crazy person who could think of nothing other than having him. Every touch made me want more. Each time he kissed me, I wanted his lips everywhere.

Then, when they were . . . I never wanted it to end.

Milo lifts his head from my breasts and looks down at me. "That was . . ."

It was the best sex I've ever had in my life. It was also a thousand lines I should've never crossed.

But when I look at Milo, still feeling his body against mine, the only word I can say is, "everything."

As rough as we were, Milo was still doing everything possible to make me comfortable. He cradled my head in his hands as we made love. He kissed me over and over, told me I was beautiful, and I felt cherished.

He pulls out and I look around at the carnage of my office.

Jesus Christ. My desk is completely bare except for our bodies.

My papers are scattered all around and I'm pretty sure the crash I heard at some point when he was going down on me was the photo of my family that looks like it's on the floor. Thank God everyone has already gone home and we don't have to come up with some lie as to how the office got this way.

Milo pulls his pants up, buttoning them, and I try to cover myself. Seriously, this is a walk of shame like no one has ever seen.

"You're not freaking out?" he asks.

"I am, but I'm not sure what has me freaking out more right now."

I want to be honest with him. It's the only way this will ever work.

"Okay, tell me."

Milo has this tough, jerk exterior, but I think inside, he's vulnerable and wants to be cared for. It's why his brother and mother's low estimation bother him so much. I don't ever want him to question what I feel for him.

"I like you, Milo. I like being around you. I like kissing you. I really liked what we just did, but I'm far from uncomplicated. I don't want to be hurt again. But then . . . I mean, I'm your boss and this is totally against company policy—I think."

Milo touches my cheek. "I know the owner."

"Funny."

I swing my legs over, letting them hang over the desk, and release a heavy sigh.

"My brother is not a problem here so cross that off your list. What's next?"

"Okay . . . what about the fact that I'm a new widow, with two kids, working full-time, who lost her shit a few days ago in the middle of a trial?"

"Yes, all of those things are true, but I don't give a damn."

"You don't?"

"No."

I look at him like he's crazy. "How is that even possible?"

Milo sits beside me, and he wraps his arm around me. "I've lived a selfish life and when I'm around you, I don't want to anymore. I'm aware of your . . . situation . . . and Parker, Ava, the trial, and anything else you come up with have no bearings on my feelings. If me working here bothers you, I'll quit."

I jerk back. "What?"

"I'll quit. I don't need this job for the money, I'm plenty rich already."

My jaw hangs open. If it wasn't about money, then why the hell is he doing this? Milo did my job for years, he's definitely the most overqualified assistant ever. It made no sense to me why he continued to show up here, so I assumed it had to be financial.

"I don't . . . I don't understand."

"I told you, I'm selfish. I wanted my job back because I never should have lost it. My brother was a prick and I wanted him to get his comeuppance. Mum was driving me nuts so I got on a plane and came here. But, no, it's not the money I need. It's the fact that he took it away, and therefore, I wanted it back."

"Screw the collateral damage?" I counter, meaning me.

"In the spirit of this conversation, I'll answer you honestly. Yes."

I get to my feet. I knew that would be the answer, but after what I did, it still stings.

His hand grips my wrist before I can walk away. "I didn't know you, Danielle. I didn't know you even existed."

I close my eyes, trying my hardest to stop the crushing emotions threatening to spill over. It's not just what he said about not even needing the job he tried to take from me, it's the adrenaline wearing off and looking around at the mess. I had sex for the first time since Peter died.

Hell, I hadn't had sex with anyone else since I was freaking twenty-two.

What the hell did I do?

Oh my god.

I grab the desk and lean back. Milo's arm is around my waist a moment later.

"Danielle?"

I look at him and guilt, shame, and regret start to fill me.

"No." His jaw ticks. "I see what you're doing and stop right now. Did you hear nothing that I said?"

"You don't get it. I liked it, Milo! I wanted it. I wasn't thinking like the adult here. I begged you." I grip my hair. "Jesus Christ. I begged you and I . . ." *I blew him.*

I was on my knees with his dick in my mouth.

I can't remember the last time I gave Peter a blow job.

With Milo, I wanted to. I was so turned on by the idea of sucking his dick that I practically begged him to let me.

"I'm not going to lie and say that doesn't make me rather happy. But so what? We're consenting adults that had sex. I don't see the problem or what has you so upset."

No, he wouldn't. Tears start to well in my eyes and I wrap my arms around my chest. It's not just about the sex for me. I've never been that kind of girl, and I don't think I ever could be. I'm no prude, but I believe that sex should mean something. I'm old fashioned in some ways, and Milo very much is not.

I know when I say this, it may not make sense, but maybe this will help us walk away at this point before I'm in too deep.

"I was married for almost my entire adult life. I would still be married to Peter if he wasn't dead. I've only had sex with one man before him. What we did . . . what we shared just now, that meant something whether you know it or not." I wipe away a tear and another one forms. "I know that it's not the same for you. We aren't anything and you owe me nothing. God, I sound like a crazy person. Please don't think I'm asking for you to share my views. I don't need for you to give me any hope for something more."

Milo takes a step forward, he wipes the tear from my cheek.

"You don't have to ask me for anything when I'm trying to give it to you," his voice is filled with tenderness. "My feelings for you aren't only sexual. Don't misunderstand, I want to continue to have sex, but I also want more than that."

My lips part as I look in his eyes to see if he's lying. "More?"

He nods. "Yes, Danielle, more. I'll be honest, I don't know what *more* looks like."

"Meaning a relationship?" I ask.

"Yes, I've never been in one before, they do seem quite fascinating."

I roll my eyes. "How are you forty-one and never had a girlfriend?"

Milo smiles, kisses the tip of my nose, and shrugs. "I never found a woman worthy of my affections." How is it that I like him so much? He's such a jerk sometimes. "That is until I found you."

And then he says shit like that and I'm a puddle.

"Well." I uncross my arms and put them around his waist. "I'll tell you this, you keep saying things like that and it'll go a long way for you."

He laughs and brushes his nose against mine. "Noted. Anything else I should be aware of?"

"Hmm," I stretch out the sound as I think. What to tell a guy about how to be in a relationship . . . "I think compliments, flowers, and affection are a must. You should also be aware that you'll probably not get what you want in the end, and the girl is always right, especially this girl."

Milo chuckles. "Is that all?"

"Well, there are other things, but they should be pretty obvious."

"No shagging other women, right?"

"That's a given."

"And you will not be with another man?" he asks with his brow raised.

"If that's what we're doing, then no. I would never betray the man I was with."

"What is it that you want us to be doing?"

With Peter, we never had time to ease into it. We started dating and then I was pregnant with Ava. There was this whole chunk of time we lost because we didn't get to really enjoy one another. Here was a chance to pump the brakes.

"I want to take this slow," I say. "Not because I'm unsure, but because I have kids to think about, and I want us to enjoy our time getting to know each other."

"You know that I'm aware of your children and that they're part of the deal?"

"I would hope so. Oh, and my friends, they're kind of a part of the package too."

I might as well get that clear now. Kristin, Heather, and Nicole are pretty much staples in my life. Not that I don't make my own choices, but I know what comes with their disapproval.

"Understood." Milo smiles down at me. "And I like your kids. Ava is a little scary, but Parker is a fantastic kid."

"Yes on both counts."

"All right, sweetheart. We take this slow. We enjoy each other's company, and for now, we take it one day at a time, sound good?"

I run my hand up to his neck and bring his lips to mine. "Thank you."

"For what?"

"For making me smile again, even if I was laughing at you some of those times."

Milo grins. "I bet I can find other ways to make you smile."

"I look forward to finding out."

twenty-two

. . .

Danielle

"SO IT'S ACTUALLY a date this time?" Ava asks as she rummages through my closet.

"No."

"But you guys are dating?"

I sigh. I decided that the best way to get Ava to stop being out of control was to treat her the way she wants to be treated. The last week has been like having my girl back who wasn't occupied by Satan's soul. I'm not sure if my new parenting approach is actually working, but I'm going with it for now.

First thing I did was tell her that Milo and I were seeing each other.

After her initial round of questions that I'll never repeat to anyone because I'm scarred for life, she actually got a little excited.

"I told you, we're taking it slow. Tonight is a business dinner. We're going to celebrate the permits and talk about the next project on the list."

She laughs. "Last time you said it was business I caught you fogging up the windows." Ava grabs the dress and starts to twirl around. "Like a couple of school kids. Oh, Milo, kiss me." She makes noises and rubs the dress against her. "Talk British to me before I stick my tongue in your mouth."

"Knock it off and give me the dress, you nut job. And you and I aren't besties or whatever you kids call it, so we're not talking about kissing."

I'm so not going there with her. There are lines, and this is one we won't cross.

"You don't have to talk to me about it, I caught you and posted it on the internet. You're welcome."

"I really should've considered adoption when I was pregnant."

Ava shrugs. "I would've found you eventually."

Yeah, she definitely would've.

"Here, try this on." She tosses the hanger over and the dress is actually not bad.

"Why the hell didn't you show me this one before the last dinner meeting I had?"

Ava doesn't even give me the courtesy of trying to look apologetic. "Because that dress was hot. This one is . . . wearable."

Unreal.

"This is classy, Ava. You don't always have to show the goods to get a man to notice you."

She bursts out laughing. "Right, Mom. Guys love it when you win them with your brains. I mean, that's what they look at when you walk by . . ."

"You know what I mean." I slip the dress on, smoothing the fabric as I look in the mirror.

This one is actually perfect. It's a maroon satin dress that cuts just below my knee. I love that it's tight around the chest and waist but gives a bit around my hips.

"Wow." Ava whistles. "You look hot."

"You think?"

"Totally. Can I do your makeup again?" she asks.

"No."

God only knows what new tricks she's learned online. I'll stick with my routine.

"Well then, can I have my phone back for more than when I'm stuck babysitting Parker?"

I was really hoping we'd avoid this fight. Yes, Ava's grades have improved, as has her attitude. It's been actually pleasant to be around her. She's being nice, even watching a movie with Parker and I the other night, and I don't want to lose that.

Part of me can't help but think it's because she doesn't have that damn phone glued to her hand.

These are the times I wish I could defer to Peter. He was really good at being the bad guy when it came to her. "No, you're doing better, and I appreciate that, but I caught you smoking, skipping school, and God only knows what I don't know."

"So I'm grounded for what you don't even know I did?"

"Ava, it takes more than two weeks of good behavior to make up for the shit you did that I do know about."

My daughter is a smart girl. She also has a manipulative side that I'm sure is working on overdrive. If I give in to her now, there will be no going back without a war.

I watch the wheels turn in her blue eyes. "Whatever."

"Trust is earned, sweetheart. When it's broken, there's no telling how long it'll take to fix it." I touch her cheek before dropping my hand.

"I'm trying."

"I know you are."

She's made strides. I'll give her that, but after the hell she's put me through the last year, she's got to run a marathon before we're on steady ground.

She heads out of the room and I release a heavy sigh. It seriously sucks having to be the adult. I always envisioned a relationship with Ava where we were friends. We would eat pizza, talk, and have a sisterhood type bond, but she never wanted that. Ava is the girl who, the minute she felt old enough, stopped holding my hand to cross the street and didn't need me to tuck her in at night.

It was hard to accept the reality of our relationship.

I head downstairs where Parker is reading his new comic book.

"Hey, buddy."

"Mom! Look!" He shows me the page.

"Wow, Thor looks pretty fierce there," I note.

Parker nods with a huge grin. "He's the best."

"Really? What about Spiderman? I thought he was the best?"

"I like him too, but Thor is cooler and has a hammer. Plus, he's a God!"

If he says so.

"Okay, I'm glad you found a new superhero."

"Thor is like Milo."

We're going to make sure Milo never hears about being like a God. I don't need to inflate that ego more than it is now.

Parker goes back to looking at the comic and I pick up some of the toys lying around. Who said motherhood isn't glamourous?

I try not to be nervous knowing he'll be here soon. Milo has been to my house, met my kids, and knows my life, but not since we had sex the other day. I'm not sure how this works now. We've sort of said we're dating but taking it slow. I just don't know how to act around him. Will my kids be able to look at us and know we had sex? Is there some weird vibe we'll give off? Do I kiss him when he comes in?

So much shit to think about.

"Mom?"

"Yes."

"Do you like Milo?"

Oh, Jesus. "Do *you* like Milo?" I repeat.

"I like him," he says. "Are you his girlfriend?"

How and why is this happening right now? "Milo and I are

friends, Parker. We work together and spend a lot of time with each other."

He nods as if that makes perfect sense. "Okay."

My heart starts to return to its normal speed and I look down at my watch, wondering where the hell he is.

"Do you kiss him?"

I close my eyes, wishing a sinkhole would open and take me with it because the only rule in our home is we never lie. Not that I think they'll always follow it, but Peter and I believe strongly in honesty. I don't know if it's because in our jobs, twisting the truth was expected, so when we came home, we never wanted to question it. Lies have the ability to take on their own life. They start off simple and small, then the next thing you know, it's bigger than you can control.

But God do I want to lie right now.

I sit on the couch beside him. "What is it that you really want to know, buddy?"

"Is Milo going to be my new dad?"

I've never been more grateful for someone not being on time than right now. "You have a dad. He might not be here with us, but he's always here." I point to his heart. "He lives inside of us and as long as we talk about him, remember him, and smile when we think of your daddy, he'll never be gone. No one will ever replace him, okay?"

Parker's arms wrap around my neck and he holds on tight. "You're the best, Mommy."

"You're the best."

He lets go, sits back as if nothing happened, and goes back to his comic.

I stand to grab my phone to see where he is and the doorbell rings.

"I got it!" Parker yells as he rushes to the door with me on his heels.

"Parker," Milo says with a grin.

"Look what I got!" Parker holds up the comic.

"Thor. Good choice."

"Mom got it for me today," he explains.

Milo's eyes meet mine and then he travels the length of my body, taking in the very tight dress. "She did very well then."

"You're late."

"I am. Do you forgive me?" He asks as he pulls roses from behind his back.

Well, that helps a little. "Maybe."

He smirks. "I didn't think you'd be an easy one." Milo squats in front of Parker. "The reason I'm late is because I had my Mum send me a package, and I was waiting for the post to come. I had her dig for something I kept, and I'd like to share it with you."

Then Milo steps out onto the porch and comes back with a bag. "This is for me?" Parker asks.

"Yup."

My son lets out a scream as he pulls dozens of comics from the bag. Not just any comics though, it's Spiderman, Thor, Batman, and Iron Man . . . the old comics. The ones that are probably worth money.

"Milo," I clear my throat. "This is very sweet, but he's six, this is too much, and he could ruin—"

"They're his to do with as he pleases. I haven't touched them in years, and I would like them to be enjoyed by someone who appreciates them."

"Still."

"Let me do something nice for your son, Danielle." He leans in so only I can hear the next part. "I'll be happy to let you do something nice for me in return."

For the love of God. "I'm eating dinner with you, that's my nice deed."

"Barely."

"Mom, can I keep them?" Parker gives me the puppy dog eyes.

Milo drops to his knees next to him, giving me the same face. "Yeah, Mum, can we?"

"You two are trouble."

"The good kind, I hope," Milo says.

I laugh at that one. "Not even a little."

We say goodbye to Parker and then he goes up to annoy Ava with his comic books. I lock the door behind me and as soon as I turn, Milo is right in front of me. His hands wrap around my body and he pushes me so that my back is pressed against the door. Then his lips are on mine.

I kiss him back, tasting the mint and loving the feel of his body against mine.

He pulls back after a few more seconds, resting his forehead to mine. "You look absolutely perfect. I couldn't wait another second to kiss you."

"Missed me that much?"

He laughs once, lifts his eyes to mine, but the humor is gone. "I wish you weren't so damn irresistible."

I rub my thumb against his lip, removing the red lipstick that was transferred. "Feeling is mutual."

We make our way to the car, both with smiles on our faces and our fingers intertwined. Milo is a gentleman, opening the car door for me and then walking around.

He starts the car and then stops to look at me. "You find me utterly impossible to resist as well?"

"I wouldn't say impossible." I don't know that I should ever let him know how much I think of him.

Mischief starts to swirl in his green eyes. "Would you care to make a wager on that?"

"On what?"

"On whether you can keep your knickers on 'til the end of our date."

I roll my eyes. "Fine, what do we bet?"

I'm totally winning this. First, Milo doesn't know the depth of my competitive side. I never lose. I ate an entire jar of hot peppers on a dare once. I skinny dipped in a freezing cold pool because Heather bet me a hundred dollars I wouldn't do it. There is nothing about this date that is impossible for me to resist. Do I like him? Yup. Do I want to have sex again? Abso-fucking-lutely. Will I if it means I will lose? Not a chance in hell.

"If I win, which means we're having some Earth shattering fucking tonight, you have to tell Callum about how good I am in bed."

Not even a possibility. "You want me to tell my boss how good you are in bed?"

"No," he corrects. "I want you to tell my wanker of a brother that I fuck better than you've ever had."

"Your brother is also my boss," I point out.

"Scared, are you?"

"Of what? You going home with some blue balls?" I scoff. "Please. If I win you have to do something equally as mortifying." I ponder what the best thing is. I could have him quit, but that's not what I want. Milo makes coming to work exciting for me.

Not just because I have these feelings for him, but he makes me smile.

During the day I get funny notes and emails, showing he cares for me. I get to spend my time with him and I learn new little details each day. Things that would seem insignificant to anyone else, but that show me who he is.

Which is why it's been so easy to fall for him.

"I'm not embarrassed by anything, sweetheart."

Such a load of shit. Everyone has limits. I try to remember something, anything, that I can use. And then I remember . . .

"But you are afraid of something, aren't you?"

"Danielle," he warns.

"Yes, if I win, you have to take a video holding a sweet, cuddly little bunny rabbit."

"I'm going to fuck your brains out tonight," Milo threatens.

Really, I wonder if I shouldn't lose just for . . . no, no, no, I must stay strong. "I wasn't planning on taking my panties off for anyone tonight, so game on. I hope you're ready for Thumper."

"Oh, I'm thumping something all right, but she's in the car right now."

I smile, my hand resting on his leg and moving towards the bulge in his pants. "Tomorrow, you can make good on that promise." I rub him a little bit. "But tonight, nothing in here is coming out."

Milo grips my wrist. "Game on, sweetheart. Game the fuck on."

twenty-three

. . .

Milo

BLOODY HELL I'm still fucking hard.

We're sitting at the table of some fancy restaurant Nicole recommended. The food is shit. They promised my favourite Italian dish, only it tasted nothing like it does in London. Not that the food is particularly fantastic there, but still.

Now, I'm sitting here, thinking of all the ways to get Danielle in the bathroom where I can sink my cock in her.

And I'm harder than I was before.

She smiles over her wine glass as if she knows it's me who is suffering with this bet.

"I'm going to wipe that smile off your mouth," I threaten her playfully.

"Whatever you say," she shrugs and then sips her wine.

If that was the case, we wouldn't be sitting at this table right now. I'd have her back at my flat, christening every surface we can find.

"Be careful of the words you use," I warn.

Danielle shakes her head. Her dark brown hair falls around her face and I would appreciate it if I didn't find everything she did fucking attractive. "I had no intentions of having sex tonight."

"Why in the bloody hell not?"

I must've said that a bit louder than I thought because she leans close, her voice is low. "Because we're going slow."

"Slow and reverse are two different things."

She sighs. "I know you're not exactly working with a manual right now, but we're on our first real date and all you're worried about is getting in my pants."

Fucking hell. I hate it when she's right. It's rather annoying because instead of me telling her to piss off, I actually have to acknowledge it.

"I'm sorry. I'll behave so we can have a proper date. And that wasn't the only thing I'm worried about," I inform her. "I'm pretty sure I've debated just about everything from the beginning."

Which is true. I don't know what the protocol on a first date with someone is. I wanted to get her flowers but worried it would be lame. Then I wasn't sure if American girls like that sort of thing or if they like a man to play it cool. Honestly, this entire thing has been a fucking nightmare.

Not the date itself. That's all gone quite well, but the lead up I could've gone without.

"Thank you." She smiles warmly, and I mash my teeth together to stop from saying something stupid.

"Tell me, am I allowed to kiss you goodnight?"

Danielle reaches her hand across the table, her fingers tangling with mine. "I very much hope you do."

"Good. I'm barely keeping myself in my seat as it is."

"Milo, there aren't rules or anything. It's that we kind of did things a little ass backwards and I want to give us the best chance at working. What you did today with Parker, meant everything to me, I want you to know that."

Her words embarrass me a bit, because it was nothing, really. My mum has been complaining about my rubbish in her home. Sure, a few of these comic books were collector's editions. I thought about keeping them, but I chose to give something that got me through a very difficult part of my life to someone who might need it.

While Ava is me, literally, at that age, Parker will eventually get there. Maybe this will help even a little.

"I'm happy to do it," I tell her.

Danielle grins at me, her lashes fluttering softly as the candlelight dances across her skin. "You keep this up, you might get lucky tomorrow."

Now it's my turn to smirk. "Let's just worry about getting through tonight. If I have my way, you'll be naked in the car."

We make it through dinner with an easy conversation. She tells me about her time at university, and I tell her about London.

I miss it.

Not just because it's home, but because Tampa is like being stuck in your bathroom after a four-hour long steam shower. It's hot, muggy, and the insects are enormous. My plan was to be here for a few months, get my job back, and then quit. I'm well aware of the faults in that strategy, but I liked the idea of leaving my daft brother with his pants down.

Of course, everything has changed now, and I don't know when or if I'll return to London.

I pay the bill and take her hand as we exit the restaurant.

"Dinner was wonderful," Danielle says as she hooks her arm around mine.

"It was."

"Have you been to the beach at night?"

I haven't been to the beach at all, really. I'm rather pale, so the idea of sitting out in the miserable heat and sun isn't appealing to me.

But the way her face lights up makes me think nighttime is different.

"I haven't had the time, why?"

She smiles and sighs. "It's my favorite. Would you like to go?"

How could I possibly say no? "Sure."

We walk a few streets over and then she slips her heels off. I remove my shoes and then we make our way onto the sand.

"I love it here," she muses as we approach the water.

"I'm not that fond of the ocean."

"Really?" The surprise is clear in her voice.

I wrap my arm around her waist, holding her tightly. "Not since my father died. He and my mother would take us on holiday to the beaches in France. We went every year, no matter what. After he died, we stopped all together."

Danielle stops walking and faces me. "I'm sorry, Milo."

"Don't be, darling."

She steps closer to me, wrapping her arms around my waist. "I wish I could meet your mom. Nicole is terrified of her, but she's an asshole, so most mothers don't love her."

I laugh. "Mum is a lot like Nicole, I think. They're unapologetic as to who they are."

"She said that."

"Which is why I think Callum fell for her so fast."

She rests her head on my chest. Without her heels, our height difference is funny. My head sits on the top of her head and we stand here.

"I feel like I fell for you fast," Danielle admits.

"You do?"

She nods against me. "I didn't want to. I sometimes still don't." Her head lifts, and the world fades away as she looks at me as though I'm worthy of her affections. "If I fall hard, and you don't catch me, I worry I won't survive the landing."

My heart aches and I see how much her words cost her. My hands hold her face, and I vow right now, I will do anything to make her feel secure. "I will always break your fall, Danielle. I want to be your safety net, and I hope I've proven that to you. Seeing you hurt, causes me pain. You're not the only one who's falling."

"I'm not?"

How is she so blind? "No. I'm all in."

She smiles, lifts up on her toes, and kisses me. "And you said you weren't a hero."

I release a breath through my nose and rest my head against hers. "I guess I needed to find a cause worth fighting for."

twenty-four

. . .

Danielle

"I'M NOT HOSTING the barbeque this year," I tell Nicole as she gives me her disapproving look.

"Why not?"

"Because I don't feel like it."

Why do I need to have a reason? It's stupid and I don't need the damn stress.

"You're full of shit." Nicole plops herself in the chair in my office.

"Thanks for dropping by, Nic."

I don't know why she's even asking about it. Each year, she'd cry and complain about having to schlep all the way over to my house, deal with my stupid husband, and leave with a renewed desire to stay single. Heather would basically threaten her to get her to come—and behave. I thought if anyone would be happy about it being done, it would be her.

"I'm not going anywhere. I fuck your boss, so I kind of have the fuck-you-very-much card."

I release a heavy sigh and bang my head on my desk. "Why have I not moved to Texas or some other state to escape you people?"

"Friendependence Day is something we celebrate. I understood why we didn't the year before because Kristin was dealing with her divorce. Then you cancelled Friendsgiving, which I accepted. I gave you another few months—"

"Oh, burying my husband that year was a good excuse?"

"Well, better than whatever shit you're coming up with this year."

"Jesus Christ, Nicole. Do you have a soul or were you always this cold-hearted?"

"Not really sure because both answers are equally scary." Nicole shrugs while looking at her nails. "This year you need to do this."

"Oh, and why is that?"

"Because your kids need to know that life goes on after loss. Ava, in all her crazy rebellion loves her aunts and cousins. Friendependence Day has been a staple in her life, Parker's, Aubrey's and Finn's since they were born—and your friends'. We did this because you fucking forced us and now you need to continue on."

She's got balls. I've always known this, but this is bold even for her. "Why do I have to host it?"

Nicole runs her hand through the blonde hair I secretly hate out of jealousy. I spent a long time trying to dye mine that color and then gave up. "Because it was always you who hosted. Kristin could, but she's traveling to see Noah for two weeks before it. Heather is talking about surprising Eli and we both know I'm the last person anyone should trust. Your house has always been where we did it."

"I really don't want to do this," I sigh.

"Why, Danni?"

Why? Because Friendependence Day was Peter's thing. Even though my friends were definitely not always nice to him, he loved it. I swear, as soon as New Year's was over, he was talking about new ideas to set up the yard.

"You know why. You know why this stupid barbeque is hard for me."

"Yes, but it's all the more reason why you should still do it."

"Should do what?" Milo asks at the door of my office.

I look to my friend to bail me out. It's not like it's a secret, but I can't exactly explain my way out of it either.

"You know . . ." Nicole grins and gets to her feet. "You're her assistant still, right?"

Milo's eyes narrow a bit. "Yes?"

"Great. We hold a big barbeque each year where the whole gang comes, the kids, significant others and all that. Danielle hosts it, and this year, she'll need some help."

"Nicole!" I hiss her name through my teeth.

I want to throat punch her.

"What? He's your assistant, he can assist so it's not too much for you. You were just saying that you were super busy. I see a problem and I fix it."

I look at Milo who is clearly confused. "You don't have to do any of this because we're not having it."

"Why ever not?" he asks.

Great, now I *have* to explain it to him? I haven't held back on mentioning Peter, but it's not been long since we started dating. Our relationship is new and I'm trying to be sensitive to how I would feel if he was always bringing things back to his ex. Last weekend was an amazing first date—and I won the bet—but we've been slammed with work since then and we haven't spent much time outside of the office.

Milo hasn't said anything or even implied it's an issue, but I happened to have mentioned my fear to Nicole the other day. Seems I'm going to pay for it now.

"Yes, why, Danni?" She smiles at me knowing I won't say it.

"I just don't think you should have to do things like this. It's not a Dovetail event so . . ."

Milo sits beside Nicole. "Bollocks."

"God, I love that word," Nicole's voice is wistful. "You say it even better than Callum. His accent is fading here and there since we've been in the states. Say fuck."

Milo chuckles. "Fuck."

"Oh." She squirms. "Say knickers."

"Knickers," Milo repeats.

"Say, I'll help Danielle with the party because I'm not a wanker."

I groan. "I'm pissed at you. It's bad enough you're pretty, but then you have to be a pushy bitch and not listen to the people around you."

She was blessed with big boobs, blue eyes, and blonde hair. Not to mention, she's skinny, smart, funny, and has never needed anyone to take care of her. Pair all that with her personality and it's no wonder it took a man like Callum to catch her attention.

"Milo will throw us a proper party." Nicole winks. "I can speak British, too."

He bursts out laughing.

At least someone finds her entertaining. "You laugh now, but I give you a week with her and you'll find her as irritating as I do."

"If Cal hasn't grown tired of her by this point, I'm sure I wouldn't."

She smirks at me with her head tilted. "I totally picked the wrong brother."

A pang of jealousy strikes me because if Nicole wanted him then I never would've gotten him.

And then a new wave of emotions flood. When did I start thinking of him as mine? Why does the idea of Nicole and Milo make me want to rip out her eyes? She's my friend. She never would do anything, but I'm sitting here, balling my hands into fists.

"Sorry, love." Milo looks at me and then Nicole. "I prefer brunettes. One in particular."

I look down at the papers on my desk, trying to hide my face. He can be so sweet sometimes.

"Awww," she claps her hands together. "You guys are so cute. Okay, about the barbeque . . ."

Sure enough, after five minutes, Nicole got her way and I'm hosting this stupid party with Milo coordinating it. Does everyone around me enjoy tormenting me? I'm sure the answer is yes. I can't wait for Ava, Milo, and Nicole to be together . . . said me never.

"Explain to me your friends' . . . whatever-you-call-it party?" Milo asks as we sit on my couch.

His arm is draped across the back, allowing his fingers to graze my arm. "It's something we started when I moved into this house. We get together, eat, drink . . . it's not a big deal."

"Then why the fuss about doing it?"

"It's . . . complicated."

"Because of your husband?"

My eyes meet his and fill with regret. "Yes. A little."

Milo scratches his cheek, seeming to ponder something. "Did you not want to tell me that?"

"I'm trying not to talk about him. I know we're in this new relationship and . . . he's gone."

Milo moves closer. "He was your life. You have children together, and whether I like the fact that another man existed before me, is irrelevant. I'm not jealous of Peter."

My throat goes dry and I place my hand on his. "I don't know what to say . . ."

"Look, I may not know anything about dating, but I know something about honesty. Have I made you feel as though I'm bothered by it?"

"No," I say quickly. "Not at all. I just know how you talking about Kandi made me feel, I don't want Peter to be that way for you."

He gives me a slow smile. "Kandi was here and a possibility. Peter is gone. He has your past. I can't ever get that time. But if another bastard wants to try to come in now and take you away from me, I'll kick the fucking shit out of him."

"Good to know," I giggle.

"But seriously, it hasn't been that long since he was killed. You're in the middle of his murderer's trial, and it would be rather unfair of me to expect it to be as though he was never in your mind, don't you think?"

The feelings I have for Milo grow deeper each day. It's crazy how much he's managed to locate the cracks in my heart and find his way through.

"You like me," I sigh and rest my head on his arm.

"I do. Quite a bit."

"I like you too."

Milo leans forward and kisses me. "I know."

"Do you now?"

"It's rather clear."

I lift my head. "How so?"

His smirk makes me want to both slap him and kiss him. "First, you can't stop looking at me, not that I blame you."

"Ass."

"Second," he continues on without replying to my insult. "You kiss me any chance you get. Again, not that I can fault you there either."

"Oh, Lord. Is there more to this?"

Milo chuckles and brushes his fingers across my cheek. "Lastly, you had me come over when both kids are at sleepovers tonight, and you're not wearing your wedding ring anymore," his voice drops low and husky.

"I took it off the other day," I admit.

"I noticed."

Of course he did, he notices everything. "I thought it was time. I . . . I want this with you, and I want my past to feel resolved, you know?"

He nods. "I didn't want to push you, Danielle."

And he didn't. That's the thing. It wasn't him, it was me. I was ready. "Maybe you were right about me liking you, huh?"

Milo grins, his finger slides against my jaw. "I have a feeling you want to show me just how much you like me tonight, don't you?"

My stomach clenches and my heart begins to race. He's right. As soon as I knew both kids would be gone for the night, I called Milo to come over. Since the desk sex, we haven't been together. He's been sweet and hasn't said a word, but I've been dying.

"Maybe. If you behave," I say.

"I'm not sure I know how to do that."

I smile. "I'm not sure you do either."

"Are you hungry?" he asks.

"For what?"

Milo's grin turns mischievous and he grabs my legs, pulling me flat to the couch. He hovers over me. "Why don't you tell me what you want and I'll do my best to accommodate your request."

I lift my fingers, grazing his face, loving that he shaved yesterday but the dark stubble is already there. "You make me feel these things," I confess.

"What things?"

He's been open regarding his feelings, and now, I'm going to do the same. Milo gives me hope again. It's something I cherish, crave, and I want him to know what it means to me.

"My heart races when you're near. My mouth goes dry when I see you for the first time in the morning at work. Everything feels easier when you're around. Since you came into my life, I've smiled again. You make me happy, Milo." Tears form, but I hold them back, not wanting to feel even more exposed.

His lips touch mine in the sweetest kiss. "I'm trying so hard not to fall in love with you."

I look up, our eyes mirroring the same thing. "I'm trying too."

"How are you doing so far?"

"Not very good."

Milo smiles. "I'm not either."

I move my thumb across his bottom lip. "What do you think we should do about it?"

He gets to his feet, hooks his one arm under my legs and the other cradles my back. "Which way to your room?"

My arms wrap around his neck and I smile. "Upstairs."

twenty-five

. . .

Danielle

MILO SETS me on the bed and I tremble a little.

In my office, it was one thing. That's not my home and it sure as fuck wasn't a bed. This is a place where I shared my life with someone. My kids live here, and I'm welcoming him into that in some ways.

"You understand this means something?" I ask, giving him an out.

"I do."

"We don't go back from this point. We're a couple or whatever you want to call it."

Milo leans onto the bed with his arms on each side of me. "I'm not going anywhere."

I really hope not.

"What about your job? What do we do about the fact that you can't continue to work for me?"

"Danielle," Milo's voice is soft. "No more talking."

My pulse is pounding like a drum in my ear. "Kiss me."

He takes his time, unlike before, measuring each inch as he gets closer. My breathing quickens as the anticipation builds. If he doesn't kiss me soon, I'm going to lose my mind.

I move toward him, gripping the back of his neck tenderly, and close the gap.

When our lips touch, I moan. He kisses me softly but still ardently. I can feel the desire coming off him in waves.

"Fuck, you're bloody perfect," he says and then pushes me back toward the head of the bed.

Milo crawls his way toward me. I lie there as his weight settles on top of me. I can feel his cock against my center and my head spins.

I remember how good he was before, and that he most definitely knows how to use it. I've craved his touch since that day, and I'm hoping I get plenty of it tonight.

"No, I'm not."

He pushes my hair back. "You are to me."

My heart swells and I bring my lips back to his. I love the way he tastes, smells, and feels against me. I love how when he looks at me, I feel strong and wanted. I love that Milo is sweet to me but remains professional with the others. It's crazy because if I told people what he's like, they'd never believe it.

Only I get the real him.

There are no walls between us. He is who he is, and I can be me.

Relationships like that don't happen to many people, let alone twice in one lifetime.

He breaks the kiss, looking down at me. "I've never made love to anyone, sweetheart, but I want to tonight."

I smile. "I want that too."

"Are you sure?"

"Absolutely."

Milo pushes up to his knees, and pulls me with him. My fingers slowly undo each button of his shirt, and then push it off his shoulders.

He lifts my shirt, exposing my breasts, and makes a low groan from his throat.

I watch him climb off the bed. "Stand up," he orders.

My chest is tight, but I do as he says.

"Take off your trousers," Milo tells me.

"I'd rather take yours off."

He smiles and raises a brow. "By all means."

I start to undo the buckle and his hands tangle in my hair as he crashes his lips to mine.

Milo kisses me like I'm the air he's desperate for. Time doesn't exist right now, and I'm under his spell.

My fingers struggle more, but I finally get the button free as his lips stay fused to mine. Milo's tongue plunges in my mouth, and we duel for power. He, of course, wins.

Milo's fingers hook in my pants and he pushes them down.

When I can't breathe, he releases me.

He drops lower, eyes staying on mine, as he removes them completely, then steps out of his.

We're bared to each other, completely exposed.

Neither of us move as we take in this moment. "Do you trust me?" he asks.

"Yes."

"Then let me make you feel good." He tucks my hair behind my ears. "Give me your heart."

"You have it," I reply.

He took it when I wasn't even aware it was up for grabs.

"That's what I wanted to hear," Milo's voice cracks a little.

His hand slides from my neck down my arm and our fingers tangle. "Do I have yours?" I ask.

"I think you had it the moment I saw you. Here was this woman, standing tall even when she felt lost. If I only knew you'd turn my world upside down . . ."

I touch his face with my other hand. "If I only knew the man who wanted to ruin me would end up being the man who put me back together, I would've never fought it to begin with."

"I'm going to make love to you now," Milo says as he lays me on the bed.

Our lips touch and the time for talking is over.

Milo's hands graze over my skin and I close my eyes, savoring every touch. He's soft with me, unlike when we went at it like kids on the desk. Now, I want to take my time with him.

I moan when his tongue swirls around my nipple before he takes it in his mouth, sucking and flicking it back and forth.

He slides down my body, trailing his tongue as he goes. I close my eyes, preparing for the onslaught of pleasure he's about to give me.

Slowly he makes his way to my core, and then Milo reminds me why I've been craving this.

"Holy shit," I pant as he starts to use pressure on my clit. My head thrashes back and forth as he continues to drive me crazy. I slide my fingers in his dark hair, trying to ground myself to Earth.

He's too good at this.

If there is such a thing.

"Milo," I moan. "Oh, God. Right there. I can't . . . I'm going to . . . . I. Oh. Yes!" I yell as my orgasm rocks through me.

He climbs back up, kissing me as he does. "I don't know that I'll ever tire of doing that."

I smile, forcing my eyes open. "I don't know that I will either."

"Well, good thing we have plenty of time for me to give you many more then," Milo's voice drips with sex.

"Lie down, baby," I instruct.

"Yes ma'am."

He flips on his back and I grab the condom off the nightstand. Once I've got it on him, I straddle his hips. My hand rests on his heart and I feel the rapid beating. He's just as nervous as I am.

It's easy to talk about what this means, it's another to do it.

"Are you all right?"

"I will be," I say as I rock forward, bringing him where I need him.

I know he's not asking about the physical part of what we're doing. We're in my home, the bed I once shared with my husband, and I can see Milo's hesitation. I don't have any, though. This isn't about anyone else but us right here. The emotions I'm feeling are because I'm overcome with hope.

Milo wasn't supposed to be anything to me. I had no plans to fall for someone. But I did, and right now, I'm happy.

I have to believe that because Peter loved me, he would want that.

If it were me who was gone, I know I would.

The tip glides in and I take his face in my hands, forcing my eyes to stay open. I start to move down, each inch filling me little by little as I go slow.

Milo's eyes start to close and I stop.

"I want you to watch this," I tell him. "I want you to feel the two of us connect physically."

"You feel too fucking good."

"You fill me up, Milo. In every way."

His hands wrap around my hips and pushes me down all the way.

I can't take it. I moan so loudly it's almost embarrassing. "God!"

He holds onto me, forcing me to move in a slow and deliberate pace. We keep our eyes on each other, not wanting to sever the connection.

Each time Milo's hips rotate a little, I damn near lose it. I rock my hips back and forth, my heart full along with my body.

The pleasure builds with every thrust.

"I want you to come again," Milo says through gritted teeth. "I want to feel you around my cock."

His thumb presses against my clit and he starts to make circles. "Right there. Milo!"

I explode again. I fall forward to his chest and then he flips me onto my back. He pushes harder, sweat dripping from his face as I hold onto his arms.

"You feel so good," he says between thrusts. "I'm almost there. Keep your eyes on me."

A wash of pleasure covers his face as he orgasms.

After we clean up, we snuggle up, my head on his shoulder as he runs his fingers against my spine.

"I never thought I'd enjoy this," Milo muses.

"Cuddling?"

"Yes." He kisses my forehead. "I always felt it was rather stupid, but I can see the appeal now."

I lift my head, resting my chin on my hand. "I'm just special."

"I don't deny that."

"When did you know?" I ask.

Milo shifts his head, his eyes narrowing as if he's deep in thought. "I'm not sure. I believe it was when I thought you were going to jail for creating disorder in the court and I wouldn't need to fight for my job."

I laugh. "You're an idiot. I couldn't believe you thought that."

"Why wouldn't I?"

"Because . . . I don't know."

Milo chuckles. "Fab answer, sweetheart."

"Fab answer, sweetheart," I mock him.

"Keep it up and you'll get a proper spanking."

I roll my eyes. "You'll regret that."

"Oh, will I?" Milo asks.

"I hit back."

He raises one brow. "I might like you when you're a bit naughty."

I laugh. "You have problems."

"You have no idea."

"Yeah?" I push him a little. "Like what?"

He sighs. "Well, I'm falling in love with my boss, which is a problem since my mission was to take her down. It leaves me in a rather precarious situation since I either need to quit my job and find something more suitable for my skill set, or stay on as her "bitch", as she so called me."

Did he just . . . did he say . . . I think he said he's falling in love with me. I swear I heard it.

After that, I wasn't paying attention to anything else that came out of his mouth. He said love. I know he did.

My heart is beating faster as I try to wrap my mind around his admission. Do I love him? Am I falling in love with him? The answer is yes to the second, but there's so much to figure out.

"Why do you look like you're ready to run?" Milo asks.

"I'm not." I shake my head.

"Lie."

I release a deep breath and sit up, pulling the sheet with me. "You said you were falling in love with me."

He pushes up, and nods once. "I thought that was rather obvious."

"Obvious how?"

"Do I look like a bloke who would want to come watch a film on your sofa rather than be at the pub? Or that I would have my Mum send my old comics from London when I wasn't feeling like more than fucking? I assure you, Danielle, that's not the man I am."

"It's just . . . you said it."

Milo watches me and then finally speaks. "I did because it's true."

I touch his hand. "I'm falling in love with you too."

He runs his hand from my shoulder to my fingers. "Now that we have that straight, what do we do about everything else?"

"I don't know," I confess.

I really don't. What can we do?

"I'll quit."

"What?" I pull my hand back. "Why would you say that's the answer?"

"Because I can. Let's be honest, I'm a little overqualified to be your assistant. Besides, you don't even make me do half the shit I forced my assistant to do." Milo grins.

I put my hand up. "I don't want to know."

"I didn't ask her to do that," he clarifies.

Glad to know.

"Still, quitting isn't the answer for either of us."

I can't quit. Milo shouldn't either. He and his brother need this time, whether he understands that or not. Their relationship has been strained for so long, and seeing each other at work has given them a small bridge.

If one would just cross it, that would be great.

"Well, I'm not going to sneak around as if we're doing something scandalous. Although . . . fucking my boss is rather dirty."

"You're an ass."

"I like your arse, sweetheart."

I roll my eyes. "You'll never see it again if you quit."

He lies back, still finding a way to touch my skin. "Then what is your plan?"

"I don't have one!" I laugh. "This is why we're talking it through."

"I'm more of an action guy. Talking is fucking boring."

How does he function in life? I wonder sometimes. But this is why he and Callum disagree. I need to have details so I can make the best decision possible. I'm not a bull in a china shop, trampling everything.

Freaking men.

"Regardless, we need to try to find the best solution. You need this job, Milo."

He scoffs. "You and my brother bloody wish I did."

"How are you working here?" I decide it's time to lead him to a real answer.

"Are you fucking with me?"

"No. I'm asking how is it that you're able to work for Dovetail?"

Seriously, I can't wait for the answer to slap him in the face.

"My brother is the owner!"

"Yes," I sigh. "And are you an American?"

Milo rubs his temples. "Clearly not."

"Right. So, again, how do you get to stay in America, Milo?"

He takes a second to actually think about what I'm saying and I then his eyes flash with awareness.

"Fuck! I have to work for that bastard because I need the damn work Visa."

Ding, ding, ding.

"Yeah, so sit for a minute and let's find a way around this." His mouth opens and I don't even need him to speak. I lift my hand to his lips to stop him before he can utter a word. "Don't even say we should get married because we are nowhere close to that."

"Fine."

I try not to laugh but his petulant face is making it hard.

"Milo, if and when you and I ever get to that point, it won't be because you don't want to hide the fact that we're dating at the office. It should be because we can't live without each other."

He grabs my arms, pulling me to his chest and I squeak. "Who says I can live without you?" he replies.

Now he's just crazy. "I don't doubt the idea of living without me is hard. I'm kind of awesome, but let's not go there, okay?"

"All right, but only if you kiss me."

Now that I can do.

twenty-six

...

Milo

"I'M HAPPY, Mum. I really like her." It's been twenty minutes of her carrying on about Callum and I abandoning her. I swear, she was never this dramatic when we were little boys. What happened?

"I'm happy for you, but that doesn't mean I want both my boys that far away," she keeps on.

"I'm not coming back to London anytime soon, but maybe you could come for holiday in a few months? There's a big barbeque you might enjoy. Plus, don't you want to come see Colin?"

Her first grandson, you'd think she would've moved in with my brother by now.

"Maybe," she sighs.

"It would mean a lot to us. I think you'd get on with her quite well. She has a daughter and son who have never had real English chocolate."

She doesn't say anything, but I can hear her smile. Mum spent twenty years working for Cadbury. Sweets are her weakness, and the idea that she can share something with them that she loves might just be the ticket.

"I guess I don't have a choice then."

I grin. "I guess not."

"You like this girl, Milo?"

I sit in my chair, looking out at the skyline of Tampa, thinking of her. "I think I love her, Mum."

She gasps. "Oh."

"I know, I don't know what's come over me, but she's amazing and brilliant. When I'm away from her I want to be near her. When she's close, I don't want to leave."

Mum sniffs and then starts blubbering. "Oh, darling. I'm so happy for you. It's just . . . it's wonderful."

"So you'll come here for a visit?"

"Yes. I want to meet this girl," she laughs. "I'll ring you soon."

"Goodnight, Mum."

"Goodnight, Milo. I love you very much, no matter what you think of me."

She disconnects the phone before I can reply, but it makes me happy to know she's on board.

I send a quick text to Callum.

Me: Mum is going to come for holiday.

Callum: How did you manage that one? She told me to sod off.

I smile at the opportunity he's given me.

Me: Because I'm the favourite. She just wanted to pad your ego by letting you think you were better than me. News Flash: You're not.

Callum: Fuck off.

Me: Mature, brother. Anyway, I'll let you know when I have more information.

Callum: Sounds good.

I have something else I need to talk to Callum about. Instead of doing it over the phone or text, I think it should be done in person.

Me: Can I stop over?

Callum: Is everything all right?

Me: Yes, you fucking nosey bastard, can I come or not?

Callum: Yes, fine, come by.

Such a prick.

I get in my car and drive the ten minutes to his house. He and Nicole live in a similar flat. He's just closer to the water.

Nervous energy fills me as I get to his door. I'm going to quit —again.

The first time went down like a lead balloon. I can't wait to see how this time goes. Even though the bastard has been hoping for this moment, he only seems to prefer it when it's on his terms.

I knock once, and Nicole answers. "The prodigal brother returns."

"Hello," I say and then kiss her cheek.

"I hear your mom is coming to see us?"

Good news travels fast. "I asked her to come over Fourth of July. She'll stay with you of course."

Nicole laughs. "Of course. Not like you have room or complete quiet. She should definitely stay here with our full house. Maybe she'll sleep on the couch?"

Callum walks in rubbing his neck. "Enough, Nic. We have plenty of room." He kisses her temple. "Plus, I get to enjoy watching you behave for once while she's here."

"Yes. I love having to be nice to you because that woman scares me."

"Our Mum? She scares you?" I laugh. "That's ridiculous."

Nicole glares at me. "Yeah, she doesn't love me like she does you two idiots."

This is true, but she's far from scary. She's sweet, when you're on her good side.

"Give her time. She's old and set in her ways," I tell her.

"Whatever," Nicole huffs. "I'll let you two talk, I'm going to take Colin for a walk."

"Be careful," Callum's voice is sharper than before. I can see the protective instinct start to rise inside him.

She rolls her eyes. "Relax, it's Tampa and . . ."

"And your best friend's husband was shot here not that long ago," Cal finishes.

"That wasn't random, babe, but okay. We'll be careful."

Nicole winks at me and then struts out of the room.

"Want a pint?" Callum asks.

"Sure."

We head inside and once again I'm amazed at the way this place looks. Mine is simple and has very little furniture, where Cal has more shit than he could ever want. I'm sure if my wife were an interior designer, I'd be living like this too, instead of the bachelor pad I'm currently occupying.

Still, no matter how many times I've been here, it knocks you on your arse.

Callum pops the top and hands it to me. This is going to be bloody painful. I drain the drink in less than a minute, almost slamming the bottle down.

"This can't be good," he says as he scratches his head. "Out with it."

"I quit."

Subtlety was never my strong suit.

"You quit?"

"Yes."

He shakes his head. "Okay. Why?"

There are a multitude of reasons, but Callum in all his faults has always been honest with me. I feel I owe him the same in this instance.

"Because I'm falling in love with my boss and I don't think it'll be a good look for us if I stay on."

"You're in love?" he laughs. "You?"

"Fuck off, mate. Yes. I don't know why you find that funny."

Callum shrugs and then hands me another bottle. "Because you've always been so against love, as if it made you weak."

"It does!" I yell. "I'm quitting my fucking job because of her."

He releases a deep breath through his nose and nods. "I moved my company to America for Nicole. But you can't quit, Milo."

"You don't get to make that choice."

"No," he agrees. "But there's another option—" His phone rings and he puts his finger up. "Hello?"

I grumble.

"Milo." Callum grips my arm when I start to walk out the room. "Yes. I understand. I'll let Milo know. Of course," I hear the panic. "Text me all the details."

"What's going on?" I ask with my heart racing.

Something is wrong. I know my brother and the last time he looked at me like this, I found out my father was dead.

twenty-seven

. . .

Danielle

"WHAT HAPPENS NOW, MOM?" Ava asks as we sit in the courtroom, waiting for the verdict to be read.

I haven't been back since my outburst. Maybe because it didn't matter in some ways. Maybe because I didn't want to hear any more lies. Or maybe because as much as I want to get closure, I found something else worth focusing on.

However, Richard called and said we should come today. He got word the jury had reached their decision.

As promised, I got Ava out of school and we came here together.

"They'll call the court to order and read the verdict. If he's guilty, they'll set sentencing. If he's innocent, you and I are leaving immediately before we're descended upon, understand?"

She nods.

Keeping my word on this was incredibly difficult. I didn't think it would be this tough. She's mature for her age in some ways, but this was her daddy. He was the first man she ever looked up to, loved, and wanted to find someone like.

He's not only gone, but now she's going to hear things that she may not want to. I'm a grown woman and couldn't handle it.

"I've never seen him," she notes. "You know, Daddy's killer."

"I never wanted you to."

My phone vibrates, but I don't look. This moment is too great to be distracted. I know that Parker is safe at school and then Kristin will take him. Aubrey apparently had big plans for their time together.

"Why?" Ava asks.

"Because he's the last person your father saw, and I hate him for taking that from our family. I wanted you to stay innocent and protected from him, but I see that you can do this. You're a beautiful, strong girl, Ava Kristin. I'm very proud of you."

Gone is the angry mask she's worn relentlessly for the past two years, and I see her again. "I'm proud of you too, Mom."

"Me?"

"Yeah, you know . . . you're dating and it's nice to see you happy. I guess. I mean, I don't care, but if I have to be around you, I'm glad you're not being a bi—"

"Watch it," I warn her.

She shrugs with a grin. "Sorry, I thought we were doing what you and Aunt Nicole do, the whole honesty is the only policy we subscribe to."

I roll my eyes. "You don't get admission to that club, kid."

Ava starts to talk, but then the side door opens and Adam McClellan walks in. I grab her hand, offering support as well as needing some of hers. Each time I see him I hate him even more.

"Just look forward okay?" Her eyes meet mine and I see the fear swimming. "You're safe, Ava. You have nothing to fear. No matter what happens today, you're safe, loved, and everything will be okay."

"He's just sitting there."

"I know." I squeeze her hand. "Eyes forward or on me."

She squeezes back and sighs. I look around for Milo. He said he'd be here, but I haven't heard from him. Which is strange because he's the one person that has always been in this room when I needed him, even when I didn't know I did.

A few heartbeats later, the judge enters and court is called to order.

"Has the jury reached a verdict?" she asks.

"We have your honor."

"Bailiff, please . . ." The judge extends her hand and he goes to get the envelope.

My stomach is in my throat as I watch her read. She makes no reaction to whatever their decision was, which I remember Peter complaining about all the time.

Being on this side, it sucks.

Each second feels like an hour passing.

Ava wraps her hand around my arm, holding on tight.

The judge hands the envelope back and then it goes back to the head juror. I swear, this is meant to make people crazy. It's not just about the murderer sitting there whose fate will be determined, it's about all of us. The people who loved my husband, our family, everyone who saw our grief and loss. This matters.

"Will you please read the verdict?" she asks as a commandment.

I could throw up. My stomach twists, my hands are sweating and I want to cry without even knowing the outcome.

It's so much.

"We the jury, find the defendant, Adam McClellan, on the count of murder in the first degree, guilty."

Relief floods through me and tears start to fall. Ava bursts out in tears, wrapping her arms around me.

"On the count of Illegal Possession of a hand gun, guilty."

I don't care about the rest of them, but this is vindication. I can breathe again. They continue to go through the rest of the charges, as I let it all out. I didn't screw up our chance to nail him. We didn't lose. We have justice for the hell this man put us through.

Ava and I sit close, holding each other's hands as they inform him of his sentencing date.

"That's it?" she asks with tears streaming down her cheeks.

"That's it."

We stand and the prosecutor walks toward us. "I'm so happy we have justice for Peter," Rachel says.

"We are too. I know that when he was alive, you guys fought on the opposite side . . ."

She shakes her head. "No, we were on the side of the law. Peter may not have been fighting for the side I chose, but he deserved justice."

"He did," I agree.

Ava wipes her cheeks and squares her shoulders. "I want to be here and speak at his sentencing."

Rachel looks to me and then back at her. "If your mother is okay with it, I think it would be helpful."

"Mom?"

I close my eyes while releasing a breath through my nose. "If you want to do that, I won't stop you. You have to behave, though. I'm not trying to give you an ultimatum, I'm asking you to think about what kind of girl you want them to see when you're standing before the judge."

This is hard, this parenting thing. On one hand you want to teach your kids they need to stand on their own feet. The other hand wants to put them in a bubble, hold tight, and never let anything touch them. Then there's the middle, where you don't know which way to go, and I hate the middle.

"I know. I just want to say some things," she explains.

"I do too, honey."

Richard comes over and hugs us both. "I'm glad we have justice for Peter."

"Me too."

"Peter would've won that case," he laughs to himself. "That's all I kept thinking. If he was the defense attorney, he would've shredded the prosecution. He was a fantastic lawyer, friend, and we miss him."

As much as I want to slap him for that being his first thought, I smile. Peter would've. He was great, and he would've gotten it done. Also, my husband was arrogant enough to have that been the first words out of his mouth. He thought he was great, and the fact that his business partner would've thought the same, probably has him smiling from Heaven.

"Yeah." I shake my head. "He really was."

"He loved you three. He talked about taking time off more, being there to see the kids grow up," Richard smiles.

"Too bad he didn't."

I see the instant regret flash in his eyes. "If you ever need anything, Danni, please don't hesitate to call us. You're family."

There was way too much dysfunction and backstabbing in the office. I would never trust any of them. Still, I can't be rude. "Thank you, Richard. We really appreciate that."

Ava tells us she's going to call her friends and excuses herself. I need to call mine, in fact, where are my damn friends? Or my boyfriend? Boyfriend. Jesus. Saying that at thirty-nine doesn't feel weird or anything.

I dig in my purse for my phone and see two missed calls and a text from Milo.

Milo: *You're not answering, but I'm at the airport heading to London. Please call Nicole when you're free. I'm sorry.*

My stomach drops. "Excuse me," I say to Richard.

I'm already dialing Nicole's number as I get outside the courtroom. It rings. And rings. "Come on pick up," I whisper.

"Hey." She answers after what feels like forever.

"Hey, what's going on?"

"First, are you okay? Did they find him guilty?"

I don't want to talk about this, but Nicole is . . . forceful when she wants something.

"Yes. Guilty. What's going on with Milo?"

She huffs. "All I know is he and Callum left for London. Their mother is sick and I guess she's been keeping it quiet, but she collapsed and they had to go right away."

"Oh, God."

"Yeah, I don't know, Danni," she pauses. "Milo was here talking about his mom coming here for Friendependence Day to meet you, and the kids. Then something about his job when Callum's phone rang. I'm not sure what their plan is, but my husband said he'd call when they had details."

I rub my forehead. "Okay, keep me posted."

This is so bad. Milo mentioned the other day about his mom being alone in London and some guilt he felt. I can't imagine how he's working through all of that.

Then another part of the conversation hits me. Milo went to Callum's house to talk about me and his job?

Oh, God. I hope he didn't quit. I swear, he just acts sometimes and I could scream. We discussed this and apparently, he doesn't listen.

Okay, getting upset isn't going to do anything. He's in London and I need to table this until we can talk.

———————————

It's been four days. Four days. Four phone calls. Four times I've found myself thinking about flying to London.

I can't go. I know this. I just want to be close to him.

Also, this temporary assistant that Kristin recommended, Sierra, is absolutely ridiculous. She has to be related to Erica, Kristin's special snowflake.

First, she put salt in my coffee, thinking it was sugar.

She then managed to spill her salty coffee on my desk, soaking a proposal I was working on. Then, she somehow, and I still can't figure out what possible way this happened, Sierra got in my inbox and deleted it all to help with clutter.

Thank God for the IT division and putting child locks on her computer.

I can't even.

I never thought I would miss Milo because of work. But here I am, once again finding a way to rationalize him coming home soon.

My video call rings and I smile when his face pops up. "Hi," I say with a dreamy sigh.

"Hello, sweetheart."

"How is your mom?" I ask.

"Not good."

He looks tired. I can see the stress in his eyes, and I hate it. Milo is always smart-mouthed, arrogant in some ways, and sarcastic. He's never sullen and I don't like it.

"I'm sorry, what are the doctors saying?"

Milo cracks his neck and flops on his bed. "I'm going back in the morning, but it's not looking good. We finally got her a proper room instead of that shit they tried to keep her in."

"I'm glad you're there though." Selfishly, of course, I'm not. He's where he needs to be, though. After losing his father the way he did, I can't imagine him not being close to his mom.

"I hate it. I wish we could throw her on a plane and take her to where it's bloody warm. I forgot how fucking freezing it is here. Tampa is a much more desirable climate."

I wish a lot of things, but I know he needs to vent a bit.

"Still." I give a sad smile. "You're where you're close to your mom. I'm sure she has comfort knowing you and Callum are there."

Milo grumbles and his eyes narrow. "He's a prick. I don't know why my mother didn't sell him when he was a boy. Such a bloody know it all. It's maddening, you know. I swear he thinks he's always in charge and I've had it. Fuck off big brother."

I bust up laughing at his outburst. "Stop it. He's probably scared too."

Now I get the look of death. "Scared? I'm not scared. I'm bloody pissed that's what I am."

"I see that."

"He thinks he can walk into any room and command it. I don't think so. I'm younger but my balls are much bigger, you can vouch for that."

My jaw drops and no words come out. He's clearly not happy with his brother, but Jesus.

"Milo, this is a chance, okay?"

"For what?"

"For you to be a fucking grown up. You and Callum need to knock it off. You know better than anyone that life is short and the only guarantee is that it'll come to an end. So, stop it. If Callum died, how would you feel? Terrible, that's what. So be the man I fell in love with. The one who is full of compassion."

Milo grimaces but then nods. "Only because you used a cheap trick to get me to bend to your will."

"Yes, I'm full of cheap tricks. Speaking of, I've decided that you don't have to hold the rabbit anymore."

"Really?" he asks with delight.

"Yes, I'm going to be nice and let you off the hook, even though I don't think for a second you would do the same."

He smirks. "Don't get upset about it. It would've been hilarious to see you walk up to my brother and tell him about my sexual competency."

"You're a mess."

"True, but together we're rather perfect."

I smile and blow him a kiss. "Go get some sleep. I miss you."

"I miss you too. How is your new assistant working out?"

"Shut up."

"Well, don't get upset about it, Callum will be back in two days. You can complain to him then."

"He's coming back?"

Since they got there, not much information has been fed back to me, which I completely understand. Milo and Callum have needed to take care of their mother, not worry about telling me crap. I've been kept in the loop by Nicole mostly. She didn't mention anything about this plan when we spoke today.

Milo nods. "Yes. He's needed back there, and I'm not exactly a critical employee."

"You are to me," I inform him.

"Sweet. However, I'm needed here."

"How long do you think?"

Milo sighs. "I don't know. I can't leave her here all alone."

"I would never ask you to."

"I know." He gets himself under the covers and I wish I could touch his face.

"The sentencing is next week."

It's been weighing on me a lot the last few days. I want this over. This is the final piece of resolution.

Milo's eyes turn sad. "I hate that I'm not there, but it all depends how the next few days go. Maybe I'll make it back."

"That wasn't why I was saying it."

"Doesn't mean that's not how I feel."

My temporary assistant pops her head in. "Did you call me?"

"No," I draw the word out. "I'm on a call."

"Oh," she giggles. "That makes sense. I thought maybe you were talking to yourself and I was going to let you finish, but then I thought maybe you were talking to me."

Oh my God.

"Thank you for checking, Sierra," I somehow get the words out.

"Of course! My job is to make sure you're all set."

My job is to wonder how we're giving the reins over to the younger generation.

Great. Now I'm one of those older people complaining about kids today.

"Good job, love," Milo answers. "Danielle loves to talk to herself, so be sure to check in."

I glare at him and then look to her. "Don't listen to a word he says."

"Oh, it's a guy on the phone? So, is he like, your boyfriend?"

"Go back to work," I instruct.

When she walks out of the room, I close my eyes and hear Milo chuckling.

"I hate you."

He smirks. "No, you don't."

"Fine, but I want to, and I should."

He laughs and then it turns into a yawn. "I'm sorry to cut you off, sweetheart, but I can't keep my eyes open. Can we talk tomorrow? I can ring you around seven before work."

"Okay. Get some sleep."

"I will," Milo promises.

Four days done, God only know how many more to go.

twenty-eight

...

Milo

"YOU HAVE TO EAT, MUM."

"I don't take orders from you, of all people," she huffs.

Indignant as ever.

I've been in London a fortnight and I'm ready to gouge my bloody eyes out. Mum is finally feeling slightly better, but then we have a night where we go backwards.

God forbid the doctor do his fucking job properly and get her the medication she needs.

"Just eat before my temper comes out."

She doesn't seem the slightest bit concerned. "When are you going back to America?"

"When you stop being a pain in my arse and eat your food."

Mum crosses her arms over her chest. "Then I will die of starvation."

"Dramatic as ever."

"I miss my sons." Her lip trembles and my cold heart starts to melt.

I don't like seeing her upset. No matter how much trouble I like to cause, my Mum is a wonderful woman who has suffered too much.

"Don't cry," I beg her.

"Don't leave."

"Mum, you know why I want to return to America."

She nods. "I wanted to meet her."

We've spent a lot of time together these past two weeks, and she has not held back on her opinions. Of course, she wants me to be happy, just in London. My hope is that she'll realize that's not likely and she'll come with us to America where her family is now.

"Why can't you meet her?"

"I'm not going there now, Milo. I'm dying."

I roll my eyes. "You're not dying. You are going to fight and win because you're too stubborn to die."

She pins me with a stare. "I wondered where you got it from."

"Look in the mirror," I laugh.

"Oh, Milo, what am I going to do about you?"

I shrug. "Get better so you can travel and see your grandson and hopefully meet the woman I'm in love with."

Her hand lifts, touching my cheek. "I don't know if that's reality, my darling. I may not get better or be strong enough. I have lung cancer. I can't fly or do much of anything."

This is what worries me as well. She looks frail and tired. As much as I want to believe she'll recover, I don't know that she can.

Then there's the worry of her being in another continent without any help.

"You will be because I can't lose you, not yet. There's children to meet and love."

Her eyes brighten and her lips lift. I know how happy that makes her. "Tell me more about Parker. He reminds me of the boy you were."

I lean back in my chair. "You eat and I'll talk. Deal?"

She nods, lifting the biscuit and I begin to tell her about his love of Thor.

"What can I do for you, Cal?" I say into the receiver as I grab my jacket.

I'm already late to get Mum to the hospital for her treatment. I'll never hear the end of it at this rate.

"We need to talk."

This can't be good. Callum doesn't ring me when he feels like having a chat. I usually get an earful of his favourite names to call me and he hangs up before I can speak. Twat.

"There's a problem in the London office."

I stop dead in my tracks. "I'm sorry?"

"Edward quit."

"Edward as in our cousin who you gave the office to instead of me?" I ask for clarification.

That's the part that Callum always seems to gloss over. Not only did he move to America, taking most of the company there, but he left an office here to run the projects we were already working on. However, he knew my feelings on leaving London, but instead of asking me, his only brother, to take over this location, he gave it to our wanker of a cousin.

Which is why I vowed to loathe my brother 'til eternity. Because he's a bastard.

Once again, the Thor and Loki comparison is striking.

"Yes, that one."

"Why are you telling me?"

He sighs. "Because I need you to take his spot. You're there and you're the only one I trust."

My heart races the slightest bit. "You want me to take over the London office?"

"Do you want to be an assistant or be the Vice President of Dovetail and run that office?" Callum asks with anger.

"And once I do this for you, what job am I going to have, huh? Filing for you instead of my girlfriend? Or are you going to punish me further?"

I'm not playing his game. I want something in writing and to be paid what I'm worth.

"No, Milo. I want you to take over the position—permanently."

I stand here, staring at the door of my flat, completely stunned. He wants me to become the Vice President of the company?

Permanently?

And why? And when? What is the sudden change of heart?

"Are you fucking with me?"

He chuckles once. "No, that's what I wanted to talk to you about when we were at my house, but then we got the call about Mum."

I don't know what to say. This is completely unexpected. "I'm trying to wrap my head around this. You want me to move back to London?"

"No," he sighs. "I don't want that, but Mum needs one of us and I want you to take the position in the company you were meant for."

I lean against the wall, feeling torn apart. "What about Danielle?"

"What about her, Milo? I'm happy you found her, but it's not like you've been together long. You're not exactly known for anything long term."

"Fuck off!"

"You can be upset with me, but there are no other options." Callum's voice is filled with remorse for the first time. "I can't move to London. I have the company here, Nicole has her company, and we have Colin. You're single."

"I'm not," I correct.

I may not be married, but I'm in love for the first time in my life. There's someone worth the effort and he's going to take that away from me.

Fuck! Fucking hell.

"No, you're not, but answer me this, when was the last time you had a serious relationship?"

I don't have to answer him because we already know it.

"Exactly," Callum answers. "I care very much about Danielle. She's a very big part of our lives here, so hurting her isn't what I want to do—or you, Milo. No matter what you may think of me, I do care about you. This is ultimately your choice, but the office is yours if you take it. And either way, you're going to need to be there for Mum."

My heart is being torn from my chest. "I need to think about this. I . . . I can't give you an answer."

Cal sighs. "I'll give you a week to give me your decision about staying on, but I need you to go there tomorrow and fix the mess Edward made."

I don't need to do anything, but I'm not going to argue that fact. The truth is, this was what I wanted all along. This company was built by the two of us. I love Dovetail as much as Callum does, and now he wants to give me what I've worked my arse off to create. I don't know that I can walk away. It was the whole damn reason I came to America.

"You'll give me whatever time I require," I reply.

"Don't be a prick."

"Don't be a bastard."

Callum grumbles. "I'll hear from you in a week."

"You'll hear from me when I decide." I smirk and hang up.

My phone pings again and it's a text from my mum, asking where I am.

I'll handle her first, then I have to call another woman I love and figure out what in the bloody hell I do about that.

twenty-nine

• • •

Danielle

"HAVE YOU HEARD FROM MILO LATELY?" Callum asks as he's at the door in my kitchen.

"No, but I'm sure I will soon, why?"

He shakes his head. "Just curious."

A niggling feeling in my gut says otherwise. Callum and I are friendly. I like him, think he's a great guy, but he's my boss. I always feel like I'm going to say something stupid and he's going to fire my ass.

"Is there something I should know?" I ask hesitantly.

"No, no. We haven't spoken in a few days, I wasn't sure how Mum was doing."

His mother has more bad days of late than good. It's been three weeks, countless phone calls, and still no Milo back in my arms. I'm starting to feel discouraged, and I'm trying hard not to. But I miss him. I hate that I do because I feel weak.

However, I can't believe he hasn't let Callum know.

"He said she was having a rough time the other night. We haven't spoken today, though."

"He hasn't said anything else?"

Okay, this is weird. "No, should he have?"

"I'm sorry," Callum lets out a nervous laugh. "It's hard being here when she's sick."

"Don't be sorry. I'll definitely tell him to call you."

"Thank you." He smiles.

That was the most bizarre conversation ever.

I grab the drinks and head out to the living room. Tomorrow is the sentencing, and my friends took it upon themselves to be here tonight. Heather, Eli, Kristin, Noah, Nicole, and Callum are apparently going to babysit me.

"Thanks, Danni." Heather smiles as I sit the wine glasses out on the table.

"You know you guys don't need to be here," I say for the tenth time.

"Yes, we do," Kristin argues.

I will never get them to leave, I might as well stop trying.

"How are you doing with Milo being in London?" Nicole cuts right to the chase.

"I'm fine. He's where he needs to be."

And I truly mean that. His mother is what counts right now. We've been dating a whole few weeks before she got sick, I know he wants to be here, but he can't.

"I'll tell you this," Eli starts. "If it was my mom, I'd be right next to her too. You can tell a lot about a man by the way he treats his mother."

I scrunch my face. "How so?"

"That's the first person to love him. If she's a good woman, which by how Cal talks about her, she is, then a man learns how to treat a woman from that relationship."

Heather nods. "I can say that the way Eli dotes on his that's true. Matt was a jerk to his, and we know why." She looks to Kristin. "How was Asshole with his mother?"

Kristin laughs. "The same way he was to everyone in his life—a selfish douche."

Noah tucks Kristin to his side a little tighter. I don't know if she realizes it, but anytime Scott gets brought up, he pulls her closer. Almost like he's protecting her from the thought of him. It's sweet, and I love seeing that their relationship is as strong as it is.

"I agree with Eli," Noah shrugs. "I would walk through fire for my mother. She pretty much did for me, and if she were sick, I'd be there."

"That's because you're a good man, Noah Frazier," Kristin sighs as she looks at him.

Nicole pretends to gag. "God you guys are so gross."

"Why because we love each other?" Kristin counters.

Oh, this is so going to get ugly.

"I love Callum more than anything. I literally would give anything for him, but I'm not all batting my eyes and sighing when he talks. He's a man. He loves his mother, but he loves me too. Milo is a good guy, and I'm happy that he and Danni found each other, but Danni needs him too."

"I don't need any of you here," I correct.

Nicole rolls her eyes. "Yes you do, it's okay."

"You guys, seriously, I'm fine. I love you all and thank you for coming, but I've got this."

"I wish we could delay filming," Heather says.

Do any of them listen? No, no they do not.

I don't want anyone but Ava with me. I know that sounds crazy, and maybe a little stupid, but we have to get through this. If they're there, I'll feel as though I have to perform. Being weak in front of others is a hard thing for me. Peter was a tough guy. He didn't love emotions and I learned to lock them up. When he first died, it was as though a dam had broken and flooded my world.

I cried more than I had in twenty years.

I cried and then sobbed and then wailed.

I thought all of it had been purged, but some must be left because I know tomorrow will affect me.

"You guys, Ava and I will be fine."

Kristin blows a loud breath through her nose. "You're being a stubborn ass."

I give her a look that says, *Maybe I am, but I'm allowed to be.*

The doorbell rings and I jump up. "I'll get it. You can continue to talk shit about me when I leave."

Nicole lifts her hand. "Oh, don't worry, we plan to."

"Bitch."

"Idiot," she replies.

I head to the door, and when I open it, my heart stops.

"Milo!"

"Hello, sweetheart." He smiles and pulls me into his arms.

"Oh, my God. You're here." Tears I swore were done falling come rushing forward. He's here. He's here now, and I'm in his arms.

I pull back, my hands touching his face. I bring my mouth to his, tasting the tears against my lips.

After a few seconds, he puts me down and smiles. "I see you missed me."

"I did. I missed you so much."

I can't explain it, but he's become such a part of my life. I felt empty, sad, and lonely without him. My heart is his and now I feel like I can breathe again.

"I know that tomorrow is important and I wanted to be here."

I clutch my chest and then place my hand over his heart. "Thank you. What about your mother?"

"She'll be okay for a few days."

"Days?" I ask, feeling dejected already. "I thought maybe . . ."

When did I become this dependent on him?

"It's just a short visit, sweetheart. Callum and I arranged for a nurse to stay with her until I can return."

I'm not going to think about him leaving again. I only want to think about what we have. A few days is better than nothing.

"I understand, I'm just so surprised." Then something else dawns on me. "Callum knew!"

"He did."

I smile. That's why he was being so weird. "Can we kick everyone out?"

He wiggles his brows. "Not can, we most definitely will."

Works for me.

I take his hand and we enter the living room. "Everyone out!" I say and they look up.

"Milo!" A few of them yell out.

Milo walks around, shaking hands, and kissing cheeks. The husbands haven't met him yet, so I give them a few minutes to make introductions. Honestly, I could care less if they never met because I want every second I have with him.

Preferably not with my friends.

Nicole walks over and puts her arm around me. "I'm taking Ava for the night. She agreed to babysit Colin for us. I asked her the other day so it doesn't look like you just want to have wild sex with your hot boyfriend."

"I didn't like you before, but now I kind of get the appeal." I smile and bump her hip. She's a mess, but it's moments like this that you remember how great of a friend she is.

"I told you, I'm a mother fucking diamond."

I laugh and kiss her cheek. "I guess you are. I'll pick her up before the sentencing."

"No worries, have a good breakfast fuck while you're at it. You can call it sausage in your biscuit."

"Nicole," I chide. "You're so vulgar sometimes."

"Sometimes?" She laughs.

"All right. All the damn time."

Good to see motherhood didn't change her.

"Milo!" Parker yells as he runs down the stairs. "You're back!"

"I am for a few days." Milo smiles as he gives him a big hug.

"I have so much to tell you," he says.

I don't know if Milo understands what this means to me. My kids liking a man I'm dating is paramount. They are my entire world, and that man has to be able to step in and become part of it. While I think I would've fallen for Milo regardless, the fact that my son came running to him says more than words.

Children are the best judges of character. I remember when Ava wouldn't go around Scott. I thought it was weird, but looking back, she knew there was something off with him. I believe children are innocent, and they can sense it.

"We'll get out of your hair," Heather says as she comes close. "Eli and I fly out tomorrow. I really do wish I could be there, even though Milo is here now, it's just . . . I love you."

"And I love you," I say, pulling her in for a hug, "I know you want to be here, but you're married to a movie star who is in high demand."

Eli chuckles. "Gotta give the women what they want."

She slaps his stomach. "You're a dork."

"You're both dorks," I clarify.

We say goodbye, and Ava comes downstairs finally.

"Milo is back." She smiles. "Are you two going to make out and that's why I'm going to Aunt Nicole's?"

"Yup," Nicole answers. "I'm pretty sure they're going to do more than that."

She should wear a shock collar and each time she says something stupid, we should get to zap her. Maybe that will teach her what is appropriate.

On the other hand, she'd probably like it too much.

"So gross. I swear."

Nicole laughs. "You asked, kid."

"Lie to me next time." Ava shivers.

"Seriously, I had no idea he was coming here. I'll pick you up in the morning," I explain.

"Sure thing, Mom. Make good choices, use a condom and all that," Ava says as she waves her hand. "I'm really too old to be a sister again."

"Oh my god."

Seriously, my kid needs help.

Nicole is about ready to pee herself. She's laughing hysterically at my dismay.

"What?" Ava asks as though she has no idea why we're horrified.

"Oh, just you telling your mother to use a condom. I thought I'd never experience this level of comedy, but . . . here it is." Nicole claps her hands. "Bravo, kid."

Ava bows. "I'm here every night, folks."

After everyone is done giving me shit, I get the kids all packed to go. Parker is having a hard time leaving Milo alone, and it's kind of cute.

"Okay, but do you say all words funny?"

Milo scoffs. "I don't say things funny, you do."

"You don't even say bathroom," Parker counters.

"Because it's a loo."

"Lou who?"

"Not Lou, loo," Milo explains.

Parker looks at him like he's crazy, and starts to giggle. "You guys are a trip. Come on, Parker, it's time to go with Aunt Kristin."

He groans. "But Aubrey will try to make me dress up and get married."

Milo chuckles and I roll my eyes. "You'll survive."

Milo helps me corral Parker and get him settled. It's as though he just gets how to be a good man. For someone who doesn't have kids or was never serious about a woman before, Milo is a great boyfriend. Here he is, for three days, to be here for me because he knew I might need support.

"Bye, Mom."

"Bye, baby." I give Parker another big hug.

Then he turns to Milo. "Bye, Milo. I really missed you!" He wraps his arms around Milo's neck and holds on tight.

"I missed you too."

Kristin grabs my hand and squeezes. Both of us know what it's like to have another man come into our lives already having children. It's scary and a leap of faith like none other. You have to hope that everyone can find their way. Thankfully, this has been seamless thus far.

And that's what also tells me it's right.

We get everyone out the door and we both stand there.

Alone.

And then, before another breath passes, we collide.

My arms are around his neck, he clutches me to him, and our lips are everywhere. We kiss hard, then soft, moving our mouths down each other's necks, then back up again. I can't get enough of him.

We both moan as our hands begin to roam each other's bodies. Every touch is better than the last.

Milo pushes my back against the wall, and his hot body and the cool wall sends shivers through me. Neither of us talk. Our mouths are fused together, tongues pushing against each other in a kiss that says so much.

He pulls me off the wall, guiding me deeper into the house. Both of us clawing at each other. My hands yearn to touch his skin, so I pull his dress shirt off, tossing it to the ground. Milo follows suit and rips my shirt off over my head as we keep moving.

"God, you feel so good," he says.

"I missed you," I breathe and then our lips collide again. No more talking.

I reach for his pants, undoing the button. He steps out of them, continuing to reach whatever bed or surface we find quickest. I want his clothes off. I want him touching me.

It's been too long that I've been without him.

I need him so much.

He pulls my shorts down as my backside hits the couch.

"I have to have you," he says before kissing me again.

"Need you, too."

His hands are everywhere. Rubbing and squeezing my breasts, my hands grip his cock, and then he moves his hand to my clit. There's no finesse to our touch. Neither of us can get enough, and yet we still need more. Milo lifts me into his arms, my legs wrap around him and he walks to the center of the living room.

Both of us are now completely bare to each other. He lies me on the rug and sits up on his knees. "I thought about you like this every day that I was gone."

I smile. "I'm glad you missed me."

"Very much."

"Show me," I request.

Milo's grin turns mischievous. "It would be my pleasure."

He hovers over me, hands beside my head, his lips barely touching mine. "Milo," I whimper.

"I have other places I want my mouth first."

And he does. He slides his tongue down my neck, moving slowly across each breast, then he travels to my pussy, licking, and flicking my clit.

"Yes," I moan as my fingers tangle in his hair.

I build so quickly, it doesn't seem possible. I don't know if it's the adrenaline, or the fact that for three weeks I've dreamed of this reunion, but I'm on fire. Each cell is alive with desire, firing off different sensations. Hot and cold, pleasure and pain, but it all feels so good.

He feels good.

I start to shake as my orgasm hovers on the precipice. "I'm so close," I yell out.

My back arches as the sensations become too much. I feel as though my body is about to shatter from the immense pleasure he's drawing from me.

Then, he inserts a few fingers, and twists. That's all it takes. I'm completely gone.

I writhe on the floor, calling out his name, and then he crawls back above me.

"Stunning."

I smile. "I love you."

The words came out so easily, and I stop breathing for a second. I knew I loved him, and I do, but I didn't know I was going to say it right then.

We've talked about how we're falling in love, but neither have fully . . . said it.

Until now.

Milo doesn't say anything, and now I feel like a total ass. He looks at me—stunned.

"You don't have to say it back," I say quickly. "It's really okay. I just . . . I don't know, it felt like the right thing to say."

Shit.

He's like a deer in the headlights. *Way to go Danielle.*

His finger covers my lips to silence me. "I love you, Danielle."

Now it's my turn to be shocked. "You do?"

He smiles. "Very much so."

"Oh." I release a soft sigh. "I didn't mean for that to . . . come out like that."

Milo's hand cups my face. "We don't do many things like we plan, do we?"

"No, I guess we don't."

Milo brings his lips to mine and then I see fear flash in his eyes. "I don't want to lose you."

I brush my fingers across his jaw. "You won't."

"God, I fucking hope not."

Milo leans forward slightly, and I open my legs to allow him in. We don't say another word. We let our bodies do the talking.

But when we're done, I can't help but feel a sense of dread in my stomach, warning me something is off. I just don't know what.

thirty

. . .

Danielle

"THAT WASN'T HORRIBLE," Ava tells us as she pops a fry into her mouth. "It wasn't fun, but I feel like Dad would be happy."

Milo nods. "I thought it was bloody brilliant. You and your mother were strong in all the right ways."

Both Ava and I decided we didn't want to talk before the judge. There was too much that we would want to say and not be able to, or we'd say things that later we might regret. Sometimes, silence is louder than a scream.

Adam McClellan took enough from me. I wasn't going to give him my words. He was condemned by a jury of his peers, and the judge provided the justice we needed.

"I think your dad would be proud as well."

"Do you think he feels bad?" she asks. "Like, he'll sit in his cell and wonder how he could be such a horrible human?"

"No. I don't think people like that feel remorse and empathy. You noticed even until the end, he didn't think he did anything wrong. When you're guilty, you have to stand up and own your mistakes. It's how we *should* conduct ourselves in life," I tell her. "Be sorry when you do wrong. Change starts with you, my darling daughter. You've made errors but look how you've responded."

Ava looks at her plate, and I lift her chin to look back at me. "I was so angry after Dad died."

"I know."

Milo clears his throat. "My father was killed and anger was the only emotion I knew."

Her lips part as she sucks in a gulp. "How old were you?"

"Your age," he tells her.

"I'm so sorry." Ava's lip trembles.

His phone rings, he looks at the screen, and silences it. "Sorry." Milo takes my hand, pulling it to his lap and returns his attention to Ava. "It's not a club I wish you joined, but I want you to know that no matter what, I'll always be a shoulder you can cry on."

Ava tilts her head with a smile. "You know, I wasn't sure about you, but you're a cool dude."

"So, we're done with you trying to make inappropriate comments?" Milo jokes.

"Probably not. I'm turning over a new leaf, but the tree is the same."

"Yeah, nice try," I laugh. "You're done. You've had your fun, now it's time to stop or I'll ground you again."

She huffs. "You're so lame, Mom. What's the fun in having a hot boyfriend if I can't make you uncomfortable?"

"Shut up and eat."

We spend the rest of our lunch laughing and telling stories about our lives before all of this. Ava asks a ton of questions about life in London. I swear she thinks it's still 1810 and they're in an Austen novel.

"We have cars!" Milo chuckles.

"And they run on gas or do you crank them?"

He rolls his eyes. "I assure you we are far more civilized than you're giving us credit for. I'm pretty sure we had most modern technology before you."

I sit as though I'm watching a volleyball match. They just toss them back and forth and I'm pretty sure one is going to spike the ball soon.

"And do you use candles or is there electricity?"

Milo looks at me and narrows his eyes. "Are you fucking with me?"

Point one for Ava.

She shrugs. "Maybe or maybe not."

"We live very much like you do in America. We have cars, electricity, fancy stores, and history. Do you really think the Queen doesn't have electricity?"

Ava bursts out laughing. "Oh, you should see your face!" She does her best British accent. "Do you bloody believe this girl? Her knickers are in a twist because of electricity."

"If we ever get married, does she come with the deal?" Milo asks.

I nearly choke on my water. "Depends how much I like her at the time."

"She is rather annoying."

"This is true." I purse my lips and tap my fingers on the table.

"Mom!"

"Ava."

She leans back with her arms crossed. "You're so mean."

"Maybe, but you're a turd on a good day."

Milo's phone pings and he pushes it back in his pocket. The look on his face gives me concern.

"Everything all right?"

He shakes his head and gives me a fake smile. "My brother."

"Is it about your mother?"

He spoke with her nurse this morning and said everything was fine. She's very ill, though. I can imagine information could change rather quickly.

"No, it's about another matter."

"Okay?" I say as more of a question.

"Oh," Ava says with her chin on her hands. "Is this like a big secret?"

That feeling in my gut is stronger. Something is going on. He's been acting strange since he got back from London.

Milo chuckles. "There's no secret. Why don't we head back and watch a film?"

I don't say anything because I'm not going to put him on the spot here and now. However, Milo and I are going to talk, that much I know. But what happens if I find out that what he's hiding is something worse that I could have imagined?

———————

We're cuddled on the couch, my head on his shoulder, his arms wrapped around me as the kids are passed out in their rooms.

Parker and Milo played video games—I found out Milo is a really sore loser—while Ava went out with her friends.

It was a nice quiet evening, and a sense of peace was everywhere.

There's something to be said about closure. I always thought it was such bullshit until I actually found it. Knowing Peter's killer will spend the rest of his life behind bars, has allowed me a chance to accept his loss.

Then, I look at Milo and I can't help but wonder if my husband isn't up there smiling down.

While he and Peter are polar opposites, Milo is exactly the man I need.

"I hate that you're leaving tomorrow," I tell him.

"I'm not happy about it either. I'm not happy about anything right this moment."

I lift my head back. "You're not happy with me?"

He shakes his head. "No, darling, you're the only thing I'm happy about."

Well, that was sweet.

"It's hard because I know you need to be there for your mother, but selfishly, I want you here with me."

Milo releases a heavy sigh. "We need to talk."

I sit up, instantly, feeling uneasy. "What's going on?"

"Do you know that my cousin Edward ran the London office of Dovetail?"

I nod. I've spoken with Edward a few times since working for the company. He's an idiot, but I couldn't exactly tell Callum that. There was always some issue that was simple to fix that Edward screwed up even worse than before.

"Right, so he did a rather shit job. I'm sure you've had to deal with him a time or two."

Then the phrasing he just said dawns on me. "Yes. But you said . . . ran? As in past tense?"

"Yes."

"Okay. Who is running it now?"

I already know the answer. I can see it in his eyes.

"Me."

My stomach drops and all the feelings I had about security and my life going in the direction I wanted dissipates. Milo wouldn't look like he's ready to lose his mind if this was some temporary thing. He wouldn't be dodging Callum's calls or texts. He would've told me, but he didn't.

"How long have you known?"

Milo closes his eyes and when they're open again, I see his guilt. "A week. I couldn't tell you, Danielle. I was dealing with my mother and you had the sentencing. I'm not even sure if I'm going to accept the position."

"What do you mean?"

He gets to his feet and starts to pace. "I don't want to live in fucking London. I don't want to go back there like this. I want to stay here, there's no other way I can be happy. The mere idea of walking away from you makes me ill."

"I don't understand. Callum offered you the company and you don't want to take it? Because of me?"

He stops, his eyes boring into mine. "That's exactly what I'm saying. I'm going to turn him down."

As much as there's a conviction in what he's saying, I can see the struggle in his eyes.

This is what he always wanted. He came back to Dovetail to fight for his job. Instead, he's been offered a chance to run the London office. I don't see how he can walk away. Whether he needs money or not, he's not happy being my assistant. Milo is far too intelligent to do that, and I don't know what job he'd take in the Tampa office. It's too small still, and . . . Edward should've never had that job.

I can't ask him to stay.

I know this in the depths of my soul. It would be selfish of me, and that's not how love works. We give up things—our own happiness—to provide another person happiness. Milo is willing to walk away from an opportunity of a lifetime for me, now I'm going to fall on the sword instead. Because I love him.

"Milo," I wait for his eyes to meet mine. "You have to take it. This is what you were fighting for. The place in the company that you deserved. Besides, you need to be there for your mom. She needs you and . . . you can't stay for me. Not like this."

"I am!" He yells. "I'll go back, get Mum back on her feet and then we'll be fine."

"Get her on her feet? She has cancer, and she needs you."

"I need you, what about that?" Milo asks.

My chest aches so bad I could crumple to the ground. I don't want to hurt him. I don't want to hurt anymore either. Why couldn't we be happy this once?

"It's just not our time." I force the words out and each one is like a knife slicing me open.

It was our time. It just got ripped away.

"I'm not giving up," he says with defiance. "We'll fly back and forth. We'll video chat every day."

He's being crazy and I have to stop this. "You and I both know that's not true."

Tears begin to form and I try with all my might to stop them before they spill over. I've loved two men in my life, and now I'll have lost them both. Only this one I have to let go of willingly.

"I love you! I love you and I don't want to lose you." Milo crouches, taking my hands in his. "I can't do it."

A part of my heart breaks inside of me. Because, I can't ask him to stay. As much as I want those to be the words that come out of my mouth, I won't let them. "You have to do this. We both know that."

"Fuck. I knew you were going to do this." He gets back to his feet. "Once I told you, no matter what, you were going to push me to go back."

"Of course I am, because it's the right thing, Milo. You're not meant to be my stupid assistant. You are meant to run that office. London is your home and your mom is sick. I don't like the reality of it, but it's what it is." The tears I tried to fight fall.

It hurts so much.

"Don't cry," he begs. "Please."

"I'm not." I try to hide my face and get a damn grip, but it's not working.

"Danielle," his voice is soft. "Look at me, sweetheart."

My head lifts slowly and I see the pain mirrored in his eyes. "I didn't want to love you," I tell him, "I didn't want to ever love another man because losing him would be too hard. But now I'm here, in love with you and I have to watch you walk away."

"We'll make this work," he vows.

I shake my head, because the reality is, it won't. Sure, we could try and maybe get a few months where we find ways, but I have kids. I can't hop on a plane and head off to visit him whenever I want. He's going to be running an empire and there's no way he'll be coming back here. Then, the phone calls will stop. We'll be too busy and time will get away from us both.

I was stupid and let myself get caught up in this whirlwind because everything felt so right.

"We have to be honest." My lip trembles as pain so deep slices through my heart. "You need to go. Your mother needs you and so does your brother. There aren't options here, Milo."

His head falls to my lap, and my fingers glide through his brown hair. I hate this more than anything. I'm doing everything I can not to break apart. This wasn't what he wanted, and making this harder on him, won't help.

When his emerald eyes meet mine, there are unshed tears. "This isn't how I wanted things to go."

"I know."

"I had a plan for us."

"Sometimes the plan we have isn't the one we're meant to follow," I tell him softly.

He cups my face, pulling his lips to mine. "Why did I have to find you only to lose you?"

I don't know why, but I'm dying inside.

Maybe Milo came into my life to get me to see that I could go on and love again. He gave me something I wasn't aware I was missing. More than that, he's made me happier than I can remember being in years.

I dared to hope only to be defeated again. But at least I know that hope is possible.

A tear streaks down my face. "I love you, Milo. I love you and as much as it's hurting me to let you go, I know it's the right thing."

"Why can't we try? Why can't we see if we can make this work?" he asks.

I push out a heavy breath. "Because it won't! It won't and we'll end up miserable and in more pain than just letting each other go now."

He shakes his head and gets back to pacing the room. "Fuck! My brother knew he was going to ruin us by doing this."

I wipe my eyes, trying to stop the immense anguish in my chest. I sit there, imagining how it will be never to touch him again. The fact that I won't be able to kiss him, see his smile, or feel his warmth. Milo is like the sun, you can't help but want to be near him.

The last few weeks have been cold. I'll feel that from now on.

Once again, my world will go dim.

thirty-one

. . .

Milo

HOW DO I say goodbye to her?

I've asked myself this question a hundred times in the last twelve hours. Yet here I am, in the back of the car as the driver takes us to the airport.

Danielle has been quiet since our talk last night. Neither of us slept, almost as though wasting the time, not being entwined, would be stupid.

We've stayed connected in some way all night. Either my hand on hers or hers on mine.

"Are you going to be all right?" I ask her again.

She tries to smile but there are tears pooling in her eyes. "I've been through this before, I'll survive."

I don't know that I will.

If this was simply about a job, I would tell Callum to shove it up his arse. My mother is the variable no one could've predicted. Someone needs to care for her and it only makes sense that it's me. The job just happened because of the circumstances.

I've tried every possible way around this and can't come up with anything. She refuses to leave London, and therefore I have to go to her.

I take our entwined hands and bring them to my lips. "I hope you know that I love you."

Her head rests on my arm. "I love you too. Wouldn't it be great if that was enough? If all of this wasn't happening and instead of going to the airport to say goodbye, it was to go on a trip?"

"Yes, it would."

"If only love could move continents together," Danielle says wistfully.

If only . . .

We pull into the airport parking and the tension thickens. Fucking hell, I'm not even out of the car and I want to go back.

I have to do what I can to make this easier on her, though. There's no other option. Danielle has to sit alone on the way back, and I have no idea how she'll be. Will she be sad and crying? Will she stay strong and break down later? Or will she hold it together the entire time?

The driver parks and I want any time I can have. "Come in with me?"

She looks at the driver and then back to me. "I don't know."

"Please," I beseech her. "I want to delay this as much as possible."

Danielle tucks her hair behind her ear and tries to hide the fact that she wiped a tear. Fuck. This is wrong. Everything about this feels wrong and I know I'm making a mistake.

Then I think about telling my Mum that I'm not coming back.

I imagine her being alone in London, no one to make sure she's okay. If it was myself or Cal who were sick, she would never abandon us. I've gone over this in my head, and I know there is the selfish choice and then the right one.

I extend my hand to Danielle, asking her to take it and give me even five more minutes.

"Okay," she says while placing her hand in mine.

I instruct the driver to wait as long as it takes and bill Callum for the extra time. We exit the car in silence and as soon as I'm close enough, I take her hand again.

Danielle stays quiet as we go through the check-in process and then find a bench before going to security.

I don't need to say a word because anyone can see how much pain we're both in. She lays her head on my shoulder and sniffs. "I swore I wasn't going to cry," she confesses.

Each one of her tears breaks me a little deeper. I shift so she sits up and I can see her blue eyes. "If you asked me to stay, I wouldn't be strong enough to walk away. If it weren't for my Mum, I was planning to quit my job and figure it out. For you, I would've given it all up."

Her lip trembles. "I can't ask you to do that. Not because I don't love you enough to want it, but because you have to go where you're needed."

And that's the worst part of all of this. If it was up to us, we would be in bed and not here. I've never seemed to get what I wanted in life. This is no different. I'm going to lay it all out there, though. I'm going to make sure that Danielle knows how I feel about her and us.

"As soon as she's better, I'm coming for you," I vow, "I know you think time will pass and my feelings for you will diminish, but hear this . . . they won't. I will love you no matter how many miles are between us."

"Don't say this," she pleads. "Just tell me you'll forget about me. Tell me this was the worst idea you ever had." Tears fall down her cheeks and I take her face in my hands. "Tell me you never loved me, please."

I shake my head. "I won't lie to you."

She lets out a soft sob and I pull her to my chest. I feel her cry harder and I hate everyone and everything right now, my Mum, Callum, my entire fucking life. I find happiness only to have to walk away from it.

I rub her back and she starts to calm herself. Danielle lifts her head, wipes her face and takes a few deep breaths. "Damn it. I swear, I was going to be strong and let you walk away."

My alarm starts, letting me know I have to go and the pain I have is amplified. "It's time."

She wipes her hands on her pants and then balls her fists. "Okay."

We begin to walk toward the security area and her arms go around my middle. "I'm going to miss you so much."

"This isn't the end."

Her lips form a small smile. "You're going to be an amazing VP. I'm really proud of you."

We stand at the entrance of the line, and I take both her hands. "I left something for Parker and Ava at the house, will you be sure they get it?"

She nods. "Of course."

"And I left you something too."

"Yeah?"

"My heart. It's yours."

Her tears form again, and I watch her struggle to stop them from spilling over. "You have mine too."

"I love you Danielle Bergen."

"I love you Milo Huxley."

I bring our lips together, pulling her tight to my chest. When we break apart, our foreheads touch and we stay like that for a heartbeat. "I have to go."

Her hand touches my chest, right over my heart, and I wonder if she can feel the pain through our skin. "Will you let me know you're okay?"

It's funny she thinks I'm going to get on that plane and never speak to her again. I wasn't kidding when I said I wasn't letting her go. The soonest I can get back here to her, I will. Losing Danielle isn't an option. Somehow, someday, I'll be with her.

There's no doubting that.

"This isn't the end," I tell her again. "I'll be with you soon."

She kisses me and then steps back. "I'll be hoping that's true."

"Believe me."

Danielle takes another step back but our hands are still connected. "You have to go."

I nod. There are no words adequate because I refuse to say goodbye. That word is too final, painful, and a lie. I won't let this be the ending on our story.

I don't know how to rewrite it, but I must.

Our fingers start to slip as we move apart.

"Soon," I say.

"Soon," Danielle repeats.

We take another step back and then our fingers disconnect.

Now I know what heartbreak feels like.

thirty-two

. . .

Danielle

"MOM?" Ava's voice is tender as she touches my back.

It's been two hours since I got home. He's on a plane heading to London right now. Each mile that the plane travels is a reminder that we're never going to be together again.

I know he thinks different, and I love that he's so adamant, but I won't keep hope alive only to be left broken. This is hard enough. False hope will only prolong my devastation.

"I'm okay," I tell Ava.

"No, you're not."

No, I'm not. I'm in pain. I miss him and don't know when I fell this deeply in love with him, but I did.

"I will be."

"Can I get you something?" she asks.

I must really be a hot mess if my daughter is being this nice.

"Is Parker okay?"

"Yes, he's watching T.V. and I'm letting him have a superhero movie marathon." She smiles.

I sit up and pull a deep breath through my nose. I need to show her how to handle heartbreak with grace, and this isn't it. My hand touches her leg. "Thank you, sweetheart. Sometimes you just need a good cry so you can pick yourself up and move on."

"You don't have to be strong in front of me."

I laugh softly. "That's exactly what I have to be. As much as it hurts, and it will hurt more, I'll survive. I can't fall apart, because life is filled with disappointment. Milo and I had this . . . special time that no one can take away from us. He made me happy." I smile thinking about him. "He gave me back the hope to love again."

"Why did you let him go?" she asks.

It's so complicated in some ways and in other ways it's not. "When you truly love another person, their happiness is what you care most about. Doing what's right for them even if it causes you pain is the sacrifice you'll make. I loved Milo enough to know that him going to London, even though it meant I would lose him, is what he had to do."

Ava scoots closer to me, resting her head against mine. "That's so sad, Mom."

"Yeah, but it's beautiful too."

"How did Milo sacrifice for you?"

My chest aches as a fresh wave of sadness crashes against me. "He offered to stay. He was willing to sacrifice his family, job, and life to be here. All I had to do was ask him."

Ava wraps her arms around my middle and holds me tight. I hear her sniffle and I embrace her. "Don't cry, Ava."

"Who the hell wants to fall in love if this is what happens?"

I'd like to know that as well. Then I think about the times we shared. The kisses, the dates, the nights where I felt as though I was floating. I remember how he looked at me when he thought I wasn't looking, or the way he looked at my children. All of that would've been lost, and that would've been the saddest thing.

"Look at the whole thing," I tell her. "I would rather have had a few days of loving Milo than never knowing that warmth."

"That's the saddest thing I've ever heard."

I chuckle and sit up. "Yeah, it is. Come on, let's go watch super-heroes and snuggle your brother."

Ava snorts. "I already told him no Thor."

I kiss her cheek. "Good call."

Who knew that Milo would also have brought my daughter back to me? No, loving him was never a mistake. It was a gift. One that I'll cherish always.

"I'm still not speaking to Callum," Nicole tells me. "Not even when he's trying to get me to touch him."

"Why? It's not his fault." I ignore the last part of her tirade.

It's been five days since Milo left. He's called me each day as he promised, and refuses to allow me to believe it's over. Two days ago, he was officially named Vice President of Dovetail Enterprises.

"The fuck it's not. He could've found another replacement." I love the whole solidarity in sisterhood thing, but it's not Callum's fault. It was the situation, and Milo should be the Vice President. He's a Huxley who helped build this company.

"And you think Milo and Callum would've ever found a way to talk again? You think that if Callum named another random cousin that things would've been better? How does that make sense? He had to name his brother, and Milo had to make the choice. But more than that, Nicole, were you willing to sell your company and move to London to care for his mother?"

That's the part that baffles me about her argument. She was never going to England. She has her life here, just the same as I do.

"That's irrelevant. You and Milo were happy and in love. He could've flown her crotchety ass here, but she refused, and they can't physically force a woman with cancer to come to America."

"And you want her close to you?" I ask, knowing how she feels about his mother.

"Fuck no, but at least you'd be happy!"

I smile and pull her in for a hug. "You love me."

"Don't remind me."

"You do." I grin. "You do because you'd rather be miserable instead of me."

"Shut up."

"I see your feelings coming through."

"Danni, shut your face before I remove my earrings," Nicole warns.

She's crazy, but it's sweet that she would take on an unwanted mother-in-law for me. Nicole hates mothers. All mothers. Her mother, her mother-in-law, the fact that she is a mother. It's actually pretty funny. I wish moving Mrs. Huxley closer was an option, but Milo's mother absolutely refused to come here, and you can't force a sick old woman to move against her will.

"Milo and I just weren't meant to be," I say as I flop on her very expensive couch.

"The fuck you're not."

"You know, Colin's first word is going to be fuck or some other curse word if you don't curb it."

"I hope it fucking is," Nicole laughs. "Then I'll know it's my kid."

"Was there a question as to the validity that Colin came from your vagina?" I ask, slightly wary of her answer.

"No, but . . . you know what I mean. Look, back to what matters. Callum is never getting a blowie again and I'm going to be sexless, which means I'll be extra bitchy, until he fixes your heart."

This is why every woman should have a squad like mine. Heather is the rational one who keeps us in check. Kristin is the mother hen who always makes sure we're okay. And then there's Nicole, the nut job who, when your heart is broken, will scoop the pieces up and make you laugh again. She reminds you that life is okay, and if it's not, she'll destroy anyone who hurt you.

"You know, in our squad of friends, Ava is the most like you," I tell her.

"Me?"

"Yeah, she's the lunatic who is a bit of a loose cannon, but when she fires, she strikes the target."

Nicole nudges me. "I'm your favorite. You can say it."

"Shut up."

"Say it," she pushes.

"No, you're not my favorite. You're like, bottom rung on the ladder."

She snorts. "Liar."

"Whatever."

"Can I ask you something?" Nicole questions out of nowhere.

"Umm, if I said no would it stop you?"

Her lips tip up. "Nope."

"Didn't think so."

She takes a few seconds, which is unlike her, and then holds my hand in hers. "Okay, why didn't you follow him to London?"

My head jerks back. "What?"

"Milo, why didn't you go with him?"

Nicole watches me and waits. I sit here, stunned by the question because it's obvious. I'm confused as to why she thinks I would go—or that I could, for that matter. I have a life here. My family, friends, kids are settled in schools, and I have a great job.

"Because . . . you know why!"

She shakes her head. "All the reasons you probably listed in your head are shit and you know it. Your parents tour Europe more than they're in Tampa. You can't tell me Parker and Ava wouldn't move because . . . they're kids and you make them."

I sit here, ticking off her counter to each point I had and hate her a little for it.

"Not the point—" I try to say but she cuts me off.

"Your job is the same damn job in England so don't go there. Also, you'd be dating the VP, so, again, shut up. Your house? Sell it. Peter is gone, and you found love with Milo. I'm not saying that it's easy or perfect, but there is not one single reason you have to be apart. It's a choice."

"What about you guys? You didn't factor all of us."

"That is the stupidest one of all. Our family isn't defined by location." She touches my face. "It's in our hearts, and we're only a plane ride or a FaceTime visit away. But your heart is in England, my friend. What are you going to do about it?"

I sit here, feeling a million things, but the one that keeps rising to the surface is longing.

I just don't know if I'm strong enough to act on it.

"Act on what?" Callum enters the room.

"The fact that you're an asshole who sent your brother to London, leaving my best friend broken hearted." Nicole crosses her legs and arms, staring at him with disdain.

Sometimes, I'm really happy Nicole is on my side. She's a little scary.

"I didn't send my brother away to hurt anyone," he sighs. "I hate that you're hurting. I hate that he's miserable. He's my brother and I love the bastard, but it was an impossible situation," Callum defends.

"Why wasn't Milo always your Vice President? Why offer him the job now?" I ask.

Callum sits beside Nicole, who gives the word frigid a whole new meaning. "Milo took off, no notice, just left for a month to go spend time in France. Then, another time he decided to rent a yacht for two weeks during the company's end of year review. Let's not forget the last time when we had no idea where he was when he found out I was going to move to America, and my wedding." He touches Nicole's hand and she doesn't move. "Milo hasn't been a consistent contributing member of this company until he came on as your assistant, Danielle. There was no way I could hand him the London office when there was no trust. But he's changed, and I thank you for giving him whatever he was lacking."

"I didn't do anything but love him," I tell him.

Callum smiles. "Well, you gave him something that neither my mum nor I could provide. He does love you, that much is clear. He's made it known each time we've spoken that he has no intentions of staying in London so I should find a replacement."

My heart swells knowing he's said this to his brother. It's one thing when he tells me, because I know our hearts are aching for each other. However, the fact that he's not afraid to let Callum know, makes me smile.

Callum continues, "I'm well aware that he's only there because of our mum. If she wasn't sick, he would've quit. Hell, he tried to already."

"He did?"

"Yes, I wouldn't let him, but he did. Because he is in love with you. Don't doubt that."

Callum's right. Milo's love is the one thing about this I'm completely clear about.

"We both love each other," I say.

He sighs and then turns to his wife. "I know you're angry with me, darling, but you weren't Team Milo a year ago."

She softens slightly. "That was before he fell in love."

"I hate that you're both struggling. I really do, and I want to offer something to you." Callum clears his throat. "If you're willing to hear me out?"

"Me?" I ask. "I'm not angry with you, Callum. I'm truly not. I understand because the truth is that he's there to care for your mom. I can't be angry about that."

"I appreciate that," he says. "Here's my offer, if you want to go to London, you can have any position in the company you want. Hell, I'll make one for you. I'll cover all your expenses to move and whatever else you need. If you want Parker and Ava in private school, I'll cover it. If you want a new home, we'll handle it. I promise, separating you both wasn't something I enjoyed doing, and if it's money holding you apart . . . that's not the case now. I want my brother to have the life he deserves, and I'm willing to do whatever it takes to give him all that he cares about . . . you."

thirty-three

. . .

Danielle

"FLIGHT ATTENDANTS, PREPARE FOR LANDING."

I'm doing this. I'm really doing this.

I'm going to be landing in London in a few minutes and I'm going to get my man.

After my talk with Nicole and Callum, I couldn't stop thinking about what they said. I was choosing to let him go. He didn't have the options, and as much as I didn't think I did, I do.

So, I arranged for Parker and Ava to stay with Heather, and I'm here.

The plane lands I turn my phone on. Immediately, it starts pinging.

Ava: I can't wait to hear what happens.

Ava: Did you land?

Ava: Were you too cheap to buy the wifi on the plane?

I roll my eyes and fire her back a message.

Me: I'm fine. Just landed. No reason to buy wifi when you're going to sleep through it. I'm not cheap, I'm smart. You're still sure about this? You really want to move?

She's probably asleep but she was the one that packed my bag and practically threw me out the door. My kids were both very excited about moving to London. Ava wants a fresh start and Parker wants to have an accent like Milo.

I was sure they'd pitch a fit, but they didn't.

So, I got on a plane.

Ava: I'm sure, Mom.

Me: Okay. I love you.

Ava: Whatever.

There's my girl.

Another series of text messages come through.

Milo: I've called and gone straight to voicemail. Are you okay?

Milo: Where are you? I've been calling for two days. Please, I need to hear your voice.

Little does he know he'll be seeing me soon.

Me: We'll talk soon. I promise. Where are you now?

Milo: I'm at my house.

Thank God. I asked Callum to send me all the info on what to ask for and how to get to his house. My nerves are frayed, but the excitement is immense.

I grab my bag from the luggage carousel and get through immigration. Then as I exit the terminal I see a driver with my name.

"Hi, are you Ms. Danielle Bergen?" he asks in his British accent.

"I am, I didn't know I had a car."

He smiles. "I was Mr. Huxley's personal driver, and he set up everything for you."

"Thank you."

"My pleasure. I'm William, by the way."

"It's nice to meet you, William."

We walk to the car, and he sits me in the back. William informs me that it'll take about forty-five minutes before we get there. I left Tampa at nine at night, and it's ten in the morning. My body is totally off kilter.

William points out some historical buildings on the ride, tells me about London, but all I care about is seeing Milo.

Me: When are you going to see your mom?

Milo: In an hour or so. Can you stop teasing me and let me see your eyes?

Me: Pushy.

I smile because in about ten minutes, I plan to let him see much more than that.

Then he sends another text.

Milo: Why in the bloody hell are you awake, my love?

Shit. The time difference.

Me: Couldn't sleep.

It's not a lie. Right now, my nerves are on overdrive. It's not like it's been that long since we've seen each other, but the closer we get, the more my heart begins to race. There's a chance he could reject me. Not that it's likely, but still. Three weeks is enough time for things to change.

It hasn't for me, but Milo has never really dealt with this. He's been alone his entire adult life, and then we fell in love only to be split apart.

"Here we are, Miss." William exits the car and my hands are trembling.

I step out of the car and look at the townhouse. It's beautiful and I haven't even stepped inside.

"This is the house?" I ask.

"Yes, ma'am, Mr. Huxley lives in the end house," William explains.

Okay. I came all this way to tell him how I feel. To give him my heart and see if this is what he wants.

I make my way to the steps and then turn. "William, will you wait . . . just in case?"

He nods.

I have an exit strategy at least. If Milo isn't ready for this step, then I'll go home, cry myself to sleep, and move on. That's the worst that can happen.

Another step closer and the door is right here. I just need to ring the bell.

I press the inconspicuous little button, my heart pounding against my chest.

The door opens, and it's as if time stands still.

Milo is wearing a pair of black slacks, and no shirt. His hair is wet from a shower, and I can smell his clean scent.

"Danielle?" his deep voice is filled with confusion.

"I said I'd let you see me soon." I smile, waiting for some kind of a reaction.

He steps closer, lifting his hand ever so slowly as if I'm an apparition and once we touch, I'll disappear.

"Are you really here?"

I touch my fingers to his face. "I am."

His lips lift, then his arm wraps around me and he pulls me to his body. Milo's mouth is on mine a second later, and I feel the pressure in my chest release since his absence.

He lifts me into his arms and walks over the threshold. I smile and turn to William. "You don't have to wait.

"Enjoy your time in London, Ms. Bergen."

Milo chuckles. "Oh, she fucking will!"

He kicks the door shut with his foot and he reminds me just how good of a time we have together.

———————————

"How long are you here for?" Milo asks as we lie tangled in the sheets.

The last two hours have been great. We've been together, happy, and kept things light. Really, we've barely talked other than a few words here and there.

Now, I guess we should get to it.

I sit up, pulling my knees to my chest. "That's up to you."

"I'm not following you."

I chew on my bottom lip, trying to think of how to say this without pretty much inserting myself in his life. Do I blurt it out? Do I work my way up? I'm not sure because Milo and I are still kind of new.

Fuck it. I'm here. I might as well figure my shit out.

"I quit my job," I say and then wait.

"You what?"

"I no longer work at Dovetail in the United States."

Milo runs his hand down his face. "Did you get another job?"

"Well, I was offered another position," I explain.

I see the anger starting to fill his eyes. "My fucking brother fired you?"

"No," I clarify. "Remember, I quit. Your brother didn't do anything."

He gets out of the bed and starts to walk around the room. "You're defending that prick? Seriously? He sends my arse over here because his life is too bloody perfect to move here, and now you're on his side?"

So, I'm doing really well here . . .

I need to stop beating around the bush, then.

"Please sit."

"No, I will not sit down," Milo bellows.

"Milo, I flew all the way here to have this discussion with you. I'm exhausted, missed you more than you'll ever know, quit my job, called a realtor to list my house, and asked my kids if they'd like to move to England, so . . . sit the hell down."

His eyes widen, and he stops moving. "You want to move here?"

"Not really, but it's where you are."

He grins. "You want to be here? With me?"

Is he listening to anything I'm saying?

"I want to be with you. If you're in London, then that's where I need to be. That is, if you want me to be."

Milo sits beside me. His hands hold my face. "If I want you to be? Are you blind? I promised you that I'd be back because this is fucking torture. I want you beside me. No, that's a lie. I need you beside me. All I think about is finding a bloody nurse to live with my mum so I can get on a plane."

"Well, it's torture for me too, and . . . there's no reason I can't live here. Each time I found an excuse, it could be negated."

"You're telling me you want to move here?"

I nod. "I'm telling you I want you more than anything else."

His smile grows wider. "And the kids?"

"Ava is already practicing her accent and Parker just wants to be close to you."

"And your job?"

"Irrelevant in comparison. I know this is fast, and maybe you're not ready for me and my kids to move here—"

"Marry me," Milo cuts me off.

Now it's my turn to be stunned. I stare at him, waiting for the punch line. There's no way he just said that. He can't be serious.

I open my mouth to speak, but his hand covers it before I can reply.

"No, hear me out. I love you. I've spent more time away from you than I ever will again. I would sacrifice everything for you, give up anything if it meant I could have you. Nothing else in this world matters. So, I know you wanted slow, but I don't. I want it all. I don't want to spend another day without the world knowing that I love you. If it's too fast, we can have a long engagement. I've spent my entire life looking for someone who would make me feel this way, and here you are, my darling. You're here and I'm right in front of you, asking you to see what's inside of my heart." He takes my hand, bringing it to his chest. Milo's heart is pounding as tears are falling down my face. "I want to marry you, Danielle. I want you to be my wife, and I your husband. So, Danielle Joanne Bergen, will you marry me?"

Through blurry vision I look at this man I love. He didn't hesitate a second. Everything he said was everything I could've asked for. Yes, it's fast, but we're not getting any younger. I married a man once who didn't make me feel the way Milo does, and I was happy, but Milo makes my world brighter than it's ever been. He tore down the old ideas of what love looked like and painted me something breathtaking.

I flew here to find a way for us to be together, and here it is.

"Yes," I breathe.

"Yes?"

I nod. "Yes, I'll marry you."

He practically tackles me, pulling me in his arms, holding me close. The smile on his face takes my breath away. There's no fear in his eyes, only love and happiness.

After a lot of kissing and smiling, he pulls me to his chest and we just stare at each other.

"I'll get you a proper ring today."

"I don't need a ring."

"Well, that's very sweet of you, but I need you to have a ring."

I shake my head. "Why?"

"So the world knows that you're most definitely not on the market."

Men.

They're all the same.

"Is this an acquisition?"

He raises one brow. "You are not property, but I do wish to acquire you."

He's such a dork. "I'm pretty sure you have—many times."

"Yes, and each time has been better than the last."

This is true. "Well, there will be lots more going forward," I say.

Milo taps my nose. "I'm very happy, are you?"

"You make me happy. I thought after Peter died, that I wouldn't be able to open myself up again." I sit up, wanting to be sure he hears this. "I thought we all get one great shot at love, and that was it. When you came into my life, I wasn't ready. I wasn't guarded enough to not fall for you, and now I've never been happier about anything in my whole life. If I was, we never would be here."

He smirks. "That's what you think. I would've worn you down, broke through every defense you had, and made you mine."

"You would, huh?"

I wonder if Milo and I met at another time, if that would be the case. Life is all about moments, and one decision can alter a major chain of events. Had I never taken the job, Milo wouldn't have been my assistant. The entire course of our relationship would've changed. Maybe we still would've fallen in love, but who knows?

"The moment we met, something inside of me was altered. I didn't know what it was until later on, but you and I were going to happen. When I thought you were still married, I remember feeling an instant hatred for a man I never knew. I didn't understand that feeling because it was foreign to me, but it was there."

"You hated Peter?"

"No," he sighs, "I hated whoever the bastard was that was near you. Not him, but the idea of him."

I smile and touch his cheek. "That's sweet."

"If I told you I was married, would you have felt that way?"

"Not in the beginning," I tell him honestly. "I was a mess when we met. It wasn't until I saw you with Kandi the hooker and wanted to gouge her eyes out to make her stop looking at you."

Milo runs his hand from my neck down my arm. "I never would've touched her. You know why?"

"Why?"

"Because you were the only thing I wanted that night."

Looking at him now, there's one thing I do believe about us. We were meant to cross each other's paths. Whatever the circumstances, the outcome would've been the same. I was always going to fall in love with Milo.

"So you really want to marry me?" I ask again.

"My favorite color was always orange. Do you know what it is now?"

I shake my head.

"Blue, like your eyes. There's nothing more beautiful in the world than this color," he says as he touches the skin around my eye. "Blonde was always what I thought I was attracted to, until I saw you. Then I realized no woman on earth could compare to you. I don't really want to marry you, Danielle. I'm really going to marry you. Now, let's get dressed, go see my Mum, tell her the good news and get you moved here."

I wrap my arms around his neck and kiss him. "I love you."

"And I love you. Now get up and get dressed before we're even later and I have to tell Mummy that I was too busy to get there on time because I was fucking my fiancé."

Oh, God, I have to meet his mother. If she's anything like Nicole says, I'm in trouble.

thirty-four

...

Milo

"I'M GLAD YOU MADE IT," Mum says as I walk in. "Oh, you brought someone."

My hand is holding Danielle's as we walk in. It was adorable how nervous she was on the way here.

"Mum, I'd like you to meet Danielle, my fiancé."

Might as well get it all out now. Give the old woman a chance to lose her rag and then settle down. I've never been a man who minces words, why start now?

"Fiancé?" she asks.

"Yes," I state. "I asked her to marry me today and she accepted."

Her eyes widen and then soften. "I see."

Danielle elbows me and then walks toward her. "It's very nice to meet you Mrs. Huxley."

"My Milo is a very special man. You must be a special woman if he's asked you to marry him."

"He is very special to me as well," Danielle tells her and then looks back at me.

As our eyes meet, I wonder how I lived before her. Everything since we've met is just . . . better. The sun is brighter, the days are more colourful, and life makes sense. I now understand why my brother packed his life to go to America. When you love a woman like this, you'll do anything to keep her.

Before Danielle, the word marriage alone would've repulsed me. In my mind, it was damnation for life. One person? Who the hell wants to eat the same flavour of ice cream for the rest of their life? Not me. Not until Danielle. There's no one else I'd ever want to taste again.

"Milo," Mum says. "Give Danielle and I a few minutes alone."

Mum is the kindest woman I know, except when it comes to her boys. However, it's sort of inevitable that they get this over with. I walk over to her, kiss her cheek and whisper. "Be nice, Mum. She means a lot to me."

Her hand pats my cheek. "Go away, son."

That's not exactly the encouragement I was hoping for.

I touch Danielle's hand and head out of the room, hoping that they both come out alive and that it goes better than her meeting with Nicole.

Once out in the hallway, I decide to call my brother.

"Is Mum okay?" he asks.

"Yes, why wouldn't she be?"

He grumbles. "Because it's fucking early and I was up all night with Colin who thought he'd become nocturnal for a change."

"Danielle is here," I tell him, ignoring his complaining.

"Yes, I know."

"She said she quit."

"Yes, again, I know," Callum sighs. "I'm assuming you didn't fuck it up when she showed up?"

I'm not a moron. I know what I'm doing when it comes to women, unlike him. "I asked her to marry me."

He nearly chokes. "You what?"

I hear Nicole in the background. "What is he saying?"

Callum moves the receiver and reiterates what I just said.

"You what?" Nicole's voice is now the one on the line.

"I proposed, do you have a problem with that?" I ask.

Nicole goes quiet for a second and then sighs. "No, it's sweet and romantic. Good job, Milo."

"Well, I love her and never wish to be parted again. She left her job, is willing to move to London, and there's no fucking way she's living anywhere but in my house."

Again, there's silence.

"Nicole, are you there?"

"I'm here," she sniffs. "Here's your brother."

Callum comes back on the line. "Great. You made her cry, now I'm going to have to listen to how you're the better Huxley again."

"Was there ever a question about that?" I joke.

"I hope you know," he starts, "I never wanted you two to be separated. It wasn't because I don't care about you or that I was being cruel. It was that there really were no options."

In a small part of my heart, I know that. But something I loved was being taken from me, without any choice in the matter. To have it be my brother pulling the strings was even worse. Was my anger misplaced? Maybe.

I'll forgive you . . . depending on the wedding present."

He laughs. "Your wedding present is that I created another senior level position where Danielle will be your equal at Dovetail."

"My equal?" I scoff. "I'm the bloody Vice President! There's no way I'll be under her again, damn you."

My bastard brother snickers. "Co-Vice President. Your soon to be wife is the other. Have a great day, Milo."

Before I can say another word, the arsehole hangs up, leaving me stunned.

Once again, Danielle is going to find a way to make me pay—forever, and that works just fine for me.

epilogue

· · ·

Danielle

three months later

"ARE YOU PLANNING TO MOVE ANYTHING?" my husband asks.

"Not really."

"So you're going to sit there on your arse whilst I carry the boxes?"

"Pretty much." I shrug.

"And here I thought we were equal partners," Milo laughs as he carries another box in.

Oh, how silly men are. Sure, we're equal—at times.

I grab my cup of tea and take a sip. I figure I should start getting used to my new homeland. In America, barely anyone drinks tea. It's all about coffee, but I actually prefer tea, so I'm happy. Plus, the tea here is really fantastic.

"I'm just doing what Nicole said to do."

He stops and looks at me. "And what was that, my darling?"

I give him a playful smirk. "Supervise."

We've been living in London for a little over a month and finally our household goods shipment from America arrived. My home sold quick, and the kids were about done with school, so we said our goodbyes and headed to our new home of London, England.

I started two weeks ago as Co-Vice President of Dovetail Enterprises. It was a little crazy, but it's been amazing. Callum wants his family to all hold board seats and now that we're officially family, it works.

Really, I think he wanted to make Milo miserable. Which is another thing I don't mind either.

Keeping him a little hostile makes him work harder.

"Could you supervise while holding a box?"

I smirk. "I could, but you didn't ask nicely."

"I'll give you nicely."

"I sure hope so, husband."

Milo's eyes fill with warmth. Each time I say husband or remind him that I'm his wife, his entire face lights up. I love that it makes him so happy. The truth is, I love it just as much.

Milo wasted no time in getting married, he said he wanted to make sure I couldn't change my mind.

Our wedding was super small, but perfect. We had a week in between the move and needing to be in London, so we hopped on a plane to the islands and were married. The kids, us, Nicole and Callum, that's it.

Of course, Nicole was supposed to get a video for us, but instead, she went live so everyone else could see. In the end, it was perfect.

"You're really going to sit there?" he asks with a chuckle.

"You could come over and make me get up."

"I could, or we can make a wager that you'll come to me . . ."

Milo and his betting.

"Are you sure you want to bet me, sweetcheeks?" I say with sarcasm. "I mean, the last time we bet . . . you lost."

Milo puts the box down and heads over to me, his arms cage me in on the couch and he grins.

"I rather think I won."

"Do you?"

He grins. "Most definitely. Besides, you wouldn't hold out on your husband, would you?"

I pretend to think about it, and sigh. "It's such a shame you're so hot. It's hard to resist you."

"That's what I thought you'd say."

"Arrogant much?"

His lips move closer. "Just hedging my bets."

Right before our lips are about to touch, Ava's voice kills the moment.

"Mom! Can you please tell Parker he doesn't get to put his crap in my room!"

Milo pulls back.

"Really? You guys are always making out, it's freaking weird," she says with her arms crossed.

"Yes, being married and in love is so weird," I toss back.

She's been genuinely happy since we decided to move here. Ava loves the arts, and London is a great place for her to study. We've already found a ballet school that she loves, and the instructor has trained some of the most renowned dancers.

Ava sits on the couch beside me.

"Aren't you glad we're married and now you get to help raise them?" I ask Milo with a brow raised.

He kisses me hard and then pulls back. "I am."

"Mom!" She covers her eyes.

I grab Milo's arm as he starts to walk away. "Kiss me again."

His lips break into a slow, sexy smile. "Happily."

"Ugh!" She huffs. "I'm going upstairs to torture Parker."

"Bye!"

Milo laughs and tucks my hair behind my ears. "I'm excited to be their bonus father. I know you worry, and I don't blame you, but I love them as much as I love you."

"I got really lucky with you."

He kisses my forehead. "I'm pretty sure I won the lottery with you, sweetheart."

I wonder if he understands how much I love him. There's something very different about my second marriage. I'm older, wiser, more understanding at the amount of work that goes into a relationship. There's no grandiose ideas on how perfect things will be. I know there will be times I'll hate him, days where I wonder what the hell I was thinking, and even times we may want to throw in the towel.

On the other hand, there will be days like this. When nothing else matters but getting another kiss from the man I love. When the kids can be stupid or his mother—whom I freaking love—will require our attention, but I'll see the beauty in our love.

He pulls back and taps my nose. "Enjoy Ava's attitude."

Yeah, there's so much fun for me there.

Ava and Parker each got their own rooms on the third level. Milo and I are on the second level. His house is magnificent, and it's truly the most beautiful building I've ever seen. He bought it when it was run down, and spent God only knows how much money to renovate it.

Their bedrooms were once a guest room and a study. He easily converted it to a bedroom before we moved officially.

"Please stop fighting," I say to them both.

"Milo said I could have this room and if I needed space for my comics that I could use Ava's room."

"No he didn't!" Ava yells.

"Okay, well, you have your room, Parker. If something doesn't fit, which makes no sense, then you'll have to throw it out," I settle that one and then look at my daughter. "And you can be nice and let him put something in there since you decided you had to have the bigger room."

I swipe my hands together and nod. That's done.

Since Milo already had so much, we sold pretty much all of

our furniture. There was no point in bringing it here, except for a few sentimental items that I couldn't part with.

I get downstairs where Milo is unpacking a box. He removes a wooden box that has my initials engraved on the top, and I freeze. Peter gave me that on the day of our wedding. He wanted us to fill it with memories. However, instead of memories, it's where his ashes are contained.

"Sweetheart? Where do you want to put this box?" Milo asks.

I step forward, touching the lid. "I wasn't sure what to do with this."

"What is it?"

"It's Peter."

Milo covers my hand with his. "Why don't we keep this on the mantle? He's part of our family, and I never want you or the kids to feel as though I'm trying to replace him. If it weren't for Peter, Ava and Parker wouldn't be. If things didn't happen the way they did, you never would've worked for Cal, and I never would've met you. I owe my entire life's happiness to him, and he's always welcome in our home."

My other hand rests on his cheek. "Why do you always say the perfect thing?"

His eyes lock on mine. "Because you're the perfect woman for me. Our hearts aren't two beating as one. They're the same heart that finally found it's rhythm. Now . . ." he smiles. "Go grab a box and get to work. I'm going to need a rub down later."

And that's my Milo. Sweet, sexy, and a smartass who stole my heart.

Thank you for reading Danielle & Milo's story. If you loved this tribe and aren't quite ready to let go, keep swiping and gain access to an EXCLUSIVE bonus scene!

bonus scene

. . .

Danielle

"SWEETHEART, we're going to be late."

"If you'd stop opening the door, we won't be," I grumble at Milo and shoo him out. It's Ava's first professional ballet gig or whatever you call it. She's dancing for the American Ballet Company in New York.

I never thought it would happen. I know that makes me a shitty mom, but out of the thousands of kids who dream of becoming a prima ballerina, I just never thought her dream would be the one that would become reality.

He knocks again. "I will leave without you. I'm not missing this." His accent is heavy since he's frustrated.

"I wouldn't have been running late if it weren't for you pawing at me as soon as Ava was out of the apartment."

We're at Ava's apartment, her very tiny apartment that Milo and I pay an arm and leg for. It's cute, very New York, and very cramped. I wanted to stay at a hotel, but she insisted she gets as much time with us as possible.

"Well, forgive me that my wife was in those tiny shorts, showing her delectable arse in my face and I couldn't resist."

I smile. "Yes, well, I'm going to need a few minutes thanks to your lack of self-control."

Milo's mouth falls open. "Lack of self-control? I've had to keep my bloody hands off of you for days! And," his voice drops low. "I'm pretty sure Ava knows exactly what she's doing by popping in when she does."

I giggle because I'm pretty sure she is doing it to drive her father crazy as well. Milo has always been affectionate, even in front of the kids, which grosses them out. We laugh and figure if nothing else, we're setting a great example of what marriage should look like, but she's been extremely attentive, giving us practically no time alone. When she did have rehearsals, she made sure we had someone to take us around the city and entertained.

No matter how much we protested.

"Doesn't mean you didn't ravage me the minute that door locked."

"And you didn't like it?"

"I never said that, husband. All I said is that's why I'm running late." Milo grins with pride. "Now, this conversation is making me even later so go sit on the couch and wait until I'm ready."

He mutters something and walks away from the door.

That means we've spent eight days with her, watching movies, laughing, playing board games, and Milo is ready to kill someone.

I check the mirror, dab more blush onto my cheeks, and then open the door. "I'm ready."

He gets to his feet. "It's about bloody time, sweetheart."

"Yes, way to add that on at the end to avoid my wrath."

He laughs. "Your wrath of what? Soft pillows being thrown as insults?"

I lean over, kissing his mouth. "I'll throw something, darling, but it won't be pillows."

Milo grabs my butt and chuckles in my ear. "We're going to the hotel tonight so I can throw your clothes to the floor without our daughter in the other room and when I don't have to hurry because we're going somewhere."

"You should not mention my wrath if you're goal is to get me naked."

"Get naked, and I'll take all the wrath you have."

"Only if you behave," I warn him.

"Let's go before we miss the ballet and we never hear the end of it."

I give him a quick kiss, tap his chest, and we head out the door.

It's been two years since we've been in New York, and I'd forgotten how much I love it here. When we see Ava, it's usually her coming to us in London. Milo and I alternate whenever we come back to the States, but she's been so busy when I'm in Tampa that we haven't been able to see each other.

For the last year, Milo has taken most of the trips back since I'm driving Parker all over for his art classes. Besides, it's good for Milo to suffer through the long flights and have to stay with Nicole and Callum while he's there.

"Has Parker called today?" Milo asks once we're in the cab on the way to the theater.

"Yes, he said your mother was behaving, but he'll let us know if the situation changes."

He chuckles. "Do you think it's wise that we let her watch him? I feel as though he's more mature than she is most days."

Those two together are trouble, but since she lives with us, it's really a no-brainer. She did exceptionally well beating cancer, but not so great with walking. After the second fall, I put my foot down and moved her in.

"We'll be home in two days, I'm sure they'll be fine."

He takes my hand in his, moving it to his lap. "I'm sure you're right."

I love how much he loves our kids. He's always doing whatever he can to show them his love. Milo is who encouraged Parker to start drawing. He was doodling a lot with different cartoon-type characters. Then he started illustrating more. Parker has now created four superhero comics that he's submitting for publishing.

My son, who is thirteen, is incredibly talented and has his own agent.

It's crazy.

The cab pulls over, and we exit.

"There you are! Jesus, way to cause an entrance," Nicole says as soon as my feet are on the sidewalk.

"Nice to see you too."

"Hey!" Kristin yells and walks over. "You look gorgeous."

"Thanks." I sigh and smooth my dress. "I'm so nervous."

"She'll do great," Heather assures me and then pulls me in for a hug.

"As much as I do love standing around four beautiful women, you are all a bit bonkers for me, are the men inside?"

Nicole smirks. "Are you saying we're crazy?"

"You missed the compliment first, I see."

I can't wait to watch this. These two are like actual siblings. They bicker and taunt each other so much that I'm surprised he hasn't pulled her hair at this point.

"The compliment gets lost when you sling an insult after," she informs him.

"It is a wonder how my brother puts up with you."

"I'm lovable."

"You're something, all right."

This is going to go downhill fast. Neither of them knows how to let something drop, and I'm too excited to allow it to go on.

"Okay," I say with a clap of the hand as if I'm talking to toddlers. "Babe, you go inside and find the men. The girls and I are going to freshen up, and then we'll meet you by the bar."

Milo walks over, kisses my temple. "I'll see you inside."

"Behave."

He grins that devilish smile that always ends with him getting his way. "I always do."

That's the biggest lie ever.

I watch him walk away, the tuxedo he's wearing is extremely sexy and trim. It fits his ass perfectly, but it isn't just the suit that makes him irresistible, it's his being. Milo commands the space around him as he walks, as though it's bending to his will. It's intoxicating, and I am so glad he's my husband.

All the years we've had so far have only made me yearn for more.

"Can you stop staring at your husband's ass?" Nicole brings my attention forward.

"Sorry, I like his ass."

She snorts. "Because he is an ass."

Kristin rolls her eyes. "And you aren't?"

Ah, to be together again. The four of us haven't been in the same city in a very long time. I've still seen them when I visit Tampa, but Heather is usually out with Eli either on set or on tour. Kristin and Noah split time while he's filming or directing. Nicole is always around, plus she's my sister-in-law, so I see her more often than anyone.

I always thought of them like family and having one actually as one has been . . . interesting. I spend every other Christmas with her in London and then we go to America to see my parents on the years she's with hers. Callum I see all the time since he's my boss and brother-in-law.

That's a relationship I've loved seeing be repaired. Mostly, the boys didn't have a damn choice since Nicole and I refuse to let up.

"So . . ." Heather hooks her arm in mine. "How's the mother of the ballet?"

I laugh. "I'm good. I'm just so proud of her, you know? She's worked so damn hard. After all the hell she went through after her father's death, I just didn't know how moving across the pond would be for her."

It was a hard choice to make, but Ava was probably the most excited because of the dance opportunities that were available to her. She also wanted a fresh start, and she was the one who wanted me happy.

"I swear someone in this tribe told you to move to London . . ." Kristin chimes in from behind. "Sometimes change is good."

"Yes, you were all right, I know." Not like they don't remind me constantly.

They were right about that and all the other things.

They were right when they pushed me to see that what I had with Milo was everything I wanted and needed. He loves me beyond reason and supports me each step of the way. Even when we disagree at the office, we find a way to leave it there.

They were right when they said I should take the job at Dovetail where I'm now the co-Vice President. He drives me nuts, but it works.

And they were right when they said that no matter the distance, we'd still be the same crazy girls we always were.

I really don't hate it when they're right.

"As usual." Nicole's voice is filled with conceit.

Well, maybe I hate it when she's right.

"You should shut up," Heather says over her shoulder. "You are almost never right, and you're the last person who listens to advice."

We turn to walk away because this will only end in disaster, but Nicole keeps up as we enter the double doors of the theater.

"I'm pretty sure I was right about all of you idiots."

I roll my eyes. "Please."

We get to the bar, but there's no sign of the guys.

"No? Really?" Nicole says, refusing to quit. "Heather didn't think Eli was a great idea, but I shoved her ass on that bus and took care of that one. Kristin over here was all hesitant thanks to the number that Asshole did on her, but again, Nicole to rescue. Let's not even go there with you, Danni and your ridiculousness about Milo. I'm the fixer. I'm the one who sees all your dumb mistakes and fixes them."

The three of us exchange a look as she waits, tapping the toe of her Jimmy Choo on the ground. "And what about you and Callum? You fixed that?" Heather asks.

"No, that was what you all did."

I smile. "Yes, yes we did."

"I'm pretty sure I was vocal about Noah and Eli, too." I remind them.

"And I was about Milo, Callum, *and* Eli," Kristin tosses in.

The thing about us is that we can see the truth about ourselves, but know what's best for the other. It's strange and fabulous at the same time.

"I missed us," Nicole says with a smile.

"Me too."

"Me three." Kristin gets all choked up and can barely say the words.

Heather gets misty too. "Me four."

"Oh, bloody hell," Milo says, coming to stand behind us. "You girls aren't going to start crying, are you?"

I slap his chest playfully. "You should shut up."

"Of course, sweetheart, but we really need to go find our seats."

The other guys come around, touching their wives in some sort of manor. I look at the three people who have been at every event in my life without question. The girls who held my hand as I cried or hair back as I got sick. They're the ones who I've never doubted would pick up the phone at three in the morning. We're sisters in every way. It's a friendship that none of us have ever taken for granted because it's once in a lifetime. Here we stand, together with people who love us, and I can't stop the tears.

I'm not a crier normally, but I'm just so happy.

"What's wrong?" Kristin asks when she sees my face.

"Nothing. Nothing, that's the thing."

Lord knows feelings bother her, but still, she watches me. "She's finally cracking."

"Shut up you turd. I'm serious. There's nothing wrong. Look at us. We're all happy, with men who truly love us and our kids are great. We're living the lives that we used to imagine."

Heather smiles and rests her head on Eli's shoulder. Noah pulls Kristin a little closer, and she doesn't even notice she melts into him. And even Nicole—the tough and doesn't need love friend—laces her fingers in Callum's. My Milo, my sweet Milo, wraps his arms around my stomach from behind, resting his chin on my shoulder.

"We're living the lives we deserve with people who deserve us." Kristin smiles and Noah kisses the top of her head.

Milo squeezes his arms around me just a bit tighter, releases me, and raises his wine glass. "Here's to the women who we somehow fooled into loving us."

The guys lift their glasses with a chuckle. Once he takes a sip, I grab it from him and lift it into the air. "Here's to the second time around and finding the men who we fooled into marrying into this tribe."

Instead of drinking, the four of us wrap our arms around each other and giggle.

Life works in mysterious ways, I'm just glad the magic was present for us.

books by corinne michaels

The Salvation Series

Beloved

Beholden

Consolation

Conviction

Defenseless

Evermore: A 1001 Dark Night Novella

Indefinite

Infinite

The Hennington Brothers

Say You'll Stay

Say You Want Me

Say I'm Yours

Say You Won't Let Go: A Return to Me/Masters and Mercenaries
Novella

Second Time Around Series

We Own Tonight

One Last Time

Not Until You

If I Only Knew

The Arrowood Brothers

Come Back for Me

Fight for Me

The One for Me

Stay for Me

Willow Creek Valley Series

Return to Us

Could Have Been Us

A Moment for Us

A Chance for Us

Rose Canyon Series

Help Me Remember (Coming 2022)

Give Me Love (Coming 2022)

Keep This Promise (Coming 2022)

Co-Written with Melanie Harlow

Hold You Close

Imperfect Match

Standalone Novels

All I Ask

You Loved Me Once

acknowledgments

If you deal with me during this process, you deserve so much more than a thank you that's back here. For real, I'm a little crazy and you know this, but . . . here it is.

To my husband and children. I don't know how you deal with me, but I can't tell you how much I appreciate you. I love you all with my whole heart.

My beta readers, Katie, Melissa, Jo: Thank you so much for your support and love during this book. I love you guys and couldn't imagine not having you. I hope I did the British parts proud.

My assistant, Christy Peckham: When I say I hate you, I'm totally lying. I love you so much. I'll totally deny this.

My readers. There's no way I can thank you enough. It still blows me away that you read my words. You guys are everything to me. Everything.

Bloggers: You're the heart and soul of this industry. Thank you for choosing to read my books and fit me into your insane schedules. I appreciate it more than you know.

Melanie Harlow, thank you for being the good witch in our duo or Ethel to my Lucy. Really you're the good witch and I'm the bad, but your friendship means the world to me and I love writing with you (especially when you let me kill characters.)

Bait, Stabby, and Corinne Michaels Books – I love you more than you'll ever know.

My agent, Kimberly Brower, I am so happy to have you on my team. Thank you for your guidance and support.

Melissa Erickson, you're amazing. I love your face.

about the author

Corinne Michaels is a New York Times, USA Today, and Wall Street Journal bestselling author of romance novels. Her stories are chock full of emotion, humor, and unrelenting love, and she enjoys putting her characters through intense heartbreak before finding a way to heal them through their struggles.

Corinne is a former Navy wife and happily married to the man of her dreams. She began her writing career after spending months away from her husband while he was deployed—reading and writing were her escapes from the loneliness. Corinne now lives in Virginia with her husband and is the emotional, witty, sarcastic, and fun-loving mom of two beautiful children.